Taking the Heat

SD Hildreth

DEDICATION

Judging a person based on what we see, the color of their skin, race, creed, religious belief, lack of religion, sex, or appearance is wrong. In my opinion, to judge a person, even for their actions, is a difficult thing to justify. Having not experienced *their* life makes it difficult to judge their actions. In short, judging a person does nothing to define them, but does everything to define you.

This book is dedicated to those who have the ability to love all creatures of this earth.

TOAD

I leaned forward and placed the folded sheet of paper on top of the headstone. I had every intention of leaving it and walking away, but for some reason I wavered. As if I expected an answer from a man who had been dead for a dozen years, I slowly knelt and stared blankly at the etched stone.

Cambio Salvadore Todelli
GY SGT
US MARINE CORPS
WORLD WAR II
May 8, 1920
Sept 16, 2003
PURPLE HEART
BRONZE STAR

"Everything's going pretty good, Nonno. Mom made those meatballs last Sunday. You remember the ones we fought over right before I left for the war? The big fuckers with the thick sauce? You remember, the ones she makes with pork? Hell, I didn't need the last one any more than you did, but I damned sure wasn't going to let *you* have it," I hesitated, wiped the dust from stone base with my index finger, and considered standing.

Instead, I maintained my kneeling position, inhaled a shallow breath, and continued speaking softly, "So we had this fella who stole from us.

1

Well, he tried to anyway. And he damned near got two of the other fellas killed; two of the main fellas from the Executive Committee. They're similar to officers in the Marine Corps. You know, it's just like the Marine Corps, Nonno, we don't do what we do for the sake of doing it; we do it for the man riding beside us. I'd die for each and every one of these men. I sure would. And they'd do the same for me. Maybe that's why I'm in this damned club, because it's the closest thing to the Corps I could find. It reminds me a lot of it to tell you the truth, the brotherhood and all."

I blew the dust from the bottoms of the chiseled letters and grinned at the thought of him actually listening to me as I continued, "Well, anyway, we took care of him. I remember you telling me when I was a kid how it was my duty to protect those who couldn't protect themselves. I suppose in a sense I was protecting the other members of the club from what he might expose them to. You know, harming them in the future or whatever. It all gets jumbled up when I think about it, really. But I know he was a terrible man, Nonno. And he almost killed two of the fellas. Well, he's gone now, so the club's a better place. I sure wish you were here to see how solid the rest of these fellas are, you'd be proud of 'em for sure. Oh, and I wrote you another poem."

I slowly stood, reached for the folded sheet of paper, and removed it from the headstone. As if rehearsed, I unfolded it and began reading.

The pages of the calendar blow in the breeze,
One by one they go.
A wounded boy stands from his knees,
The scars of war heal slow.

Wind at his face, dead men blow past;
The warm breeze dries the tears.
The sound of thunder fills the air,
And days fade into years.

With a watchful eye the boy checks his six,
For a ghost rides in his wake.
As the apparition weaves through the mix,
A second glance the boy must take.

He blinks his eyes in disbelief,
There is no need to fret.
An exhaled sigh, one of relief;
The wraith's a combat vet.

The ghost rides past, his face is clear.
The boy grins and nods his head.
He rides without an ounce of fear,
For Nonno is not dead.

I folded the paper, placed it on top of the headstone and wiped the tears from my eyes, "I like that one. It's better than the one I wrote last year, isn't it? You give me the courage to stand up against evil, Nonno. And I know you've got my back. I appreciate you, old man, and I miss you. I miss you a lot. I better get back, it's a long ride. Take care, and I'll be back to see you real soon."

My grandfather passed away after my first tour in Afghanistan. I felt as if he had waited for me to return from the war before he allowed himself to pass. As I knelt at his bedside, he held my hand and explained how he would continue to watch over me after his death.

"While I fought in *my* war, my grandfather watched over me; it's what grandfathers do. I can't keep a good eye on you from down here, the earth is too damned flat for me to see you with these old eyes. It's time for the good Lord to drag my old ass up to the heavens so I can look over you. From up there I'll be able to see it all, so don't worry, I've got your six. I'll tap your left shoulder if I ever need to forewarn you about anything life threatening. And if I don't warn you, fight without reservation, Cambio. *Capisce?*" he whispered.

Outfitted in my Marine dress blues, I held his hand and attempted to force a smile. The thought of him dying was devastating to me.

"*Capisco,*" I nodded, "I'll make you proud, Nonno."

He closed his eyes and grinned, "You already have, Cambio. You already have."

The next day he passed away. I went on to serve half a dozen tours in the war, and did so without much fear of death or even injury. According to those who fought beside me, I made some very courageous decisions; saving the lives of many Marines while I risked my own life in the process. As far as I was concerned, I was simply doing what I was capable of. Although I knew my grandfather wasn't *really* going to warn me, I continuously told myself the absence of his warning tap on my left shoulder was reassurance there was no *real* risk in my decisions or actions while in combat. The entire time I was in combat I felt as if I had a sixth sense.

I have since left the war, but the war has never left me.

I doubt it ever will.

TOAD

When exposed to the brutality and horror of war, a man's mind must decide how to process the terrifying experiences so the memories may be carefully filed away into the chosen portion of the frontal cortex of the brain; saved for long-term recollection. Some men seem to dwell on the horrific events, and allow them to chisel away at their life for all of the years which follow. Others become somewhat immune to the events of their past, or any similar circumstances which may present themselves in the future. I don't believe the decision to either lose sight of the past or allow it to inhabit our mind is a conscious one, but more a matter of a person's chemical assembly. The men who don't seem at all bothered by their exposure to the atrocities of war are often perceived as evil, immoral, depraved, or wicked.

Hardened.

I've heard some describe me as hardened.

I couldn't say I enjoyed what I witnessed in combat, nor could I accurately describe it as something I found to be horrifying. War happened and I was present. My mind processed the events, and for whatever reason, they were placed on a shelf along with chapters from various graphic books and scenes from B rate horror movies. I'm not so shallow that I perceived the war as a fictitious event, nor did I dwell on it as an absolute fact which required my continual approval or constant embrace. I did, however, realize my exposure to certain violent events had caused me to become *less sensitive* to any and all things life now offered me; sex included.

In short, I needed tremendous mental stimulation of the violent variety incorporated into my sex. I needed it to be aggressive, rough, and unrestrained, or I wasn't able to perform. My war-torn mind which had been pickled by the savagery of combat now needed violence to become aroused. There was no doubt in my mind I was a sexual misfit, and I realized my tastes and desires weren't shared by the masses. The considerate side of me – the side my Catholic parents raised – often viewed my sexual side as a walking contradiction. I saw my sexual self as nothing short of a disaster. As much as I had tried to change it, I couldn't. So, I simply considered myself damaged and decided to embrace it.

"Stop flopping the fuck around," I sighed.

Considering my sexual tastes and lack of specific boundaries when it came to a *sexual* relationship, I was very thorough in my explanations of what my sexual partner and I were planning to do. The event, entirely, must be 100% consensual. If after discussing my sexual intention an agreement could not be reached regarding the intended event or events, the plan was changed until it was agreed upon. I may not be as compassionate as most men when it came to sex, but my partner's knowledge of the situation and expressed consent was a *requirement*, not a recommendation.

I continued to wrap the Saran Wrap around her head at a rapid pace, covering her mouth, ears, and eyes with several layers. Too little of the plastic may allow her to force her tongue through the slit I intended to provide for her to breathe through; but in my opinion there was no such thing as *too much*. As I made one last revolution for good measure, her arms began to flap like a bird attempting to flee from a captor. Aggravated at her inability to hold still, I gripped the plastic wrap in both hands and pulled, stretching the material until it snapped. I pressed the loose end against the back of her head and grinned at my handiwork.

I quickly grasped the wrists of her flailing arms, pulled them behind her back, and wrapped them with several layers of the plastic, hoping to prevent injury. Now completely naked with her entire head and forearms wrapped in Saran Wrap, she collapsed onto the floor of my bedroom. Although her body began to convulse, I knew from experience it was mostly show and not solely from lack of oxygen.

Satisfied, I tossed the remaining roll of plastic wrap beside the bed.

I pulled my knife and flipped the blade open with my thumb. As it snapped into locked position with a pronounced *click*, she began to whimper and squirm on the floor. I knelt beside her and pressed against the back of her head with the palm of my hand, tilting her head slightly to the side. As I positioned my mouth against her plastic covered ear, I spoke clearly and with a tone of authority.

"I know you can hear me, this isn't my first time doing this. Just listen. You're fine. It's only been about twenty seconds. Now, I'm going to poke a hole in this shit with my knife, which will allow you to breathe a little. The opening won't be very big, but it'll be enough for you to survive. If you flop the fuck around while I'm trying to poke this hole, it'll just cut your face, and I don't want that. I'm going to let go of your head, but you need to hold still, okay?"

As soon as I lifted my hand from her skull she nodded her head eagerly. Although she continued to moan and sob, she was otherwise motionless. Gripping the knife with one hand and holding her head with the other, I carefully poked the tip of the blade against the material which covered her mouth. A small slit roughly an inch long developed between her lips. As I tossed the blade on the floor beside the roll of Saran Wrap, I watched the plastic heave inward and outward with each labored breath she took. Her muffled sobs only added to the excitement of it all.

Fuck yeah.

This is the good shit.

This not being my first time at doing this, I knew *for the most part* what to expect. All people are different, and each one will react differently to the same situations. I did know the small slit would allow her to take in enough oxygen to survive, but her attempts to breathe with an elevated heart rate while I fucked her senseless wouldn't be easy. Probably similar to running a full out one hundred yard race with your mouth covered and one nostril plugged, she'd be convinced each breath would be her last. In the end, she'd realize she was far more resilient than she originally thought.

As I stood and unbuckled my belt, I felt my cock rapidly rising against the fabric of my jeans. Prior to seeing combat, the mere *mention* of sex made me hard as a rock. After the war, the thought of simply having sex no longer made my cock hard; regardless of whom my potential partner may be. As past-war fate would have it, the notion of tying someone to a bed and fucking them into a whimpering pile of flesh excited me greatly. Additionally, the thought of a blowjob no longer aroused me. However, grabbing a woman's skull firmly in my hands and face fucking her until the eyeliner ran down her cheeks provided me tremendous satisfaction.

I suppose in the eyes of many, I had become a casualty of war. I, on the other hand, looked at it as a blessing. I no longer had the luxury of even being able to muster a stiffy if the anticipated sex was going to be mundane or simple. For me it was a gift; God's way of weeding out the few who may be unwilling; or women who were satisfied by simplistic sex. If there was a drawback, it was that I was always seeking someone who was able to withstand my sexual punishment. My definition of *rough sex* as compared to the opinion of the women I had fucked was in clear contrast.

As a result of my past problems with women and their inevitable gasps of, *oh my God, you're an animal,* I made it a point to explain in great detail what it was I expected, wished for, and intended to do; sexually speaking. If someone wasn't willing, neither was I. If women weren't absolutely eager to attempt to out-fuck me, I never felt it was my job to convince them to do so. A person needed not only to be willing, but eager. Somewhere in the mix, I always made it clear early on that I wasn't into kissing. Kissing, as far as I was concerned, was the definition of intimacy, and intimate I was not. At least not to the women I was fucking.

Lastly, I made it crystal fucking clear there was no possibility of a future relationship. I didn't doubt *my* ability to be faithful to a woman; in fact I knew I was more than able to do so. However, I was quite uncertain of my capacity to be faithful to a *typical* woman. At some point in time, boredom would surely set in. For me, adventurous sex was a must; and nothing was more satisfying - long term - than the thought of wild sex with countless willing women.

"If you keep breathing like that, you're going to pass the fuck out," I said as I reached down and grabbed her bound wrists in my hand.

As I lifted her to her feet by her wrists, she struggled and groaned against the unforgiving food storage wrap which encompassed her head. When she finally stood on her own, I grasped the inside of her hip on the right with my fingers, and placed my left hand against her upper back. As I pushed my lips against the plastic which covered her ear, my warm breath condensed to moisture on the surface.

"Settle the fuck down, you need to pace yourself. Just like we talked," I breathed into her ear as I kicked my jeans to the side and bent her over the bed.

Using my right foot, I swept her feet outward, forcing her to take a wider stance. I was tall at 6'-2", but Sloan's legs were much longer than mine. Standing, her pussy was naturally even with my belly button. Lowering it down to a place where I could pound it into a swollen mound of flesh was crucial to the success of this little romp.

While she grunted and whimpered, I guided my cock between her upper thighs. As I felt the warmth and wetness of her pussy encompass the head of my cock, I shoved her full of every inch of my throbbing shaft. It wasn't my intention to simply fuck her and fuck her hard; I wanted her to feel as if she was going to die from what I was doing to her. I pressed my hand against her back of her plastic wrap covered skull and pushed her face into the comforter as I began to work myself in and out of her pussy without so much as an ounce of mercy.

I watched my cock disappear in and out of her glistening mound repeatedly. The sound of flesh on flesh motivated me to continue until my breathing was labored and I felt weak. Considering my physical conditioning, this was quite an accomplishment. Although I hadn't checked the time, I suspected I had pounded away at her doggy style for no less than fifteen minutes; and not one second of it was slow or sensual. I beat my throbbing cock in and out of her as if my life depended on it. As I finally became conscious of what I was doing, I pushed my cock deep into her and held my hips against her ass cheeks. She arched her back and moaned as I felt myself bottom out.

"You young little bitch. You really thought you could keep up with me? I warned you. Ten inches of cock *real slow* is one thing. Getting your shit beaten to a pulp is another. Now I'm going to fuck you into a coma," I grunted as I held my cock deep inside of her.

I pressed my hand against the back of her head and shoved it deep into the bedding. Again, I pounded my cock inside of her as fast and I was able. My balls steadily slapping against her clit with each stroke began to become hypnotic. A low groan as I tilted my head back and studied the ceiling was confirmation of my deep feeling of satisfaction.

As I continued to force my cock in and out of her dripping wet pussy, I released her head from my grasp and gripped the twelve inches or so of hair draped from underneath the plastic which covered her entire head. As I pounded my swollen shaft in and out of her, the sound of my hips slapping against her ass echoed throughout the sparsely furnished room. I pulled against her hair, forcing her to arch her back and lift her head to an elevation where I could see her face.

She arched her back to relieve the pain, moving her head toward my hand. In response, I pulled her hair downward, forcing her head to the side. As she turned her face upward, I could see the plastic stretched over her mouth was covered in moisture from what were certainly her continued efforts to breathe enough to survive. My continuous pounding of my cock deep into her soaking wet pussy wasn't helping her situation at all. As I stared down at her face, I wished I could clearly see her eyes as I fucked her mercilessly.

"Kind of tough breathing through that little hole, isn't it? My guess is when we're done, you'll decide you don't want to do this again. But that little twat of yours sure loves it. I just love filling you with this big fucking cock," I looked down as I pulled my hips rearward, watching my entire length slide from inside of her.

I slowly thrust my swollen cock inside of her until my balls were against her clit, held it for a moment, and then began pounding away furiously, "And God damn your pussy is fucking *tight*. Too bad your face is covered in plastic."

Her muffled moans provided the fuel for me to continue.

"I'm really diggin' the thought of covering your pretty little mug in cum," I growled as I gazed down at her face.

I shifted my gaze to the cheeks of her well rounded ass and watched my thick cock continue to disappear in and out of her swollen pussy. Although her mind might have been telling her she wasn't enjoying this torturous event, her pussy was conveying an entirely different story. As her juices dripped from my tightening ball sack, I released her hair and slapped the right side of her ass with all my might. I smiled at the red hand shaped welt as it began to rise on her pale skin.

"Fuck yes. That fat little ass of yours loves being slapped," I howled as I raised my hand in the air.

As her knees bent in anticipation, I slapped the side of her ass and shoved my throbbing cock as deep as I could into her pussy. As my balls pressed against her swollen clit, I moved my stinging hand toward her head and grasped her hair in my fingers.

"Something about pulling this black hair of yours keeps my cock stiff. Maybe it's that you can't do a God damned thing about it because your fucking hands are bound," I breathed as I pulled her hair tight, causing her to arch her back again.

She lifted her chest from the bed, and her monstrous dangling tits reminded me of the fun I previously had while titty fucking her. Slowly,

I pulled my cock from her pussy and tugged against her hair. As she twisted her body to the right, I gave my verbal command.

"Roll onto your back. I'm going to titty fuck you while I watch you try to breathe," I groaned.

I pressed my right hand into her left shoulder and forced her to lie on her back. After realizing she was half on the bed and half off, I slid my hands under her armpits and shoved her body onto the bed. Seeing her otherwise very attractive face covered in Saran Wrap was both satisfying and sickening at the same time. As I climbed on top of her torso, I positioned my cock between her tits. Grasping her nipples in my hands roughly, I shoved her tits together, squeezing my cock between them. As I slowly began to fuck her mounds of flesh, I lowered my head and spit between them and onto the shaft of my cock.

"Nothing like a little natural lube," I chuckled as I began to forcefully fuck her chest.

Watching my cock work back and forth between her massive tits was a huge turn on. By itself, it wasn't that big of a deal. Combined with the fact I was able to watch her gasp for breath as I did so made everything much more enjoyable. As the plastic wrap flexed back and forth with each breath she struggled to take, I alternated glances from her face to her tits.

As I felt my cock begin to swell, I knew I'd reached my limit.

Covering her tits in cum didn't seem so appealing, considering all of my options. As I felt myself coming close to climax, I lifted my weight from her chest and thrust my index finger through the small slit in the mouth of her plastic binding. As I tore the hole larger, immediately she gasped for air as if she had just rose from the bottom of the ocean.

"Oh my God…" she gasped through the opening I provided.

I blinked my eyes and looked down at my semi-rigid cock, "You were far from dying. Did you see how hard my fucking cock got? God damn that was hot."

"Untie me," she whimpered through the torn plastic.

I rolled to the edge of the bed and toppled over the end. As I stood on the floor stark naked, I gazed for a short second at her plastic wrapped head and bare body. In realizing the sexual event was over, I began to feel much more compassionate about her requests for being free from her plastic prison.

"I'll be right back, I need to get some scissors. It'll be safer than a knife," I said over my shoulder as I double timed it toward the kitchen.

I grabbed the scissors and ran back into the bedroom. As I stepped to the end of the bed, I reminded her of what we had spoken of earlier, "Lay still and I'll cut this shit off. If you thrash around, you'll end up cut and I don't want that, okay?"

"Hurry," she sighed.

I slid the scissors underneath the plastic, against the back of her head, and lifted them slowly. Without much effort, the bottom blade sliced through the material, freeing her from the translucent confinement. I tossed the scissors aside and carefully pulled the multiple layers away.

"Okay, that was freaking scary," she gasped as I pulled the material away from her face.

"If it wasn't it wouldn't had been such a turn on," I shrugged as I relaxed beside her.

She rolled over on the bed and propped the side of her face against her palm, "It might have been a turn on for you, but for me it wasn't. That shit scared me. I can't believe I wanted to try it."

I narrowed my gaze and studied her pale face. It seemed much whiter than before we started, "Your pussy was dripping wet. It might have scared you, but your subconscious mind loved every minute of it."

I leaned over and hugged her, holding her until she pushed me away. As she pressed her palms against my shoulders, I gazed into her eyes.

"I love it when you screw me Toad. You were screwing me, so I loved it. That whole," she paused and tossed her hand toward the pile of Saran Wrap.

"The uhhm…covering my mouth thing…that was just freaking *scary*," she breathed as she shook her head.

"Well, we can add it to the list of shit *not* to do in the future," I said under my breath.

She rolled her eyes and lifted her head from her hand, "That's for sure. Now that I tried it for you, can we like *date*? Like be *official*?"

I sat up on the bed and stared at her as if she had just slapped me. In some respects, I suppose she had.

"Say again?' I snapped.

"You know, be official? Like exclusive?" she grinned.

I stared at her as if she was out of her mind, "Because you *did this for me*, you think we should be exclusive?"

"Uh huh," she nodded.

I turned my head, rolled my eyes, and stood up. I guess I should have known, regardless of the size of her tits and the fat ass she was packing, she was no different than any of the others. Facing away from her, I pulled on my jeans and buckled my belt. Still having a difficult time believing she could be *that* forgetful over what we had discussed, I glanced over my shoulder in her direction.

I raised one eyebrow in true disbelief, "You're fucking serious?"

She nodded her head eagerly.

"What part of *I won't be in a relationship* didn't you understand? I didn't say I *might*. Or *I'd consider it*. Or *if* you *do something for me* you may convince me, did I? Fuck no, I didn't. I said, and I quote, *there is no chance we will ever be in a relationship. None*. To which you responded, *that's okay*. I asked if you were sure. You said *yes*, " I shook my head as I scanned the floor for my boots.

"I didn't mean to make you mad," she whined.

I shifted my gaze from the floor to where she sat, still naked on the bed, "You didn't. I'm not mad, I'm just done. Get dressed, I'm taking you home."

She scrunched her brow and stared, "What do you mean, done?"

"The *done* kind of done. You know, finished? Like *over*? The *I'm taking your ridiculous ass home* kind of done. Get dressed," I snapped.

"Toad, I'm sorry. I didn't mean to…" she blubbered.

"Sloan look, the last thing I need is some crazy bitch thinking I'm hers. If you're hoping we're going to be exclusive after the speech I gave you a few weeks ago, you're already half way there. I'll save *you* some confusion and *me* a hell of a lot of headaches. I'm done fucking you. And just so we're crystal fucking clear, I'm done fucking you forever. Get dressed," I said as I bent over and picked up my boots.

"Oh my God, like *forever*?" she screeched as she slid her legs over the edge of the bed.

"Roger that. Forever. The *forever* kind," I nodded as I laced up my boots.

"Oh my God Toad, I didn't mean it. I was just kidding," she sniffled.

"Well, I'm not. Get dressed," I said as I leaned over and picked up my knife.

While she cried and complained, she slowly found her clothes and

17

got dressed. Disappointed somewhat at the fact I would no longer be able to explore my sexual desires with Sloan, I found a little humor in knowing more than likely one of the other Sinners would.

I realized through my mental therapy at the Veteran's Administration that a man's feelings become real only when shared. It would stand to reason sharing my sexual escapades with the fellas would make my feelings of satisfaction from fucking her for the last three weeks even more profound.

After hearing details of all of my sexual adventures with Sloan, one of the fellas would surely want to give her a try. Which one it might be would be anyone's guess. Most of the men should be a little more forgiving than I was, and she may even find one who'd put up with her juvenile behavior.

As I held the front door for her, she sniveled and walked past. My patience for her behaving like a sixteen year old high school girl was wearing thin. After standing on the porch and watching her blubber as she stumbled toward the bike, I guess what little sympathy I had for her must have vanished.

"I'm sure one of the other fellas will throw you a little cock," I shrugged as I raised my leg over the seat.

Through the sniffles and sobs, she wiped her face with the back of her hand and gazed my direction. After wiping the final tear from her face, her mouth curled into a half-assed smile.

"You really think so?" she asked in a broken voice.

"Hop on, I'll haul you over to Corn Dog's house right now. The Dog will fuck anything that'll hold still long enough for him to finish," I responded sarcastically.

"I'd really appreciate it," she sighed as she climbed over the rear fender and onto the seat.

Holy shit, bitch. Have a little self-worth.

I reached for the hand controls and started the bike. As the sound of the engine echoed against the garage door and through the neighborhood, I stared along the driveway and realized my thoughts of women and their inability to be sexually adventurous, loyal, *and sane* were accurate.

There was no such thing.

TOAD

"Now I'm not saying this as any means of disrespect to Stacey, you all know this. But good fucking God men, I shouldn't have to remind you of shit like this," Axton paused and stood from his seat.

"If you're sitting at a God damned stop light in the fucking dark, and you see the lights of some cage rolling up behind you, and the son-of-a-bitch is *coming in hot*, run the fucking stop light. Shit, you're on a bike, fellas. There isn't much of anything more nimble or agile than a bike. Run the fucking light, speed into oncoming traffic, ride the bastard into a ditch, but do *something*. Don't sit and stare in your rearview mirror and wonder if that dumb drunk fucker's gonna hit you. Because odds are if it's three o'clock in the morning, and he's driving the fuck around, he's either drunk or stupid," Axton crossed his arms and exchanged glances with most of the men.

A few days earlier, Stacey was at a red light waiting for the left turn signal, and a car rear ended him, killing him instantly. The police declared the driver drunk, and claimed he was traveling at a speed in excess of sixty miles an hour when he hit Stacey's bike. Several times I had been in a similar circumstance, and I had sped through the red light to make distance between my bike and the dip-shit in the car that wasn't paying attention. I believed riding a motorcycle was similar to being in combat; your head must remain on a swivel at all times.

Axton uncrossed his arms and pressed the palms of his hands onto his belt, "As you all might have guessed, the special election was called today to fix this mess in our ranks. I'm the President, so I can't make a motion, but I'll God damned sure entertain one if you make it. I have a Vice Presidency slot open, and a Road Captain spot I need filled. Any of you fucking brain surgeons have an idea of what I should do?"

As far as I was concerned, a man would have to search the entire earth extensively to find a person with as much heart, spirit, and compassion as Axton Bishop. He was as solid of a man as God had ever created. To an outsider, Axton might seem like a heartless prick, but to the select few who knew and understood him, he was truly a man amongst men.

"Well, none of you fuckers will probably agree, but I say we move Otis to Vice President," Pete said under his breath.

"Speak up, Pete. You sound like an indecisive little girl," Axton growled.

Pete fixed his eyes on Axton, narrowed his gaze, and cleared his throat, "I say we move Otis to Vice fucking President, Slice."

"I need a motion," Fancy sighed.

"Son of a fuckin' bitch," Pete rolled his eyes and pulled against his long beard with his right hand.

"I *make a motion* we move Otis to Vice God damned President," he bellowed.

"Second," Mike chimed.

Fancy scribbled onto his note pad and tilted his head slightly, "All in favor?"

The entire room responded, "Aye."

"Opposed?" Fancy asked as he looked down at the pad.

The room fell silent.

Axton raised his hands in the air and shook his head, "Well fuck me running. Thanks fellas. Now I need a God damned Sergeant at Arms *and* a fucking Road Captain. We made zero progress. Why do I have a feeling we're going to be here all God damned day?"

Otis turned to face Axton, "Boss, I'm all for moving into the VP spot, but I can't say I'm real comfortable leaving my position of SAA before I know who's filling it."

Axton lowered his hands and crossed his arms in his signature pose, "I've got to agree with you, Otis. There's a clear problem now with you as Vice President. At least in *my* opinion, there's only one motherfucker who I'd trust to do what needs done in the SAA position. Feel free to correct me if you think I'm wrong, but remember, I can't make a motion or influence your vote. Let me refer to the bylaws in an effort to remind you pricks of the duties of the Sergeant at Arms."

Without a doubt, every man in the club respected Axton. A good percentage of them feared him. Almost all were intimidated by him, and I'd never seen one man clearly oppose him. He reminded me of a Marine Corps Drill Instructor. Intimidating as hell, and never had to demand respect; he earned it through his actions and the respect he gave the men who respected him.

"You can read all that precedes this if you want," Axton hesitated, turned toward the wall, and began to read from the posted bylaws.

"The Sergeant at Arms is responsible for the safety and security of the club, as well as *the protection and defense of all club Members and Prospects*. He shall keep and maintain a record of all data pertinent to the safety and security of the club, its Members and Prospects. Upon becoming aware of any real or perceived threat to the club, its Members, Prospects, or events, he shall immediately notify the Executive Committee of that information," he slowly turned and faced the somewhat somber group.

"Who here is mean enough, tough enough, and has not only the heart, but the *ability* to protect this entire group of men?" Axton raised his eyebrows and waited for a response.

I gazed down at the toes of my boots, feeling somewhat uneasy about Stacey's death, Axton's frustration, and the fact I didn't necessarily trust *my* protection and defense in the hands of anyone except Axton, Otis, or myself.

"I make a motion we move the Marine into the Sergeant at Arms spot, Slice. He's the only one big enough and tough enough to fill the shoes. Well, besides you and Otis," Mike offered.

I glanced upward. Axton shrugged his shoulders in an exaggerated fashion as he shook his head, "Jesus H Christ. I swear to God almighty. I need a fucking *motion* and a God damned *name*. Come on, Mike."

"I make a motion we move Cambini Toad-a-relli or whatever his fucking name is, otherwise known as *Toad*, who's the only fucking Marine in the club to Sergeant at Arms," Mike grunted as he raised his hands into the air.

It's Cambio Todelli, but you were close.

"Can I get a second?" Fancy asked.

It seemed as if the entire room responded, "Second."

Fancy scribbled onto his notepad, "All in favor?"

"Aye!"

I gazed at Axton, who now stood fifteen feet from me with a grin on his face. He rarely smiled, and when he did, there was no hiding the fact he was either amused or extremely satisfied. I hoped his smile was one of sheer satisfaction. I inhaled a shallow breath, lowered my cupped hands along the seams of my jeans, and stood proud as I waited for someone to oppose the motion.

"Opposed?" Fancy asked.

Complete silence.

"Well, I feel better about the welfare of my beloved Sinners. Welcome to the Executive Committee, Toad. Now all we need is a Road Captain," Axton sighed as he extended his hand.

As I gripped his hand in mine, I bit my lower lip slightly and gazed beyond Axton and toward the group. Without a doubt, I'd never let any harm come to the club, the club's welfare, or any of the Members or Prospects. Although I was appreciative and humbled by the motion and the expressed opinion of the club in voting me into the Executive Committee, I didn't dare show it. Being in the club was similar to being in the military or in doing a stint in prison. Showing emotion was a perceived as a sign of weakness. I released my grip on Axton's hand, crossed my arms, and stood stone faced as if I didn't give two fucks about the promotion.

Nothing could have been further from the truth.

I felt as if I was finally where I belonged. Protecting those who were incapable of protecting themselves was what my family had practiced for centuries. I came from a long line of Todelli's who had risked their lives to make sure the incapable or unwilling didn't have to stand up against a potential foe. As a US Marine, I risked my life to protect my brothers and preserve this country. For the club, I would certainly do the same. As any former Marine knows, there are no *former* Marines.

Once a Marine, always a Marine.

TOAD

The tales told by men in a Motorcycle Club are less accurate but far more entertaining than the events inspiring them. Over time, the stories grow, become more interesting, and always develop an ending that's either funny as hell or unbelievably grotesque. I've always believed they started out as the truth, and become polished to perfection over a period of time. Some men are typically more truthful than others; and considering my capacity to digest lies and bullshit, I was close friends with very few of the men in the club. I loved them all as my brothers, but I chose not to befriend each and every one of them. The club decided through the process of being a Prospect who was allowed in, and I determined through my own means and methods who I felt I could *truly* trust. In the end, I had a short list of people I called my friends, and Otis was on the top of the list.

Otis leaned onto the edge of the table and pushed his cup of coffee to the side, "So, you wrapped her head in plastic, fucked her until she was damned near unconscious, shoved your cock down her throat, dumped a load of cum in her gut, and then told her to kick rocks?"

"Yep," I nodded as I tipped the bottom of my coffee cup up, draining the little remaining liquid from the bottom.

"You're such a fucking romantic. Think maybe that was a little harsh?" he asked as he leaned away from the table and into the back of his chair.

27

"Fuck no, it wasn't harsh. She was a childish bitch. She started talking about being *exclusive* as soon as I cut the shit off her head. And I'd already gave her my speech about *all we're doing is having sex,* and she agreed. I fucking swear, finding a good bitch is impossible," I hesitated and leaned into the edge of the table.

"But I did give her dumb ass a ride to Corn Dog's house. Left my place, rode to the Dog's, and dropped her off in the driveway. Fucking bitch waved as she walked up the drive like I was doing her a solid," I chuckled.

Otis picked up his cup of coffee, shook it, and rolled his eyes, "That's some funny shit right there, I can't believe you did that. Well, I really can't believe *she* did it. Heard from the Dog yet?"

I shook my head, "Nope. Not a fucking word."

"Probably still fucking that poor girl. Been five years without pussy, he's got some catching up to do," Otis laughed.

I grinned at the thought of Corn Dog taking five years of frustration out on Sloan. Maybe his personal sexual taste combined with the absence of pussy in his life for the five years he spent in prison would mesh well with Sloan's desire to be filled with biker cock. As I stood from my seat and tossed the empty cup in the trash can, I shook my head and laughed.

"You ready?" I chuckled, still laughing at the thought of Corndog and Sloan.

"Suppose so. Damn this sun feels good," Otis said as he stood.

Sitting outside at the local coffee shop was a guilty pleasure of ours. People walking into the store always admired our bikes, and the more brave souls would often ask questions about the club, our bikes, or our cuts. Spending time watching the customers go in and out provided confirmation of just how fucked up Wichita's east side Starbucks coffee drinking society really was.

I tilted my head toward the bank on the other side of the street. "We're just going right over there. I need to get this shit deposited as soon as they open. You can sit on your bike while I go in if you want."

I had taken the majority of my pay, tax free combat pay, and what little money I hustled from side work and invested roughly half of it into a barbeque joint and two rental houses in Winfield. I purchased the rental houses after bank foreclosure, and got one for $7,500 and the other for $9,000. By my calculations, each should provide between $400 and $500 a month of income. The barbeque business was already established, and it came complete with everything I needed from wait staff to meat smokers. $50,000 wouldn't buy much of anything in a large city, but in a town the size of Winfield, it had potentially purchased my retirement. Income from the restaurant and rentals, combined with what little work I did on custom bike building allowed me to enjoy my days without necessarily having a job.

As we pulled out of the parking lot of the coffee shop and into the street, the light at the corner changed from green to red. As we slowly rolled to a stop at the intersection I tossed my head in the direction of the light above and twisted the throttle. Age and level of maturity always seem to be tossed aside when two men are riding side by side on motorcycles. Otis alternated glances between me and the light as he nodded his head and revved his motor. The sound of the obnoxiously loud exhaust being thrust into the cars behind us would support their thoughts of bikers being obnoxious tattooed pieces of shit. As the light turned green, I released my grip on the clutch and twisted the throttle tight. Two clear advantages I had over Otis were the high performance engine I had built, and the weight of my bike. At nearly nine hundred pounds, I didn't have to worry about the front tire coming up off of the ground under hard acceleration. As the rear tire screeched and the bike lurched forward, I watched in amazement as Otis shot past me as if I were parked.

What the fuck?

After shifting through two more gears at full throttle, I pulled in the clutch, released the throttle, and slowed down to a responsible eighty miles an hour. There was clearly nothing I could do to catch Otis. Like a little boy who had just been beaten handily on his own playground, I slowed the bike down and pulled into the parking lot of the bank; aggravated and ashamed.

"What the fuck, brother?" I complained as my bike rolled to a stop beside Otis.

"New cams," Otis grinned.

"Cams?" I shrugged.

Otis nodded his head.

"When?" I asked.

"Put 'em in last weekend. Surprised you couldn't *hear* the difference. She's got a real *rumpity rump* to her now," he said as he stepped over the seat and stood staring at his bike admiringly.

I flipped the switch on the hand controls and killed the engine. Still pissed off at the quickness of Otis' bike, I leaned over and unlatched the left saddlebag. After stepping off the bike and to the side, I opened the lid and removed my deposit pouch. Generally, I kept a week of earnings at home in a safe, and rode to the bank once a week for deposits into my business account. Gripping the pouch of money in my hand, I turned toward Otis and lightly shook my head.

"Wallow in it for now, you big prick. I'll tear mine down this afternoon, and we'll go at it again. Fucking asshole," I hissed.

"Runs like a beast now. Shit brother, I waited all fucking morning for you to try something. Go ahead, get your cams in, and we'll race for that little bag of money you're carrying," Otis chuckled as he tilted his head my direction.

"Afraid not. I need to get this in the bank. That fucking Junior is eating me into the red. I'm going to have a talk with that mother fucker," I laughed.

"The big black kid?" Otis shrugged.

I nodded my head, "Yeah. My meat cost has gone up almost ten fucking percent. He's either eating ten percent of the meat, or making the meals ten percent larger. Either way, we're going to have a talk."

"Well fuck. Kid probably weighs what, four fifty? I bet he can eat a shit load of barbeque," Otis chuckled.

After I purchased the restaurant, a few of the employees immediately quit. I put up a *Help Wanted* sign on the window and almost instantly a local kid approached me about employment. He had just dropped out of school and was trying to help support his family. He explained his mother was having a difficult time supporting him and his five younger brothers and sisters with no father at home. Although at the time he was only sixteen, I hired him on the spot. He was polite, had a great sense of humor, and seemed very responsible for his age. Initially, a perk of employment was free meals for the employees. Later, due to plummeting profits, the perk changed to *one sandwich* per employee. Now roughly eighteen years old, Junior weighed in excess of four hundred pounds, and it appeared he was eating me into a daily deficit.

"Yeah, he probably weighs four hundred something anyway. So you going in or staying out here in the sun?" I asked.

"I'll sit here if you'll make it quick," Otis responded as he turned toward his bike.

A newer model BMW pulled alongside Otis' bike as I turned to walk across the parking lot and toward the bank. The gorgeous blonde riding passenger caught my immediate attention, and I craned my neck her direction until I reached the sidewalk leading to the entrance. As I slowly shuffled my feet toward the steps, I watched her out of the corner of my eye until she got out of the car. I continued to make a conscious effort to meander to the door slowly, hoping to hold it open for her and the shit hat she was riding with so I could get a better look at her.

I stepped onto the top landing of the steps, reached for the door, and hesitated as I grasped the handle. As they began to walk up the stairs, I pulled the door open and held it for them to enter, looking over my shoulder as I did. She was wearing nice jeans, conservative heels, and a sleeveless silk top that looked like it had a thousand wrinkles in it. He was wearing slacks, a dress shirt, and a jacket three sizes too large. She shifted her gaze to meet mine, smiled, and immediately looked down as if embarrassed. He, on the other hand, focused his nervous eyes on the deposit pouch I held, eventually broke his stare, and forced his mouth to form a half-assed smirk as he looked upward.

I have always seemed to possess an uncanny knack for reading people. She appeared to me to be apprehensive or as if she felt out of place. He seemed nervous and quite anxious. My efforts to make eye contact with him as they walked past me and into the bank were unsuccessful. As soon as he entered the otherwise empty bank, his eyes began to nervously shift back and forth throughout the lobby. He either had a plan and was too damned nervous to implement it, or was assembling one quickly in his mind. Either way, I stood by the door and watched his every move with interest. As he walked into the center of the lobby, she remained at my side; standing beside the door.

A man's physical size may have something to do with his capacity to intimidate other men, but in all honesty, size has very little to do with actual ability. Although I was a good six inches taller than he was, and clearly physically larger and stronger, something about him made *me* nervous. I was in no way intimidated by him or scared, but his nervous behavior was beginning to make me feel more and more uneasy. As my eyes shifted between him and her, his plan became crystal clear.

You've got to be fucking kidding…

"Nobody fucking move; and if anyone pushes a panic button, I'll kill every motherfucker in here!" he screamed as he began waving a pistol at the bank tellers.

Immediately, my military instinct took over. I damned sure wasn't new to fighting, combat, gunfire, or stupid fuckers armed with guns, but I wasn't so self-centered that I didn't realize he was twenty feet from me and armed with a pistol while I had nothing more than a knife and a pouch full of money. If I could only get him close enough to touch him, I knew I could disarm him before he knew what happened. Having received my black belt in the Marine Corps Martial Arts Program, or MCMAP, I could have remained in the states and been a Marine martial arts instructor. Instead, I opted to go to war. As I studied him and his manner of holding the weapon, he turned my direction and began nervously screaming.

"Toss your deposit bag. Throw it over here, you big fucker…" he stammered as he waved the gun my direction.

If this motherfucker thinks he's going to rob me, he's either going to have to get a dozen more men or a hell of a lot more firepower.

"Throw it on the fucking floor," he demanded as he shifted his gaze back and forth between the bank tellers and me.

Sorry, shit hat. Come and get it.

Nervously, he shifted his eyes to the row of tellers, "Every one of you motherfuckers better get the money out of your drawers *right now*. Put it all in deposit bags, and don't sound an alarm. If a cop comes in here, I'm going to shoot every one of you bitches before he shoots me."

As he quickly turned away from where I stood and faced the tellers, I tilted my head to the side and whispered, "Stay right here by the door. Don't move, understand?"

His female accomplice nervously nodded her head.

While he faced the other direction, I took two steps toward him. As he turned around, he blinked his eyes a few times and once again demanded I drop the money.

"I told you to toss that bag on the floor, big boy," he snarled as he pointed the gun toward me.

Did you just call me a boy?

I figured my best bet was to coerce him to come to me and attempt to *take* the money. All he needed was a little encouragement. I rolled my shoulders forward, stared down at my boots, and tried to appear as small as a six foot tall 190 pound Marine could possibly look. Luckily, I was wearing a tee shirt that did a pretty good job of covering my Marine tattoo.

"Can't do it. I *need* to deposit this money in the bank," I said sheepishly.

Come over here motherfucker, I've got a little trick I want to show you.

"Toss it on the floor," he barked as he motioned to the floor with the barrel of the pistol.

"But it's damned near fifty grand. I really need to deposit it," I lied as I raised my left hand toward my chest in what he would perceive as a fearful posture.

As I had hoped, the claim of fifty grand got his attention. With widened eyes he quickly began walking my direction. As he approached, he held his pistol with his arm extended and elbow locked. Contrary to what was typically shown in movies and television, holding a pistol in this manner is an invitation to have it taken away by anyone with an ounce of training. As he took his last step, the gun was mere inches from my chest. With my left hand raised and my palm outward, I loosened my grip on the bag of money with my right hand and waited. If possible, I needed him to raise the pistol just a little…

"Drop it," he grunted.

I attempted to make my voice seem shaky and nervous. Nothing could have been further from the truth. I enjoyed situations like this and truly missed the adrenaline rush I received from being in combat.

"It's all I…it's all I got…I really…can't…" I mumbled.

He slowly raised the pistol toward my head. In firearm disarmament training, I'd disarmed a man no less than a thousand times in the exact same situation. Taking his weapon would be no different. I released my grip on the deposit bag, and before it hit the floor, I swung my left hand toward the barrel and gripped the slide as my right hand simultaneously swung into his right forearm, just above the wrist. Instantaneously, the pistol snapped out of his hand.

In a move which took a fraction of a second, the pistol swung 180 degrees and was now in my control. Unarmed, and with his mouth wide open, his eyes were filled with a combination of sheer surprise and *oh shit, what just happened*? I raised my right foot and planted a front kick into his left lower hip – bringing my heel down against his upper thigh. He fell to the floor and landed flat on his back.

"Don't fucking move or I'll plaster what little brains you have all over the floor, you fucking idiot," I growled as I pointed the pistol at his head.

I tilted my head toward the tellers as I stepped on his chest.

"I'll hold him here until the cops arrive," I shouted toward the three tellers.

I turned my head slightly toward the woman standing at the front door.

"Come here," I said through my teeth.

As far as anyone in the bank was able to discern, the woman could have entered with either of us. From the time he stepped in the bank and began demanding money, she stood by my side at the door. Additionally, as I had held the door for them to initially enter, it was never clear if she was with me or with him. I wanted to give her an opportunity, a way out, but only if she wanted it. Nervously, she approached. As she got within a few feet of where I stood, I said what little I had to say.

"I'm giving you a way out of this. He'll do a 20 year mandatory minimum in Federal Prison for this stunt. You'll do at least half that much for being with him. Cops will be here in a matter of minutes if not sooner. I'm willing to say you came here with me. You married to him? Or tied to him in any way?" I asked under my breath.

Clearly nervous and shaken up, she shook her head.

"Now, I'm *asking* you, who'd you come here with?" I whispered.

"Uhhm, I uhhm. You?" she stammered as she glanced toward him anxiously.

"Don't look at him; he doesn't have a fucking thing to do with this. He's on film robbing this bank, he's fucked. Now, who'd you come here with? Make a decision *right now*," I whispered.

She swallowed heavily and bit her lip slightly, "You."

"But…" the would be robber whined.

"Shut the fuck up," I grunted as I stepped down on his chest.

"What's your name?" I asked.

"Sydney. Sydney Shephard," she whispered.

"Cops can't tie you to him?" I asked.

She shook her head.

"I'm Toad. You rode here with me from Winfield on the back of that bike out there if anyone asks. Where's your car?" I asked.

"In Old Town. At the Pump House. I seriously just met him," she responded.

"I met you at the Pump House last night, picked you up, and you came home with me on my bike. Understand?"

Tears began to roll down each cheek. She bit her quivering lip and nodded her head.

"Have anything in his fucking car that has your name on it? Anything that'll tie you to him?" I asked quietly.

She raised her purse and shook her head from side-to-side.

"Get outside. Go to the big guy sittin' on the bike. His name's Otis. Walk out to the bike right now, and say these *exact* words. '*Toad told me to tell you to take me to Biscuit's house right now. The Devil looks after his own.*' He'll do it. If the cops show up before you get to the bike, tell them you're with me," I said under my breath.

"Otis take me to Biscuit's house. Devil looks after his own," she stammered.

37

"Good enough," I nodded.

I watched out of the corner of my eye as she pushed the door open and ran toward the parking lot. The entire event, from our walking into the bank until she left took roughly two minutes time. I didn't know much about robbing banks, but I did believe regardless of his demand to the tellers, they would have probably sounded a silent alarm. I exhaled a sigh of relief as I heard the sound of Otis' new cams rumble in the parking lot. As the exhaust note faded away, I wondered if one of the overzealous Wichita cops would shoot me as soon as they entered the bank. Considering the fact I was tall, muscular, holding a weapon, covered in tattoos, and wearing a 1%er cut - and the robber was wearing slacks, a dress shirt, and jacket, I stepped into his chest harshly and pushed the pistol into the waist of my pants.

After picking him up from the floor and placing him in a choke hold, I tossed the pistol toward the front door. It came to a stop a few feet from the threshold. As I stood fifteen feet from the door choking the fucktard who tried to steal my money, I laughed to myself at what the police would think when they learned the Sergeant at Arms for a 1% club stopped a bank robbery in progress.

Ten seconds later, when what appeared to be the entire S.W.A.T. team broke through the front door, I got a good idea of what they were thinking.

"Release the man, take two steps backward and slowly interlock your hands behind your head," the man with the H&K MP-5 pointed at my head barked.

Suddenly I wasn't in the mood to try to explain anything. After tightening my choke hold - bringing shit-for-brains a little closer to unconsciousness - I slowly released him from my grasp and swept his legs out from underneath him with a quick right foot, dropping him to the floor. As soon as his body came to a thud at my feet, I grinned, raised my arms, and interlocked my fingers behind my head.

"The guy on the floor is the one who tried to rob us," the teller shouted.

The immediate look of surprise on the faces of the over-dressed and under trained officers removed what little wonder I had in what they were all thinking.

I can see it in your eyes, asshole. Oh shit, the biker didn't do it?

Considering how much I disliked cops, the fact Otis beat me in a street race, and some brainless thief tried to steal my deposit money, I wasn't in a very pleasant mood. I stared at the cop whose face was covered in disbelief, and I couldn't help myself.

"Sorry fellas, at least this time, the biker didn't do it," I chuckled.

TOAD

As I pulled the bike into the driveway, Otis, Biscuit, and Sydney were all standing by Otis' and Biscuit's motorcycles staring out at the street. Two hours of questions, interviews, and a short spot on the local news was a little more than I had planned or was prepared for. Luckily, the city cops were the only law enforcement who showed up, and I didn't have to argue with or talk to the Fed's. City cops are typically so poorly trained and out of touch with real world reality that bullshitting one of them goes unnoticed by even their best trained idiots.

"I expected you'd be here an hour and a half ago," Otis shrugged as I pulled alongside the parked bikes.

"See me on the news?" I laughed as I stepped off my bike.

"Seriously?" Otis chuckled.

"Afraid so. Did a pretty long interview. Fuckers asked me to take my cut off. Can you fucking believe that? She asked if I'd interview in my shirt. I fucking laughed. Told the little bitch *listen up, a Sinner stopped this robbery, and a Sinner is who you'll interview*. She finally agreed. I thought it was fucking hilarious," I hesitated and reached toward Biscuit with my right hand.

"How's it hangin' Biscuit?" I asked as I shook his hand and patted him on the back.

"Ain't nothin' goin' on here but the rent, brother. That and harborin' fugitives," he chuckled.

41

"You were the closest Sinner I could think of," I nodded, "Appreciate ya, brother."

Biscuit released my hand, leaned back, crossed his arms and grinned, "The life of a Sinner, it's always interesting if nothin' else. So, we heard *her* side of it, let's hear what *really* happened. She said you whipped some of your martial arts bullshit out, took the fuckers piece, and karate kicked his ass to the floor. Sounded like she was watching the entire show through rose colored glasses."

Although Otis knew she had ridden to the bank with the guy in the BMW, he wouldn't necessarily know *he* was the one who was robbing the bank, unless Sydney had told him. Otis had no way of knowing how many people were inside before we arrived. If for some reason she had told Otis, Otis wouldn't have said anything to Biscuit without talking to me about it first. One thing I admired and appreciated about the club was that a man's business was just that, *his* business. The shit talking and storytelling about any activities aside from what was common knowledge didn't exist. I decided to tell *my* version of the story, leaving out a few minor details, but being cautious not to actually lie.

"Well, I walked into the bank to deposit my hard earned money, and some cock sucker decided to try and rob the motherfucker before I had a chance to get out of there," I hesitated and exchanged glances between Sydney and Otis.

No reaction so far.

"So this fucker starts screaming and waving his Ruger 9 millimeter around like he's gonna get the money and head out without any problems. I acted like I was scared and convinced him to come try and *take* my money. When he got close enough that I could reach him, I grabbed his weapon and pushed his ass on the floor. Pretty simple stuff," I shrugged.

As I spoke, Otis stood without much expression. Sydney, on the other hand, seemed somewhat nervous at first but calmed down as I finished speaking.

"It ain't every motherfucker who's gonna take a man's piece when he's tryin' to rob a bank. You act like it's no big deal. You're a wacked out war hero. I like her version better," Biscuit chuckled.

Otis raised his hands and began rubbing his head, "So what about the cops and the news? Slice's gonna *love* the news coverage."

I was pleased with the fact Sydney hadn't spoken so far. Not that I wanted to try and bullshit my club brothers, but the fewer people who realized what *really* happened, the better. A handful of people knowing something like this was a handful too many.

"Cops questioned me for an hour or so. Fuckers couldn't believe I disarmed him. One of 'em was a real prick, the senior officer. He acted like it couldn't have gone down like that, even after the tellers told him how it happened. Finally, I told the cocksucker to pull his piece and I'd take it from his ass too. So anyway, the news showed up; it was the little brown haired girl from the ten o'clock news on channel 10. They originally came to interview the tellers, but when they found out a civilian stopped the robbery, they decided the Toad man was a better story," I shrugged.

"What'd you tell 'em?" Biscuit asked.

"Same fucking thing I told you. Kept it simple," I grinned.

"So how the fuck's she fit in?" Biscuit asked as he tilted his head toward Sydney.

I decided to answer in an abbreviated version of the truth, and see what everyone's response was.

I shifted my gaze toward Sydney and maintained my focus as I answered, "Well, she was scared and I really couldn't see her sticking around for the cops to harass. I told her to hop on with the big O and get a ride out of there before the fucking cops showed up."

Biscuit crossed his arms, studied Sydney for a long second, and lifted his chin slightly, "So, what now? Should we kill her or fuck her first, and then kill her?"

Biscuit was the most serious practical joker in the club. He was a master of keeping a straight face while telling a joke or bullshitting someone. Until the very end of a story, you never knew if what he was telling you was the truth or a lie. He was an honest man and could be trusted one hundred percent, but he got great satisfaction out of bullshitting people just to get a reaction out of them. As soon as he spoke, *I* knew he was joking, but I waited anxiously to see how Sydney responded. Keeping an expressionless face was difficult, but I didn't have to do it for long before she reacted.

"Definitely fuck me first. Hell, maybe gang bang me right here in the driveway before you cut my throat, huh? And just to forewarn you, you may want to get a warm washcloth and a little soap, I haven't cleaned my twat in a few weeks," she responded in a serious tone.

Damn, she's got a little guts.

Although Biscuit tried, he couldn't keep himself from laughing for long. Within a few seconds of silence from Otis and me, he erupted in laughter.

"There's no bullshittin' you, is there?" he chuckled.

She shook her head from side-to-side as she rolled her eyes, "You've got no reason to kill me, I don't put your club at risk. If anything, I provide corroboration to Toad's story."

Otis glanced in my direction and raised his eyebrows comically.

Biscuit uncrossed his arms and hooked his thumbs into the front pockets of his jeans.

"Keep using words like that and I just *might* cut your throat. You sound like a fucking cop, sayin' shit like *corroboration*. You a cop, little girl?" Biscuit grunted.

"Far from it. Right now I'm a jobless, homeless, hopeless, penniless bitch that needs a ride to my car. And this isn't my first time around 1%ers. My brother's in an outlaw club, *Hell's Fury*. Is, was, whatever. He's doing life in Big Sandy now," she snapped.

Damn, no wonder she kept her mouth shut.

Biscuit widened his eyes, crossed his arms, and took one step back as he studied Sydney, "Hell's Fury, huh? Don't think I won't check him out. I know a few of those fellas in the Fury's Colorado Springs Chapter. What's his name?"

"Jackson Shephard, same last name as mine. Road name was *Killer*. Just Google him. If you all remember the ATF infiltration of the Fury and the conspiracy to commit murder charges, well that was him. And if you want to read the piece of shit, they wrote a book about it," she explained.

"I remember it. Fuck, *everyone* remembers it. Chicken-shit undercover ATF agent rode with 'em for a few years, got patched in and everything, and then tried to set the club up on murder charges. When they couldn't get 'em to kill anyone, they made up some bullshit about a contract killing for another 1%er club and railroaded a few guys. And fuck, Big Sandy's no joke. That's a shit-hole penitentiary, even for the Fed's. Tough time to do, right there," Otis nodded.

"You got it. Undercover ATF agent fucked them over big time. Set my brother up like a bowling pin. Since they shipped him to Big Sandy, he won't even let me visit, but that's a whole different story," she sighed.

Biscuit took one more step rearward and narrowed his eyes. After a long pause, he began to speak, "So, lemme ask you a question. If you're homeless, jobless, penniless, and what else did you say? *Hopeless*? If you're all that, what the fuck were you doing in a fucking bank of all places?"

"I was going to rob it, but the other fucker beat me to it," she responded without expression.

Biscuit glanced in my direction.

I shrugged my shoulders and grinned.

"You truly homeless?" I asked.

She rolled her eyes and nodded her head, "Somewhat ashamed of it, but yes I am."

After her confirmation, it appeared no one really knew how to respond to her. As the three of us stood and stared, she broke the long silence, "See this top? Doesn't it look like I dug it out of the dirty clothes? Know why? Because everything I own is in the back seat or trunk of my car. I live out of it; have been for about a month. Now I'm down to no money and only a little bit of gas. Hopefully I'll find a job in the next week or so."

As I considered what to say, Otis and Biscuit both reached for their wallets at the same time. She turned her hand up and shook her head.

"Sorry, fellas. I don't take handouts. Call me whatever you want including stupid, but I can't do it. I'll die first. I work for my money. I just need to find a job," she said in a voice full of emotion.

"Do you use dope?" I asked.

She shook her head, "Never have."

"Liar, thief, cheat, or anything of the like?"

"Nope, I've never stolen anything in my life. And I don't lie *or* cheat. I'm actually a great person who was dealt a shit card in life," she responded.

I crossed my arms and examined her. Other than the fact her top was covered in too many wrinkles to count, nothing about her really bothered me. She certainly didn't *appear* homeless. In fact, she was a very well put together woman. The blonde hair hanging well past her shoulders was beautiful and full of body, and although she wore minimal makeup, her skin appeared to be blemish free and healthy.

"Can you wait tables?" I asked.

"Never tried, but I'd be willing to give it a go," she said.

I lowered my chin slightly and uncrossed my arms. As I raised my hand to my chin I grinned slightly, "I tell you what. I can give you a job at my restaurant in Winfield. It's thirty miles from here, but you can start tomorrow if you want. I pay minimum wage plus tips, which is more than most restaurants. Tips aren't much, but with your looks and attitude, you'll probably do well. It's the least I can do for a 1%er who's locked down; or I guess for his sister. Maybe you can put some money on his books; get him some zoo zoos and wham whams."

"I can't make it that far on the gas I've got in the car. If you want to give me a ride by my car and let me grab a few things, and then if you could maybe give me a ride to Winfield, I'll sure start tomorrow," she smiled.

It dawned on me as she spoke that she was actually *homeless*. Not homeless in a broad meaningless sense, but truly without a place to stay. Her car full of personal belongings was all she had. She had no money, no means, and certainly had no possibility of even doing something as simple as bathing. Seeing someone like her in the condition she was in made me angry with society. I wanted to know what happened to cause her to be destitute. Before I had a chance to water down a question and make it seem less invasive, Biscuit beat me to the punch.

Still standing with his wallet in his hand, Biscuit cleared his throat, "So, if I can ask, what happened?"

"You sure can, and I'll tell you. The aircraft plant laid me off. I had a high school education and ten years of experience when they did. I went quite a while looking for another job and couldn't find one because I was pushing 30 years old, and had no experience other than pounding rivets. I couldn't pay my rent, and eventually got evicted. I lived in and out of cheap hotels for almost a year delivering flowers part time, but lost that job when they found out I didn't have a license to drive."

"Son-of-a-bitch, you can't catch a fuckin' break, can ya? What happened there?" Biscuit chuckled.

"I got three parking tickets for leaving my car sitting in one spot too long. Working part time, it got down to either eat or pay my tickets. I chose food." she shrugged.

Everyone on this earth requires money to survive. Unless a person is born into wealth, they must work to obtain the money. Realistically, we all must drive to our place of work. Society dictates we need a license to legally drive a car. At some point, we must park that car. To think Sydney was given a ticket or multiple tickets for parking a car she wasn't able to drive because she couldn't afford to do so, and was then relieved of her license for failure to pay the tickets angered me to no end. Thinking of the rules, regulations, and requirements of society often angered me to a point of being furious. I stared down at my boots for a long second and attempted to collect my thoughts.

"I tell you what," I said as I looked up.

I raised my hands and rubbed my temples with my fingertips, "I've got a little rental house Otis and I have been working on for a while. It didn't cost me shit, and I was going to rent it at the end of the summer when we were done painting and making a few cosmetic repairs. Rent's cheap in Winfield. Probably go for $350 a month. It's a shitty one bedroom in a shitty part of town, and it doesn't have a garage. I understand the pride thing, and not wanting a handout. How about this; pay the rent at the *end* of each month instead of the beginning? You can pay me the rent in four weeks. One catch, you'll be responsible for making the repairs."

Her face lit up like a Christmas tree, "I don't know what the repairs are, but I'll do my best. Seriously?"

I nodded my head as I exchanged glances between her and Otis, "Just minor painting and stuff, and yes, I'm serious."

"Please tell me it has running water," she breathed.

"Sure does. I turned on all of the utilities when Otis and I started doing the work. I gave the city a few hundred bucks for the bills. What I've paid in advance will probably get you to September if you don't run the air conditioner too much, but after that the utilities are on you," I nodded.

"You've got a deal," she smiled, "Holy shit. This is crazy. Oh my God. Are you for real?"

As I nodded my head, Otis and Biscuit both grinned. What satisfaction they received was not from my helping her. They, I imagined, were more concerned with the fact her 1%er brother was doing life in a federal penitentiary for some bullshit charge fabricated by a lying undercover ATF agent. In their minds, helping her was helping him, or as close as they could come to doing so. The legal case she spoke of received a lot of attention by 1%er clubs all over the nation. In fact, the Selected Sinners modified their bylaws as a result. When the ATF agent co-wrote a book about his experiences in infiltrating the club, further lining his pockets with money, it sickened each and every one of us even more.

For me, it was a little different. I wasn't necessarily *helping* her in my mind, I was *saving* her. And, saving her was something I felt I *had* to do. I didn't have a choice. This wasn't the first time something like this had happened. Giving Junior the job at the restaurant was a similar circumstance, at least according to my psychiatrist at the Veteran's Administration.

A facet of my Post Traumatic Stress Disorder was a severe case of Survivor's Guilt. Until I was diagnosed with PTSD, I believed I should not have lived when so many Marines in my battalion died. I often wondered what I could have done differently, and questioned if I had made other choices, whether or not some of the dead would have survived. In short, I felt guilty - subconsciously - for surviving when so many other Marines did not. The human mind provides its own therapy in receiving satisfaction from *saving* others from a traumatic situation. Saving a life *now*, in a sense, for the ones I couldn't save in the past.

Impossible for me to totally understand, my PTSD caused me to lack compassion in some areas, and be far more understanding and sympathetic in others. I realized I couldn't save the world, nor did I wish to. For some reason I had attached myself to *certain* people and their needs, feeling tremendous guilt if I didn't step forth and extend my hand to pull them from whatever it was they were drowning in.

Sydney, for some reason, was one of those people.

TOAD

The tone of Axton's voice didn't have to change, the look in his eyes told the entire story. We had been arguing about the concept of good versus evil for nearly twenty minutes. He was clearly aggravated and so was I. As he pushed himself away from the table and maintained eye contact, he raised his hands to his face, tilted his chair back on the rear legs, and spoke.

"Stop being so fucking philosophical, Toad. Answer this, would you kill a man if he crossed you? Let's say if he really, really did you or your family wrong?"

I pushed against the edge of the table, sliding my chair back a few feet, "You know I would."

Axton gripped the edge of the table in his hands and flexed his forearms, "So let me ask you this, how can you say you stand up for all of what is good if you'd kill a man for simply doing something *you* perceive as wrong?"

I crossed my arms in front of my chest and exhaled. I shifted my gaze to meet Axton's, inhaled a shallow breath, and responded, "Because it's in defense of or in support of what's good. I wouldn't kill someone for the sake of simply killing them, Slice. I'm not a cold-blooded fucking killer. That's my point. They'd have to be a really bad person or be doing something pretty fucked up."

Axton shook his head and stood from his seat, "I think that's the

51

Marine in you, Toad. You've been reprogrammed to think because of your abilities that you're *required* to stand up against evil. Society might see it as good *or bad*, but you don't give two fucks. If *you* see it as bad, you're going to stand up and speak your mind. If it requires physical intervention, you'll intervene. If it requires killing a motherfucker, you'll do it. I guess I'm damned near done arguing about it, but my point is this. Just because *you* believe it to be right doesn't make it right. You're a good man, Toad. Make no mistake about it. But you do, you've done, and you'll continue to do what's evil when you feel it's necessary."

I looked up at Axton for a moment, and eventually stood. Having him stand over me made me nervous. The conversation began over discussing the bank robbery, and my interview with the news media. After the editing of the interview, several of my long responses were cut down into a few short remarks. One of the longer statements ended up edited to nothing, with my stating, *I stand up against evil.* The original question was regarding the MC, and my statement in whole was, *although I'm in an Outlaw Motorcycle Club, I'm not a criminal. A common misconception is that men in Outlaw clubs are criminals, and we are not. I've always made an effort to stand up against evil.* The woman interviewing me said, *so you stand up against evil?* And I responded, yes *I stand up against evil.* The changes they made to the interview took what I said out of context, and the entire thing, including Axton's questioning me, was beginning to irritate me. Now somewhat frustrated and standing across the table from Axton, I crossed my arms, mimicking how he was standing.

"A man's *abilities* do not define who he is. His choices, and the application of those abilities, however, do. Life is not only about the choices we make, but *why* we make them. If a man commits an act

52

and it is perceived by the masses as evil, but it is done to support all of what is good, or it was administered with good intention, the man *and the act* are good," I uncrossed my arms and rubbed my palms together, convinced I'd made my point.

"All evil acts aren't preceded by a conscious thought of evil, Toad," Axton sighed.

"What are you saying?" I shrugged.

Axton turned his palms up and shook his head, "I just fucking said it, Socrates."

I stood silently and continued to glare Axton's direction.

Axton exhaled loudly and rolled his eyes, "Some people commit acts of evil without *thinking* the act is evil. Or, they don't consciously believe they're preparing to commit evil before they act. That doesn't necessarily make the act just or right."

"I'm done arguing about this," I said as I turned away.

"I was done a long fucking time ago," I heard Axton chuckle.

"Where the fuck are you going?" he asked.

"Out to the shop," I said over my shoulder.

"Don't get all butt hurt, Toad. I wasn't attacking *you*," Axton said.

I continued to walk toward the door, opened it, and hesitated.

"So let me ask *you* a question, Slice. If a man crossed you, or let's say really, really did Avery wrong, would *you* kill him?" I asked under my breath.

"Without even thinking about it," he replied.

I released the door handle and turned to face him, "So why are you crawling all over me for having the same reaction?"

Axton reached behind his head with both hands, placed his fingers against the base of his skull, took a deep breath, flexed his biceps, and exhaled.

"Because I *know* I'm evil, Toad. I'm pretty fucking certain if there's a heaven and a hell when we're all done here, I'm going to the place with the warm climate. And I'm not the man stopping bank robberies, being interviewed by the news, and saying I stand up against evil. Hell, you walk around this motherfucker all the God damned time making reference to the Bible. And unless I'm going completely crazy, that night you got your patch - when we killed the child molester - you cited the Bible chapter and verse to that prick before you killed him."

I stood staring his direction blankly as I considered what he said. In actuality, he wasn't worried about me being who I was or believing what I believed, but he damned sure wasn't pleased about my news interview while wearing my Sinner's cut. To be honest, I wasn't either.

"You pissed off about the news segment?" I asked.

"Can't say I'm real happy about it, Toad," he sighed.

I stared down at my boots and thought about what had happened and how it may have an affect on the club. Before I had a chance to speak, Axton began to walk my direction. Without turning and facing the bylaws, he began to speak from memory.

"The Sergeant at Arms is responsible for the safety and security of the club, as well as the protection and defense of all club Members and Prospects. Upon becoming aware of any real or perceived threat to the club, its Members, Prospects, or events, he shall immediately notify the Executive Committee of that information," he paused and smiled his shitty little smile.

I smiled in return.

"Toad, you're on the Executive Committee now. Be as nice or as fucking evil as you feel you need to be. Personally, I wish it was me who would have taken the gun from that shithead in the bank. Hell, I'd have probably shot the prick just to save taxpayers a little money. More than likely would have taken the homeless girl home too. But what I wouldn't have done was agree to do that *fucking interview*. They never put them on the news the way they're recorded. Always think of the best interest of the club," he said as he extended his hand.

As I reached for his hand, he pulled me through the doorway and slapped me on the back, "You're a good man, Toad. I'm proud to have you as my Sergeant at Arms, I really am. Consider the club first in all you do."

"Aye aye, sir," I said, using the Marine acknowledgement that an order had been received, was understood, and would be carried out.

"Carry on," Axton said as he released my hand.

"Sorry boss," I sighed.

"No apology needed," Axton replied.

I turned and walked into the shop as Axton quietly followed. Unlike many of the other Sinners who continuously spoke until interrupted, Axton was a master of knowing when to speak, what to say, and when to be silent. I stopped a few feet from my bike, placed my hands on my hips, and stared. After what seemed like an eternity of silence, I looked over my left shoulder toward Axton.

"I'm thinking the interview with the news was me being a little selfish. You know, wanting the recognition and such. I'm not using this as an excuse, but I'm thinking it might be part of my PTSD; the Survivor's Guilt. I think I thought if the entire city believed I saved those people at the bank from harm, then maybe that would have made up for all the Marines my battalion lost in Afghanistan. Either way, it doesn't matter now. I'll talk to my shrink at the VA on Friday when I go to mental health," I said.

After a short pause, Axton pushed his hands into his front pockets, nodded his head slowly, and spoke.

"I've never been in the military or fought in a war, nor am I trained medical professional," he paused as he chuckled slightly.

"But in my opinion, and it's only that, an opinion..." he slowly walked over to his bike and leaned against the seat.

He pulled his hands from his pockets and rubbed them along the thighs of his jeans, "You're a good man, a damned fine one to be honest. Part of the problem is you're too damned good, raised by good Italian parents in the Catholic church. You grew up believing your understanding of God's will. You went to war, just like your father, grandfather, and your great-grandfather. And now you struggle with what happened and the lives of your Marine brothers that were lost. You wonder why you didn't die instead. You wonder what you could have done differently. Now you live your life trying to make up for what happened as if it was your fault, or you had some control over it. I've got news for you, it wasn't and you don't. Let me ask you something. You don't have to answer, and I know this is a sensitive subject, but tell me this if you can; were any of the Marines in your battalion who died on your immediate left or immediate right? You know, within an arm's reach?"

I didn't really have to think for very long to answer. It seemed odd talking to Axton about this type of thing, but I felt strangely comfortable, "No. Not so much. They were close, but not *that* close."

"So moving one way or another you couldn't have made a difference by taking a bullet for them or anything like that?"

I crossed my arms and I shook my head.

"Well then, what happened to them was *God's* will. Not yours,

God's. And for you to think you had or have some control over what happened is to think you're God. I got news for you Toad. You're one solid motherfucker, but you're not God," he said as he stood.

He took the few steps which separated us and slid his hands back into the pockets of his jeans, "I think your struggle is with God. In the civilian world, you continue to do what most perceive as evil. It allows you to think the atrocities of war weren't so evil. It puts things into a different perspective, so to speak; making this life and that life seem similar. If your civilian world was full of butterflies and rainbow barfin' unicorns, you'd clearly see the complete contrast between life and war. But, if your life resembles war, there is no contrast. Not much anyway. So, considering your upbringing and your relationship with God, you struggle. You *know* the difference between right and wrong. Do you regret being a Marine?"

"Fuck no," I snapped.

"Marines kill, Toad. And Marines die. It's what they do. Stop trying to make peace with God for something he's already accepted as being part of his master plan. He's moved on to hurricanes, earthquakes, that crazy prick in North Korea, and making sure those flowers Avery planted at my house don't die. He's over it. Now it's your turn," he pulled his hands from his pockets and stretched his arms wide.

One thing I never expected from another man until I was in the MC was to be hugged. I learned in my introduction to the club as a *Hang Around*, and later as a *Prospect* that all of the members hugged each other. It seemed strange seeing it at the time, but now it was common practice for me. It was part of the brotherhood, the bond, and a means of expressing our closeness to each other. As he slapped me on the back, he exhaled and spoke in a low tone.

"God, Country, Corps, Family, and Self. In that order," he breathed.

I broke the embrace and stared, "Where'd you hear that?"

"Read it on the internet, along with all the other shit we just discussed. I want you to get better, so I've been researching. You're the Sergeant at Arms for this club Toad, I want you at your absolute best," he responded.

As I studied Axton in an odd admiration, I realized in spite of his attitude, rough exterior, and harsh way of making himself clear, he did almost everything for one reason and one reason only.

The betterment of the club.

And it was time I do the same.

SYDNEY

"Peanut butter, bread, 2 dozen eggs, and toothpaste. Is that going to be it for you?" the sixty-year-old cashier asked as she carefully placed the groceries in a bag.

"Yes ma'am," I smiled.

Inside my head, a song was playing. Not one from the radio, but one my brain had just made up in celebration of earning my tips. *I can pay for my own groceries. I can pay for my own groceries.* I grinned as the words continued to repeat themselves.

She looked over the top of her glasses toward the register, "That'll be $13.20."

Watch this. I'm going to reach in my purse and grab money.

My money.

I pulled my wallet from my purse and thumbed through the bills as if I were looking for something small enough to give her. In actuality, I was looking for a $20 dollar bill, and I knew I only had one. The remaining $1's and $5's littering my wallet made me look *and feel* as if I was on top of the world.

In all respects, I was.

"Here," I said as I pulled the $20 bill from my wallet.

"Are you new in town, Hun? I haven't seen you in here before," she asked as she accepted the money.

"Yes ma'am. I just moved here a week or so ago. I couldn't find a

59

job in Wichita, and was offered one here at a restaurant. So, here I am. I'm Sydney," I smiled.

"I'm Gladys. Well, it's nice to have you come in. We try to keep our prices down, but I can't get as cheap as those places in Wichita. But we're sure convenient," she said as she opened the register.

As she handed me the change, she smiled, "So, which restaurant are you working at?"

"Randy's Rib Shack," I responded.

She raised her hand to her mouth and leaned over the counter as if telling me a secret, "Randy doesn't own it anymore. Some hoodlum bought it, but he kept the name."

I wanted to shove the groceries to the floor and tell her to fuck off. Having grown up in a small town, I knew small towns were generally filled with people who had far less exposure than larger cities. The lack of experience with various races, religions, beliefs, and cultures caused many people in small cities to turn their noses up at anyone who even *appeared* to be different. As much as I wanted to scream, in my opinion it was always better to educate than argue. I swallowed heavily, tapped my toe on the floor lightly, and smiled.

"I certainly didn't see him as that. He was very kind to me. I was unemployed and homeless. He offered me a job, gave me a ride here from Wichita and offered me one of his rental properties for free, or at least until I could pay him," I said as I reached for the bag of groceries.

She covered her mouth with her hand as her eyes widened, "You don't say?"

No, actually I just did.

I smiled and nodded my head, "He was very sweet."

She lowered her hand from her mouth tilted her head slightly, "Well,

60

George said he rode motorcycles with that group of hoodlums down south. There's a bunch of 'em over there at that old warehouse Torn Mattern used to own, and they all look dirty."

I shrugged my shoulders, "I have no idea. All I know is he was very nice to me, and he was far from dirty. Actually, he was clean cut, and had a military haircut. Oh, and I caught a glimpse of a Marine tattoo on his arm, so I asked him about it. It seems he's fought in the war for this country, they awarded him a few medals for bravery as well."

She leaned back and scrunched her brow slightly, "You don't say. Well, George was a Marine. Those guys are as thick as thieves, you know. I'll have to pass the word. Well, Sydney, it was nice talking to you."

"Likewise," I smiled.

After I walked the three blocks home, I used *my* peanut butter, *my* bread, *my* knife, and *my* plate to make the best peanut butter sandwich I'd ever eaten. After I finished eating, I took a shower, brushed my teeth, and relaxed on the bed I was so graciously provided by one of the Sinners. As I stared up at the ceiling and waited for the sleep fairy to take me away, I thanked God.

For hoodlums like Toad.

TOAD

I had been sitting on my bike outside the back door of the restaurant waiting for the lunch rush to end. Junior and I had a long talk about his eating habits, and as a result I had changed the rules for all employees. The new allowance was one sandwich of their choice, one side dish, and as much as they wanted to drink per 8 hour shift, free. I had my doubts about Junior adhering to the rules, and I wanted to catch him in the act of eating lunch. Generally he ate lunch around 1:30, and I hoped to stop in and find him eating. If I didn't get to the bottom of my steadily increasing meat costs, I was going to go out of business.

I raised my leg over the back of the bike, locked the ignition, and walked to the back door. I gripped the door handle lightly, held it in my hand and pressed my ear against the door. The faint sound of whistling was all I heard. Just as I had hoped, Junior was either eating or cleaning the kitchen. I twisted the handle and yanked the door open.

Junior turned to face me, his eyes opened to an almost comical width, and his mouth agape. In front of him on the prep table sat a plate of various meats stacked ten or twelve inches high. Beside the meat was what appeared to be the upper and lower portion of the bun we used to make sandwiches. My experience in the few years I had owned the restaurant told me the plate of meat probably weighed three pounds. Our typical small sandwich was to include 4 ounces of meat, and the large 6 ounces. This wasn't a sandwich or a meal, it was a family feast.

63

"Gorgeous day, Junior. What's going on?" I asked as I stepped into the kitchen.

"Just cleaned the kitchen and I's going to eat me some lunch, Mr. Toad. Worked me up a powerful hunger, we was busier'n a bunch of bees at lunchtime," he grinned.

I stepped a little closer. As I glanced at the plate and inventoried the meat, Junior walked over and picked up the plate, whistling the entire time.

"Do you remember our talk about the eating? How it was dipping into profits?" I asked.

He nodded his head as he reached for the plate, "Yes sir, Mr. Toad. I remember it clear as a bell."

I shook my head and tried not to laugh, "Well, if you remember it clear, why don't you explain to me what you're eating for lunch?"

He looked down at the plate he held, twisted it and tilted it as if looking to make sure he was holding what he'd prepared. As he glanced upward, he smiled, "A sandwich, Mr. Toad."

I rolled my eyes, "That's a *sandwich*?"

"Sure nuff is, Mr. Toad," he grinned.

Although I tried not to, I chuckled slightly, "Junior, that's *not* a sandwich. A sandwich is two pieces of bread with meat in the middle."

He looked down at the plate for a long second. As he shifted his gaze to meet mine, he widened his eyes, "Zactly what we got right here, Mr. Toad. It's sure nuff two pieces of bread and some meat. I can't get it in the middle like you say, 'cause the dag nabbed thing always falls over. It's tough to stack it up that high without droppin' it on the floor."

"Junior, if you stacked that meat up on the bun, it'd be three fucking feet high," I shrugged.

He nodded his head, "That's zactly what I'm sayin' Mr. Toad. A three footer'd fall over fo sho. So, I's using the brain God give me to lay it down flat so we don't have us a meat wreck."

It was all I could do to keep from laughing. "A meat wreck?"

"Yessir, Mr. Toad. That's when she all falls over on the floor. *A meat wreck*. It's just like a train wreck, but with meat. So to keep from havin' em, I flatten my sandwich out," he explained as he waved his hand over the plate.

Still standing beside the prep table with the plate in his hands, Junior stood and grinned. I motioned toward his plate with my right hand, "What all's on that plate Junior? Just what have you got there?"

He looked down at the plate and recited every type of meat we sold, "There a little bit of the pulled pork, some sliced brisket, some chopped brisket ends, a slice or two of that brown sugar smoked ham, a little chicken, got me a couple slices of turkey, and some of them ribs. Oh, and there's a few of them hot links down there, but they's hidin' under the rest. And the bun. The bun makes it a sandwich, Mr. Toad."

Junior appeared to have gained twenty pounds since I'd seen him a week prior. Easily pushing four hundred plus pounds, he was huge. Without a doubt, at his size he needed to eat considerably more than most to simply stay alive. I shook my head and smiled, "Looks like a fine sandwich Junior, just try to keep it down to one a day. No nibbling on the side."

"I'll do me just that. One a day, and no nibblin'. And thank you Mr. Toad, I takes me some pride in my work."

"Well it shows," I chuckled.

I couldn't bear to watch him eat the mess on his plate. I glanced around the spotless kitchen, down at the well cleaned floor, and recalled the condition of the kitchen before I hired Junior. It was a catastrophic mess. If Junior was nothing else, he was prideful and clean.

"Have a good day, Junior. I'm going to go fuck me some bitches," I chuckled.

Junior looked up from his plate as he pulled a stool to the edge of the prep table, "Mr. Toad, my momma says your tallywhacker's gonna fall off if you keep on with those women like you do. Offer she made still stands for goin' to church with us. She says that's the only place for a man to meet a good woman; in the church before God."

"Appreciate it Junior. I'll think on it," I nodded.

"You do that, Mr. Toad," he grinned as he sat down.

As I turned toward the door, I realized I had made zero progress for the day. Slowly I sauntered toward my motorcycle. Although I felt a slight desire to go by and check on Sydney, I decided I really had no right to do so. Having provided a place to stay and a job gave me no privilege to stop in and see her, no matter how much I wanted to. There was something about her attitude, gorgeous looks, and take no bullshit personality that not only intrigued me, but provided me with comfort. It was almost as if I felt spending time with her would allow her gratuitous nature and strong will to rub off on me. Knowing seeing her without an invitation could seem creepy, I began to consider what other options I might have.

Sometimes I felt having nothing I was *required* to do during the day, while most all of the other Sinners worked, was more of a curse than a blessing. As I relaxed into the seat of the bike and turned on the ignition, it dawned on me it was Thursday, and my new cams should be in.

Now I had something to do; modifying my bike, which would hopefully allow me to beat Otis in our next race. As far as I was concerned, nothing was more important than beating Otis. Not only in my eyes, but in the eyes of most of the Sinners, Otis was somewhat of a God. It seemed he was incapable of doing wrong. Although Axton was always willing to listen, sometimes he held a strong opinion and came off as a bigger prick than he really was. Otis, on the other hand, was always reasonable and willing to discuss anything at length with any of the club brothers. He never seemed to lose his cool or come unraveled, regardless of what life tossed his direction.

Hopefully after I got my new cams in my motor, I could change all of that. Nothing would satisfy me more than beating Otis in a race and having him explode with anger. Highly unlikely to happen, but it would prove to me he was just as human as the rest of us.

Either way, I was ready to find out.

SYDNEY

Being placed in foster care at the age of four wasn't something I wished for as a three year old child. Having been shipped around from foster home to foster home and never being adopted caused me to feel unwanted and alone. Eventually, we ended up in a permanent foster home, but I never felt as if we were part of the family, because we weren't adopted. The father a minister, and the mother a codependent housewife, the home was an extremely strict one. Although we weren't the only foster children in the home, we were the youngest.

The biological children of the couple were treated differently, and the foster children were considered outcasts. The father kept the cupboards locked, and I remember always being hungry. The older siblings, be them in foster care or the biological children of the parents, raped the younger children; me included. I didn't tell my brother until we were out of the home and adults - for fear of losing what little family we had. As I grew older and found out I had aunts and uncles who *could* have adopted us - but didn't - the sadness I felt was immeasurable. I remember at the time feeling as if my suspicions of not being wanted by *anyone* were confirmed. As an adult, I became grateful my brother and I were never split up, and I was able to at least grow up with one member of my blood family by my side.

As children, we were as inseparable as two orphaned siblings could be. As adults, we were equally as close, but his involvement in the MC separated us more and more as time passed. Eventually, I saw him less frequently, and came to understand the difference between being without parents and actually being alone. For me, being alone as an early adult was extremely difficult. As a result, I attached myself to any man who would give me the time of day, and always kept my mouth shut for fear of them leaving if I chose to oppose their thoughts, ideas, or principles.

In the end, I had four failed relationships, a tendency to attach myself to abusive males, severe codependency, and daddy issues. If I had an advantage over all of the other fucked up women on this earth, it was that I was knowledgeable of my deficiencies, weaknesses, and patterns of behavior. There is not a day that passes where I don't ask myself the same questions I have since adolescence.

What would be so bad to cause a murder/suicide by our parents?
What did I do wrong?
Why did no one want me?

My brother's absence in my life, and knowing he would never be free from prison caused me a tremendous amount of grief; so I did my best not to think about it. Inevitably, I did have thoughts of his imprisonment, and in a short period of time I was filled with sorrow knowing I would live my entire adult life without a family member by my side. I do believe, considering all things, I am a strong woman and I do a reasonable job of masking my true feelings and faults. Having a sense of humor is the best gift God ever gave me.

"Are these racks big?" he asked.

"Huge," I responded as I extended my outstretched arms.

"How many ribs on a rack?"

"Eight," I responded.

The man questioning me appeared to be in his early sixties. He had explained he was from out of town and was working at the refinery twenty miles away. He had come to the restaurant for *rib night* because racks of ribs were on sale for $10.99. His concern was the *size* of the rack, and more importantly, how many ribs were included.

"Eight? There ain't eight ribs on any cow I ever seen. How can you call eight ribs a *full rack*?" the man complained.

"Yes, eight. The owner raises the cattle outside of town at a special top-secret ranch. They're genetically altered to have eight huge ribs instead of thirteen reasonably sized ones. As long as he continues to breed eight ribbed cattle to eight ribbed cattle, he has an endless supply of racks of ribs that are massive. The only downfall, if you can call it one, is there are only eight ribs to a rack," I said straight faced.

"No shit? Ain't never heard of such a thing. These cows are big ribbed fuckers, are they?" he asked.

I nodded my head and tried to keep from smiling, "Sure are. But something about the genetic alterations makes the meat orange and kind of fishy tasting. We slap enough barbeque sauce on 'em you should never notice though."

He narrowed his gaze and wrinkled his nose as he looked up from the menu, "Fishy tasting?"

"Most say they taste like barbequed Halibut, I don't know. I won't eat 'em personally," I shrugged.

He sat and stared as if he'd just witnessed a train wreck.

"I'm sorry, I couldn't help myself. I was *kidding*. Our rack of ribs includes eight beef ribs. At least *here* that's a rack. And you're right, cows have thirteen ribs, but depending on the butcher, some are left on the shoulder, and the little ribs at the end are cut off and used as riblets. You don't want those little guys anyway," I paused and twisted my mouth to the side.

"I tell you what. It's not *policy*, but I've worked here long enough to take this risk without fear of losing the bet. Order the rack of ribs. If you finish the entire rack, two sides, the Texas Toast, and want more, I'll give you as many as you can eat afterward for free," I shrugged my shoulders and waited.

"But you was kiddin' about the fishy thing, right?" he asked.

I grinned, "I was, I'm sorry."

"Damn, you scared me with that fish deal. Yeah, sounds fair, bring 'em," he grinned as he handed me the menu.

"Sides?" I asked as I pointed along the list of side orders on the menu.

"Beans and slaw," he responded.

I shifted my eyes to the man accompanying him, "And for you?"

"Gimme the same deal?" he chuckled.

I nodded my head, "Beans and slaw?"

"Sounds good," he nodded.

I scribbled down the order and pulled the page from the pad, "You won't be disappointed. Our ribs are huge. I'll have 'em here as soon as they're ready."

Both men smiled and nodded their heads.

Although I had never waited tables when I started, my small amount of experience taught me if I was polite and interacted with my customers, they were appreciative of my personality and humor, and rewarded me in a reasonable tip. The customers themselves were a real pleasure of my work. Either by design or sheer luck, there were never really any problem customers in the establishment, even at the bar. Although I couldn't be certain, I suspected it was because Toad was the owner. He appeared to me to be the type of person a man wouldn't want to cross. As I walked into the kitchen, I grinned toward the other pleasure of my job, Junior.

"Two full. Beans and slaw on each," I said as I pinned the order to the carousel.

"Comin' right up, Miss Sydney," Junior grinned.

In the short period of time I had worked at the restaurant, I had talked to Junior quite a bit. After finding out he grew up in a home with no father, I felt a little closer to him. His mother had raised him, three brothers and sisters, and two other children he called his siblings. In reality, he had three siblings and the other two children, the youngest, were his cousins. All told, there were six children, Junior included. They ranged in age from 6 to 19, Junior being the oldest. I admired the fact he still lived at home and worked for the sole purpose to provide for his family.

"Busy night, huh?" I asked as I grabbed a plate of ribs for another table.

"Sure nuff, Miss Sydney. Busy as a bunch of bees, we are. Makes the time pass real quick like, you know. I like it when we's busy. When we slow down, I get bored after I clean the kitchen. When I'm bored, I want to eat me some of Mr. Toads barbeque. If'n I eat like I used to, Mr. Toad's gonna put that big boot in the middle of my black ass. So busy is good," he chuckled.

"I still haven't had my sandwich for the day, Junior. You can have it later, how's that?" I asked as I pushed my butt against the kitchen door.

"I could sure nuff use it, Miss Sydney. I'm a feelin' faint," he laughed as he raised his hand to his forehead.

I rolled my eyes and pushed my way through the door. As I walked through the dining area and toward the gentleman who had ordered the ribs, I passed the table of the two refinery workers and paused. As I held the plate under his nose, the man's eyes widened.

"Good God. Now *that's* a rack of ribs," he said as he reached for the plate.

I slapped his wrist with my free hand, "Sorry, these aren't yours. I just wanted to show you what you're up against."

"Think I'll manage just fine," he grinned.

After dropping off the ribs, it seemed as if the next thirty minutes or so was nothing but delivering food to tables. Again, I had nothing to compare it to, but it seemed taking orders and delivering food came in completely separate waves. After taking half a dozen orders or so, I would be caught up on orders, and then the delivery would start. After the delivery of food to each of the tables, dropping off the bills came in another wave, and then cleaning the tables. In fractionally more than a week, I felt I had the system down to a sheer science.

I glanced at the table of the two refinery workers. Both men were leaned against their chair backs talking. Each of their plates still had what appeared to be two untouched ribs. A precursory glance around the restaurant produced no one needing a refill on drinks or napkins. I grinned as I walked toward the table.

"So, how many more ribs you want?" I asked as I flopped down in the empty chair.

"Shit. I can't finish these. Biggest fuckin' ribs I ever seen," he moaned.

"Can we get a doggie bag or a box or something?' the second man asked.

"Sorry. We take the uneaten ribs back to the kitchen and serve them up all over again. It helps keeps cost down," I shrugged as I stood.

Both men stared as if in shock.

"Just kidding," I laughed, "Can I get you anything else? Other than a couple boxes, that is?"

"You know," the first man began, "We eat out every damned night. Have for what, John? Ten years?"

The second man nodded his head as he picked his teeth with a toothpick.

"We work turnarounds in the refineries. Have for a decade or so. After work, we eat out. I'm from Texas, but I've eaten in restaurants every fuckin' day for the last ten years. Hell, from Pennsylvania to Wyoming, and from Texas to South Dakota. Anyway…" he paused and narrowed his gaze as he studied my nametag.

"…Sydney. I just want to tell ya, you're the best damned waitress I ever had," he grinned.

I smiled, thanked him, and walked back to the kitchen to get boxes for his ribs. His comment made me feel so good, so excited, that I literally felt as if I was going to vomit. I'd never been so excited or felt so good about doing anything in my life.

I often wished I could have a second chance to live my childhood. There were so many things I wished I could do over. The last few weeks of my life, however, seemed nothing short of perfect. I was beginning to feel as if all of my regrets of yesterday were slowly being washed away by my gratitude for what I was fortunate enough to have today.

After I dropped off the boxes and exchanged a few niceties, I made my rounds cleaning tables. A few trips to the kitchen with dirty dishes, followed by Junior's jokes, and I was back out in the dining area. Sadly, the two refinery workers were gone. Although he said they would be back the next week, I had hoped to say goodbye. As I reached for the bill holder, I noticed the receipt was under the holder, not inside. I picked up the holder and looked down at the credit card receipt. Under the space marked *tip*, he had written the number 0 and placed a line through it. I had learned this was not uncommon for people who left cash for a tip. I opened the bill holder to drop the receipt inside. A crisp one hundred dollar bill was inside with the words, *Best waitress ever. Thanks Sydney,* written across the top.

As I felt my eyes begin to well with tears, I slapped the holder closed and looked around the restaurant at the diminishing crowd. There was no doubt in my mind; I would never spend the $100 bill. I'd frame it for sure. When I started the job at Toad's restaurant, I wondered how long I would last. As time passed, and certainly at that particular moment, I knew one thing for sure.

I was where I belonged.

TOAD

A man's character can almost always be determined by two things: the cleanliness of his belongings, and how he treats animals.

I knelt down and looked at my freshly detailed bike. Not much was more satisfying to me than having my bike free of any road debris, bugs, or water spots. No doubt it would be filthy in another week, but at least for now, it was gorgeous; gorgeous and ready for Otis with a new set of cams. As I admired the black paint and glistening chrome, my mind wandered to thoughts of Sydney.

As much as I wanted to stop by and see her for the last few days, I had fought the urge and refrained from doing so. The sensible side of me told me a girl like her would have very little interest in a man like me. Regardless of her knowledge of bikers, understanding of clubs, and the fact her brother was doing time in the pen for his club, she seemed to me to be a person who wanted more out of life than a good hard fucking.

Generally speaking, I was a good judge of character. Although I would typically look at a woman like her and wish she was different than my opinion or expectation, I found myself looking at Sydney and hoping I was in fact correct in my assumptions. The thought of her being wholesome and basically off limits appealed to me more than the thought of her being otherwise.

If any one thing bothered me about her it was that I found myself thinking differently about her than I was accustomed to. For me, *not* wanting to fuck a woman was something that hadn't happened since childhood. Sydney intrigued me; her homelessness, her attitude, and her savvy personality alone were enough to make me want to know more about her. Her living on the street, in itself, made me want to sit and talk to her about her experiences. My not-so-typical feelings about *not* wanting to have her succumb to my sexual wishes provided even more reason for intrigue. All things considered, I was beginning to feel I was spending more time thinking about Sydney for some reason or another than I spent thinking about anything else.

As I gazed at my bike and fought the urge to ride to her house, the sound of an approaching Harley caused me to stand and peer over my shoulder. Biscuit was coming down the street at a rate of speed well in excess of the speed limit. As I began to wonder if he knew which house was mine, the suspension on his bike compressed as he applied heavy brakes. After releasing the brakes and twisting the throttle one last time, he shot into the driveway between where I was standing and my bike.

"What's shakin', motherfucker? You got any Red Bulls around this camp?" he asked as he flipped the ignition off.

"Don't fuck with the stuff. Sorry, Brother," I shrugged, "What's going on?"

"Quite a bit, got a minute?" he asked as he stepped off the bike.

"I got as much time as you need, Brother Biscuit," I responded as I tossed my polishing rag in my saddlebag.

"Let's go inside," he said as he tossed his head toward the house.

"So what's up?" I asked as I followed a few steps behind his brisk walk.

"Need a beer if you ain't got any Red Bulls. Fucking ATF, FBI, DEA and every other motherfuckin' Fed agency paid me a visit. Oh, and the

US Marshall's were with 'em. Cocksuckers," he huffed as he stepped onto the porch and reached for the door handle.

"What the fuck, are you fucking serious?" I snapped back.

"Sure as fuck am. In the fridge?" he asked as he walked toward the kitchen.

"Grab me one too," I nodded as I sat down at the kitchen table.

As he sat down and handed me a beer, I attempted to resurrect every gun deal I'd been involved in for the last five years, and if there was anything inherently wrong with them. As I mentally struggled to assemble a spreadsheet in my head, Biscuit began to explain his visit.

He tipped up his bottle of beer, drank half the bottle in one swallow and slammed the bottle down on the table, "So I was at the house dicking with my bike in the garage, and about four fucking Suburbans come rolling up. Two of the pricks pull in the drive, and the other two behind the drive. I fucking looked up, and the suits start piling out."

I widened my eyes, took a drink of beer, and gasped, "What the fuck?"

"Precisely what I said, I'm tellin' ya. If there's two motherfuckers I hate, it's people who text and drive, and fucking cops. And there ain't a cop on this earth worse than a fucking Fed. So anyway, I stand up, toss my rag on the seat, and say *how's it hangin' fellas?* One, found out later his name was McCreary, he responds. He says *like a hammer.* Fuck I couldn't believe it. So I ask these pricks as their steadily filing into *my* garage if they're at the right place. Now this is where it got kinda scary. This McCreary fella looks at me as they're all gatherin' around like a bunch of fuckin' ducks, and he says *you're Biscuit, ain't ya? You ride with the Sinners, right? We're at the right place, ain't we? This is 9310 Shannon Way, ain't it?"* he paused, drank the remaining beer from his

79

bottle, stood and walked to the refrigerator.

As I sat in a state of shock and waited for him to return, my mind continued to race.

"So what the fuck did they want?" I asked over my shoulder.

"Hold up, I'll get to it, Brother," he responded as he sat.

He opened a beer and placed two more in the center of the table.

"Now I ain't wearin' my cut or anything, so it ain't like these walkin' turds are readin' my patches or something. These fuckers are *in the know*. So, I say *let me see some identification*. And it's like a scene from that movie with Tommy Lee Jones, you know the *Men in Black* movie? They all yank out ID wallets and flash 'em at me, and that's when McCreary hands me his business card. Card says he's the Special Agent in Charge. If you ask me, there wasn't nothin' special about any of them pricks. Anyway, so that's when they start askin' questions," he wiped the sweat from his brow, downed half the bottle of beer, and exhaled as he gazed down at the floor.

I took another drink of beer and leaned into the table, "God damn, Biscuit, get to the meat of the story, what were they after?"

"Well, this little short prick, I didn't get his name, he's a DEA or ATF, I don't remember. He starts in on the bad cop side of things, actin' all tough. Little fucker's about 5'-8" and maybe about a buck and a half, and he ain't wearin' his government issue black suit. No sir, he's dressed like you and me. He's covered in tats, got a two foot long goatee, and about ten ear rings. Little prick steps between McCreary and me and says *when was the last time you seen Toad?"* he paused nodded his head, and took another drink.

"Motherfucker. What'd you tell 'em?" I asked.

He slapped the table with his hand and chuckled, "Well, that's what pissed this little bastard off. I said I ain't seen a *toad* in a bit, but I was fishin' the other day and I seen some *frogs*."

"You said that?" I laughed.

His eyes widened as he took another drink from his bottle. As he rested the bottle on the table, he raised his hand to his chin and began to rub it with his palm, "Them exact words. And get this. Motherfucker looks at McCreary, and McCreary says *Cambio Todelli. Toad. When did you see him last?* Now fuck, I don't even know what you're fuckin' name is for sure, so I'm shittin' razor blades at this point, and I look up at the ceiling of the garage and act like I'm thinkin' real hard, and I look down and nod my head a couple times. I say *oh, Toad? Fuck fellas, I seen him just the other day*."

I shook my head and rolled my eyes, "Fuck me. Was it about the bank?"

He raised his index finger in the air, "Hold up, almost there, Brother."

My insides felt all jumbled, and my mind was going in about ten different directions. As I battled with my nerves, considered what I might have done to deserve a Government investigation, and attempted to drink my beer, Biscuit nonchalantly sipped his beer and held his free hand in the air to silence me.

After he finished his beer, opened another, and took a sip, he continued, "So he said *was it the day of the Rock Road Bank Robbery?* Now I look at this McCreary fella and I blink a couple of times and I respond *fuck I don't know, when was the robbery?*"

"And this little ATF or DEA fella with the tats starts squealin' *cuff him, let's take him in. We'll pick up the others later.* And McCreary says *no give me a minute with him* and he takes me off to the side. That's when the good-cop-bad-cop shit *really* starts. McCreary's askin'

81

questions, and ATF boy's hollerin' to round up the entire bunch of us and haul us in. Say's somethin' about the girl, Sydney, and how you got her out of there so she wouldn't talk. Said he thought the Sinners orchestrated the whole bank robbery deal. Now about this time, I'm just done listenin' to this little prick, and he don't know much about ol' Biscuit if he thinks I'm gonna drop a dime on the fellas, and I turn to this little sawed off cock sucker and I say *shut the fuck up you sawed off little midget, you're making my head hurt*. And I didn't realize it until McCreary starts pulling on my arm, but I'm steady walkin' toward little ATF man with my hands doubled into a couple of fists. I'm about two seconds from droppin' this little fucker right there in the garage, and he pulls out his government-issue Sig Sauer 40 cal. and points it at me. I stare him in the eye, and say shoot me you gutless worm. Just like that. Hell, everyone starts screamin' and I'm screamin' and this little fucker starts shakin' like a dog shittin' peach pits. Fucking pussy. So, I'm screaming for him to shoot me, and steady walkin' toward him, six other fuckers are hollerin' for him to holster the piece, and McCreary starts pullin' on my leg, tryin' to get me to stop. And he's pullin' on my leg, and pullin' on my leg, and pullin' on it. And…" he lifted his beer bottle and began to laugh.

"Just like I'm a pullin' on yours," he raised his bottle in the air and grinned.

"Huh?' I shrugged.

"The whole story, I was pullin' your leg," he chuckled.

I raised my hands in the air and stood from my seat, "What? What happened? What did you do? What did they say about Sydney? The club?"

He raised his bottle of beer and tilted it toward me, "I was pullin' your leg. ATF didn't stop by, brother. I was shittin' ya. I just wanted a beer and to see if you wanted to roll with me back to Wichita. I stopped in the shop to talk to Brother Slice, and I was bored. We was out of beer at the shop, so I thought I'd stop in and see what ol' Toad was up to. Heard you got your cams in, and wondered if you wanted to try her out, you know, take her out on the highway."

I crossed my arms in front of my chest and shook my head. I should have known, the club practical joker, playing jokes and having fun at my expense. Feeling as if I was a few seconds form a heart attack, I picked up my bottle of beer and drank the remainder of it.

"You prick, I about had a fucking heart attack," I snapped as I slammed the bottle of beer onto the table.

"So you fuckin' that girl yet?" he asked as he stood.

I shook my head, "Nope, and I won't. She's too civil for me."

"Oh, she don't like havin' shit poked up her ass or a rope around her little neck? Damn shame, she's a looker. Cutest little bitch I seen in a bit. Damn shame about her brother, too," he said as he opened another beer.

"Sure is. No, I think she's going to make me a good waitress, though. People have been commenting about her already, and it's all been good. Still can't believe you came over here to get me all pissed off with that bullshit story," I said as I picked up the empty beer bottles and walked toward the trash.

"I come over for free beer, dumbass. Let's roll," he said as he tilted his head toward the door.

"Fuck it, let's do it," I nodded as I walked back toward the trash can and removed the liner and twisted it closed.

I followed Biscuit through the door and onto the porch. As I turned to lock the house, my mind drifted to thoughts of Sydney and I began to wonder how she was doing.

"You know, we need to get Sydney's brother's address and information so we can get some money on his books. Anybody's guess what his club's doin' for him," Biscuit sighed.

"I'll get on that," I said over my shoulder as I carried the trash to the container beside the house.

As soon as I made sure my cams were going to provide the power and torque I expected them too, I knew I'd do just that, see Sydney.

All I needed was a reason to do so.

And now I had one.

SYDNEY

Absorbing the sun's rays had always been a guilty pleasure of mine. When I sunbathed, it was never for a short period of time; but became an event in itself. Generally I baked in the sun, checking my watch every fifteen minutes or so, rotating in thirty minute increments. Every half hour I would tell myself *just one more thirty minute session, and I'll stop.* Typically it turned into a four hour long period of wasted afternoon. Afterward, I felt guilty and spent the remaining portion of the day doing things around the house to make up for my lack of accomplishments during the availability of the mid-day sun. In the last year or so I hadn't been able to sunbathe much. Something about seeing a homeless woman in a bikini lying on the sidewalk or in between cars in the parking lot didn't appeal to the Wichita police.

I opened my eyes at the unmistakable sound of a Harley coming down the block. After introducing me to my new home, surprisingly Toad hadn't reappeared. Not that I necessarily expected him to, but I hoped at some point in time he'd simply stop by to check on me. The fact he hadn't so much as peeked in the door left me wondering if he had no interest in me whatsoever or if he was simply being polite and giving me space. Either way, as much as I appreciated him allowing me to live a life of solitude, sharing his company would have been enjoyable. It seemed no matter how much I tried, I couldn't force myself to associate him with a 1% motorcycle club. His boyish good looks, Marine haircut, and his lack of prison tattoos made me think of him as more of an attractive actor than an attractive biker. As the sound of the exhaust got increasingly closer I closed my eyes, recognizing it as not being the sound of *his* motorcycle. I'd been around enough Harley baggers to know the unmistakable sound of the low steady rumble of the exhaust. This one seemed louder and more along the lines of a performance model. As I decided it was probably one of his brethren in the neighborhood on an old school chopper, the sound echoed through the space between the neighbor's house and mine along the fence separating the front yard from the driveway. I sat up, pulled off my sunglasses, wiped the sweat from my eyes, and tiptoed to the fence.

The small home I was renting from Toad had no garage, only a short concrete driveway leading from the edge of the house to the street. A new wooden privacy fence encompassed the entire back yard, allowing me to sunbathe in the back yard without feeling like a total skank. With the added privacy I was able to walk out the back door to little corner of the yard without the neighbor's seeing me, which made sunbathing in my yard an acceptable option. I may have been an orphan and homeless, but I was a far cry from Whiskey Tango. As if my footsteps could have been heard by the visitor, I tiptoed to the fence and peered over the top into the driveway. Toad's bike sat behind my car.

Shit.

I crouched down behind the fence and hid. As I considered my options of presenting myself to him, I remembered I had left the front door of the house open. Earlier in the morning while eating breakfast and drinking a cup of coffee, I had enjoyed the cooler morning breeze in the front room. Now, the wide open door would be an invitation for him to walk in. It was, all things considered, Toad's home and Toad's investment.

I peered through a small knot hole in the fence and watched as he walked up the drive, looked in my car, and turned toward the house. Dressed in a white tee-shirt, baggy jeans, boots, and his cut, he looked identical to the way he did the day we met – with the exception of a light, very sexy beard.

Soft core biker porn.

After a short pause, he placed his hands on his hips and looked around the yard. I smashed my face against the fence and stared as he began walking toward the front door, eventually disappearing in front of the house.

I heard his muffled voice echo through the house, "Sydney, you home?"

The back door was also open, and the front and back door were in line with each other; allowing someone to potentially stare in one door and out the other. If Toad was standing at the front door, he'd be able to look right out the back door and into the yard. Although I was at the side of the house and out of sight of the doorway, if I attempted to walk into the house he'd immediately see me if he remained anywhere close to the front door.

Shit.

I stood from my knot hole and ran to the rear of the house, standing to the side of the back door. If anyone were to see what I was doing, I would no doubt appear to be some psychotic oil slathered maniac in a bikini. I'd grown up around bikers, so I didn't feel threatened at all by his biker persona, but Toad was intimidating to me. More than likely not only was he intimidating to me, but to every other woman who had an opportunity to admire him - as long as she had blood pumping through her veins. His strong jawline and high cheekbones helped make him a very attractive man, and his muscular body didn't make him any less appealing. His dark complexion caused his muscles to appear even more pronounced, and it was difficult not to survey his body attempting to find a fault.

To see him walk was interesting in itself. Undoubtedly an extension of his Marine Corps training, his walk was methodical and his perfectly paced. It seemed in watching him that he had a detailed plan on where he was going, how he was going to get there, and exactly how many steps it was going to take in doing so. He didn't have a swagger, nor did he saunter; his walk had purpose. Not only did it propel him, it was a portrayal of his discipline.

He was a walking aphrodisiac; an approaching reminder it was time for me to masturbate.

"Sydney?" The sound of his voice came from the front of the house.

I crouched and ran back to my knot hole and peeked through the fence.

Nothing.

I squatted down and attempted to make myself as invisible as possible. After a short pause and an unsuccessful attempt to quiet my labored breathing, I pressed my eye to the hole and gawked as he stood in the driveway rubbing his bicep as if it were sore.

Jesus. Is that really necessary?

I watched in a trance-like state until he released his bicep and began walking toward his bike, temporarily disappearing behind my car.

I slowly stood and peered over the fence. My mild curiosity immediately turned to shock. He stood a mere twenty feet in front of me, walking my direction. Startled, I immediately ducked down behind the privacy of the fence. After realizing I looked like an idiot, I stood and smiled.

"Oh wow, I must have fallen asleep out here in the sun; I didn't even hear you pull up. You on your bike?" I asked with an exaggerated tone of curiosity, trying not to sound like a complete liar.

He nodded his head as he approached the fence, "Surprised you didn't hear it. It's loud as fuck now. I put in new cams and removed the baffles from the exhaust."

On my tip-toes and stretched to my vertical limit, my eyes barely cleared the top of the fence. He stepped to the edge of the fence and rested his elbows along the top. Without the need to hide behind the cover of the fence any longer, I stepped back and sighed lightly.

"I'm anxious to hear you fire it up," I grinned.

I raised my hands slightly and shook my head, "Not that I want you to leave or anything. I just meant I'd like to hear it. I love bikes and the way they all sound a little different."

"You look a hell of a lot different now than you did at the bank. Damn, you work out a lot?" he asked.

I glanced down at my glistening thighs.

"No. Well, yeah. Kind of, but not so much lately," I responded as I looked up.

He narrowed his eyes and stared, "You look like a gym rat."

"I'm a runner," I nodded.

He leaned away from the fence and inhaled a shallow breath. As he exhaled, he raised his hand to his chin and smiled, "You know, I've always said people who run are running *from* something. What are you running from?"

"Cellulite, high gas prices, the cops, outlaw bikers, and…" I looked down at the ground and paused.

"And the reality that after each day passes I don't get a chance to redo it, live it over, or make any changes," I said as I looked up.

Be it a strength or be it a weakness, it really had never mattered to me who was in my presence, I acted the same way around everyone; as if I were alone. I was a true take me or leave me type of woman, and there was no place in my life or my routine to try and be someone or something I wasn't. So, I acted like myself at all times and held nothing back. People could see me for what and who I was and either accept me or cast me aside. The advantage, if there were one, was if someone accepted me they generally did so because they truly found value in *me*.

As he moved his hand from his chin, his mouth curled into a smile, "You talk fast. Actually, you don't *talk* fast, you *respond* fast. You're a quick thinker, aren't you?"

"Quick thinker, quick runner, quick learner…" I quickly responded as I looked down at my thighs again.

"And quick to burn in this hot sun. It's been too long since I've been outside, I'm fried. Want to come in?" I asked as I motioned toward the rear door.

"Sure, if you don't mind," he responded.

"It's your house," I sighed.

He shook his head lightly as he stepped away from the fence, "No, it's yours."

After he disappeared, I ran to the back door, into the house, and took two long strides to the bathroom door – hoping to get there before he made it to the front door. Quickly, I dried off with a towel and pulled on my shorts. As I was pulling a tee-shirt over my head, the doorbell rang.

I have a door bell?

"Come in," I shouted in a high pitched voice.

Although the front door was open, I recalled the outer screen door was locked. I opened the bathroom door and leaped the three steps to the front door, bouncing into place and unlocking the door. Toad watched intently as I pushed it open slightly and smiled. I stood in front of him feeling like the little girl I never had an opportunity to be. The look on his face confirmed it really didn't matter to him how I acted. After stepping into the front room, he simply stood and grinned as I pulled the screen door closed.

"Do you drink tea?" I asked as I turned toward the kitchen.

"Sure," he responded.

As I walked to the kitchen, I realized it had been almost a month since I had moved in, and he was probably coming by for one reason and one reason only – he was hoping for the rent. I sighed as I pulled the refrigerator door open and reached for the tea.

"It's funny. Unless you're in the country, houses don't have screen doors. Hell, most of the new ones don't even have windows you can open," he said flatly.

As I placed the pitcher of tea on the counter and pulled two glasses from the cupboard, I thought about his statement. I'd never lived in a house that *didn't* have a screen door; at least not that I could remember.

"Really?" I said over my shoulder as I filled the glasses with ice and poured them full of tea.

"Absolute fact," he nodded.

"Sugar?" I asked.

"No thank you, I try to stay away from the stuff," he responded.

I should have known.

I couldn't choke down a glass of tea without sugar if I had to. As he walked up beside me I poured about two inches of sugar into the bottom of my glass.

"The only place to sit is the little table," I said as I nodded my head in the direction of the table he so graciously left in the home.

"Otis and I sat there and solved the world's problems while we were working on this beast," he responded.

The home was small and had an open floor plan, one bedroom, a utility room, a bathroom, and the main body of the house which consisted of the dining area, kitchen, and living room. If I was a guy, I'm sure I could stand on one side and piss to the other. It was small, but it was perfect for me.

"You need to get some furniture," he said as he sat down.

"I know. I need a lot of things. I've only been working a little more than a month. A little at a time," I sighed as I stirred my tea.

He raised the glass to his mouth, took a small sip, and raised his eyebrows as he did. My tea making abilities were apparent. Eyebrows still raised, he downed half the glass.

I noticed as he relaxed into his chair he had a small skull patch on the bottom of his cut. Motorcycle clubs have assorted patches for various accomplishments and goals, and although each club was different, most had similar patches for certain achievements. A skull or skull and crossbones meant one thing in most any club. The patch holder had killed for the club. Some clubs added a knife or a gun under the patch to indicate how the killing was done. I couldn't decide if I was *much* less impressed with him or only a little less. I decided as I looked over his cut I would have to know all of the details to make an accurate decision. For now, I decided I didn't like it.

"Damn. That's good tea. Oh, and another thing. Your four weeks comes up in the middle of the month, so let's just go to the beginning of the following month for rent. Say, the first of next month, how's that sound?" he said as he lowered the glass to the table and smiled.

Killer or not, you are gorgeous, aren't you?

"How's that sound?" he asked again.

"Oh, uhhm, yeah. Sorry, I heard you, but that's like six weeks without paying rent. You're saying not to pay rent for six weeks?" I asked.

He shook his head as he surveyed the empty home, "Nope. I'm a fucking weirdo. I like even numbers and shit like that. I'm kind of a neat freak, and paying in the middle of the month on a random day seems sloppy to me. So, let's make it the first day of September. And then the first of the month every month after that; it makes it easy to remember," he said as he smelled the glass of tea.

"Okay, sounds great. Is there something wrong? Does it smell funny? Taste funny?" I asked.

"No, it's really fucking good. Like *really* good. I'm trying to decide what it is I taste in it," he responded as he licked his lips.

I had received very few compliments in my life. When I did, I remembered them for a long, long time. Having spent the majority of my life with nothing, compliments included, allowed me to truly appreciate each and every thing I obtained or achieved in life. To me, a compliment was similar to payment for a job well done. Slowly, Toad was making up for his little skull patch.

"It's my special recipe, half Lipton, half Golden Monkey Organic Black. Two ounces of water to one gram of tea. Add half an orange peel to the pitcher. Let it sit for four hours in a glass pitcher. Not three, not five. Best tea ever," I nodded.

"No argument from me, that's for sure. I'm not much for hot tea, but

I sure like the cold stuff. My mother drinks tea and my father hates it and detests the fact she even drinks it. He's old school Italian. He drinks espresso before bed," he chuckled.

"So you're Italian?" I asked.

He nodded his head, "Cambio Todelli. It's where the name Toad comes from."

"Are you *really* Italian? Do you speak Italian?" I asked.

"Yes, I'm *real* Italian, and I speak Italian," he chuckled, "My great-great grandfather brought my great grandfather here as a baby in 1887. He fought in World War I, my grandfather in World War II, my father in Korea, and me in this war. I come from a rich Italian heritage and a long history of Marines. You know it's funny. Everyone else was coming here *before* the Italians. If you look the Italian immigrants before 1887, they came at a pace of about 10 people a year. Some years there was like 30 or something. This went on for almost the entire century. Then, in about 1887, there was like 50 thousand. After that, the numbers increased every year until there was a quarter of a million per year starting in around 1900."

"I didn't know that. That's interesting. What caused the initial influx of Italian immigrants? You know, once they started coming in droves," I asked.

"Poverty. Most came from the *mezzogiorno,* or southern Italy. A man in southern Italy would make roughly $2 a week in wages. In the US, the same man would earn $20. It may not sound like much of a difference in dollars, but that's 10 times the pay to come here. It made good economic sense for families to migrate here," he explained.

Although I hadn't had similar feelings in the past, I felt a little jealous that Toad knew his family history and had actual parents. He knew about my being homeless, and I had explained to him how I met the man in the bank, but I failed to tell him of my being an orphan. Generally speaking, it wasn't something I liked to make common knowledge or brag about.

"Okay, I've got a question," he said under his breath.

Oh Lord.

Fine, ask.

"Okay," I shrugged.

"So when we were outside, what did you mean about not getting to redo your yesterdays? Do you have regrets?" he asked.

Grateful that he hadn't asked about my family, and that he was actually paying attention to what I said - and remembered it - I grinned like a cat eating a canary.

I'm not going to completely forget about the skull patch, no matter how nice you become.

"Well upon the arrival of tomorrow, today, which is the most important day of all of them, will be just another yesterday. I will only have the memory of it and I'll either toss it in the satisfaction pile or regret pile when I look back on it," I shrugged.

He shrugged his shoulders slightly and narrowed his eyes, "Regret pile?"

"Yes. *The regret pile.* I see life like this. The days, after we're finished with them, build a big puzzle. I mentally snap them into place after I'm done, making a huge puzzle depicting my life. You know, where we've gone, what we've done, things we've seen, some days are filled with pride, and some with regret. Individually, none of those things are earth shattering. Looking back at a day and saying *I wish I would have*, or better yet, *I wish I wouldn't have* isn't that big of a deal. But as a whole, if you have a few thousand days in your regret pile, it makes for a lifetime filled with regret. I don't want that," I shrugged.

He raised his hand to his face and stared down at the table as he rested his chin in his hand.

"Interesting concept," he said as he shifted his gaze upward.

"It's not a concept. It's the truth. A day of regret is like a coin; a quarter for instance. Individually, so what? Right? But what if you have four of them? It's a dollar. And what if you have three solid years of shit days? That's $250 bucks. You see? They add up. I don't want *any*. I've made a few mistakes and a few bad choices, but I've learned from them. I won't make the same ones again."

With his chin still in his hand, he studied my face for a long moment.

"You have any days you regret?" he asked.

I grinned and nodded my head, "Individually, yes. But so far I'm building a pretty awesome puzzle."

"Hopefully this little job will help you keep you tossin' your days in the right pile. You enjoy working there?" he asked.

"I love it. I really do. And Junior? He's the best. He makes the good days great with his humor," I grinned.

"He's a good kid. I'm going to have to talk to him again though. Fancy went in for ribs and one of the ribs on his rack had a huge bite taken out of it. He saved the rib and brought it to me. I had it in the fridge at the shop until today. You know there's really only one way that rib could have had a bite taken out of it," he said as he stood.

"You mind if I get a little more tea? I'm sorry, but it's addictive," he asked over his shoulder.

You keep being sweet, and I'm going to completely forget about that patch.

"Not at all please do. And please tell me I didn't serve that rib," I said as I stood from my seat.

"Nope, it wasn't you. It was Sarah. I've already had a talk with her. And I'm going to see Junior when I leave here," he said over his shoulder as he poured his glass half full, drank it, and poured another full glass.

He turned around and started walking my direction. As he looked up and noticed I was standing, he stopped as if startled. Gripping the glass of tea in both hands, he smiled and continued, "The main reason I stopped by was to tell you there'd be a group of us heading to Austin for a few days. Maybe a week, I don't know. We've got a chapter in Austin, but most of 'em will be going on a mandatory run that weekend. A new club is trying to start up down there, and they're having a meeting with the local clubs to get permission. Axton needs to be there and he wants me and Otis to go. Anyway, so I won't be around the restaurant if there's anything that goes to hell. You know Junior's been there the longest, and he kind of runs things, but if you really need anything my number is posted on the wall in the kitchen."

"Okay, I'll remember that," I smiled as I looked down and realized I hadn't so much as taken a drink of my tea.

I silently wondered how much time had passed since he had shown up. More often than not when I was enjoying myself, time escaped me at an extremely rapid rate. The company of a gorgeous Italian biker made matters much worse.

"Do you know what time it is?" I asked, not wanting to try and find my inactive cell phone.

"I was just getting ready to leave. It's 1:00. You want to ride to the restaurant with me?" he asked.

"I'd love to," I grinned.

"Do you have an apple?" he asked.

I shook my head, "Sure don't, why?"

"I need one. We'll have to stop and get one on the way," he said as he finished his tea.

"I'm not even going to ask," I shrugged.

"Oh and one other thing before we go. Can you write down that recipe for the tea? My mother will love it," he said.

Okay, so you have a skull patch on your cut. What does that even represent, anyway?

TOAD

The quickest way to get to the bottom of something is to dive in headfirst. The rate of descent is determined by the resistance of the matter between your point of entry and the final destination. In this particular situation, I was dealing with an extremely thick and variably resistant substance.

"I don't remember taking no bite of a rib I didn't go on and finish eatin', Mr. Toad. Sure nuff that don't sound like me. You know how Junior loves them ribs, Mr. Toad. No sir, sounds like someone else mighta done that," Junior's eyes widened to the point they looked like white orbs against his black skin.

I stood on the edge of the kitchen holding the grocery sack containing the apple I had purchased and the half-eaten rib Fancy brought me. After Sydney went into the dining area to talk to the other waitresses, I had started questioning Junior regarding the rib with the teeth marks in it. I wasn't angry with Junior, but I was disappointed one of my customers had received a partially eaten rib. It was fortunate for me, Junior, and the restaurant that the rib was served to Fancy - and not some local customer who was blabbing to everyone else in the small city. Even though this seemed like an isolated event, I couldn't help but wonder who else this may have happened to.

"So you're thinking it wasn't you who nibbled on the rib?" I asked.

"No sir, Mr. Toad. I ain't so much thinkin' that at all. No sir, I'm *knowin'* it. Yessir, sure nuff I'm standing here knowin' it," he nodded.

I stood for a long moment holding the sack. I consciously changed the tone of my voice from an accusatory one to one of curiosity, "Junior, do you like apples?"

"Apples, Mr. Toad? Likes the kind that grows on trees?" he shrugged.

"Yes, Junior. Apples," I nodded as I lifted the sack.

Junior rubbed his hands together and smiled, "Oh I love me some apple pie. And you know what the doctor man says about them apples, Mr. Toad."

"What's that?" I asked.

He grinned and widened his eyes as if he were revealing some loosely known medical secret, "An apple a day keeps the doctor man away."

"Well, I've got one left here, do you want it?" I asked as I pulled the apple from the sack.

Junior shrugged and nodded his head once. I tossed the apple in the air and couldn't help but grin as Junior caught it mid-air and took a bite before even looking down at it. I expected considering his constant state of hunger he wouldn't be able to help himself. I attempted to make myself seem preoccupied, and began walking toward him. As soon as I was within a few feet of where he stood, I looked down at the apple he held.

"Damn Junior, you flat took a bite out of that poor apple didn't you?" I chuckled.

"No need in beatin' around the bush, Mr. Toad. I knows I'm gonna eat this here apple, so taking me a little nibble don't make good sense. Fewer bites I take, the quicker I can get back to work," he smiled and slowly lifted the apple to his mouth.

I studied the apple curiously and slowly reached for it. As I did, he tilted his head to the side and shifted his gaze to meet mine.

"Do you mind?" I asked.

His face filled with wonder, he released the apple into my hand.

I turned to the prep table, placed the apple on the table and removed Fancy's half-eaten rib from the sack. I placed the rib beside the apple and stared. Junior stood in awe as I compared the two identical bite marks.

"Junior, it looks like we have us a match. Those were *your* teeth that took a bite from that rib my friend was served," I said as I pointed down at the prep table.

Without complaint or explanation, Junior walked toward the table and stared down at the rib. After a few alternating glances between the rib and the apple, he looked upward with his eyebrows raised.

"Oh *that* rib. I recognize it now, Mr. Toad," he exclaimed.

"You recognize it?" I chuckled.

I purchased my meat from the same butcher every week. Consistency is one of the key elements to the success of a barbeque joint. Every *rack* of ribs looks the same, and after trimming them into individual ribs, every *rib* looks the same. To identify a particular rib would be impossible.

"Sure nuff," he nodded.

"You see. I'd cut a whole bunch of ribs that night. It was rib night. I was cuttin' 'em like wildfire. Girls was sellin' 'em and I was a cuttin' 'em. Goin' out of this here kitchen like hot cakes. And after the dinner rush, I looks down. One lone rib was sittin' there lookin' back at me. The kitchen was a mess, and you know how I hates me a mess Mr. Toad. So I commence to cleanin' this here kitchen, just like you taught me. Cleanliness is right next to Godliness, Mr. Toad. So when I gets the kitchen spotless, I looks over at the prep table, and I realize ole Mr. rib is still sittin' there. Now I know I done messed up. I can't serve that poor rib to a customer, because he's done cooled off," he paused as he shook his head and raised his hands in the air.

I stood, attempting not to smile, and waited for the remainder of the story.

"It gets mighty hot in this here kitchen, but it sure nuff ain't 140 degrees, Mr. Toad. Meat gots to stay at 140 degrees to keep them bacterias from developin'. You taught me that too. So I looks down at that poor Mr. rib, and I knew I couldn't sell it. But my big belly is like a trash can, I don't get sick from no sammy-nilla or no bacteria. So, I stares down at the rib, knowing I can either throw him in the trash or I can just eat him instead. It'd sure make me sad to toss it in the trash can, so I picked it up and took me a bite. As soon as I did," he paused and pointed toward the door leading into the kitchen.

He tossed his hands in the air as if he were shocked, "Miss Sarah comes in with a dag nabb rib order."

"So, I pulls me a rack, fills the order, and sends 'em out of here right fast. But when I looks down at the prep table after Miss Sarah was gone, ole Mr. rib was gone too. I remember thinkin' at the time I musta ate him and clean forgot. But seein' him layin' there now, I know I done made me a mistake, Mr. Toad. I sure nuff did, didn't I?"

I bit my lower lip slightly to keep from laughing and nodded my head.

"I'm powerful sorry Mr. Toad. Is you gonna fire me?" he asked.

I shook my head slowly. I'd already given the rib incident and the previous problems with Junior's eating habits much thought. Considering my continual rising cost of meat and Junior's physical size, I was going to make him an offer which would help me and could potentially help him considerably. The presentation of my offer was crucial to his accepting it.

"No Junior, I'm not. You know…" I paused and raised my hand to my chin.

"Right now I have other things on my mind. You're a problem solver, aren't you?" I asked.

"Yes sir, Mr. Toad. I try and nip them problems in the bud," he grinned.

"Well, you know Mr. Greely at the corner? He sells the used cars?"

"Big white fella with the long hair on the side of his head he flips over to the top. Yessir, I knows Mr. Greely."

"Well, he has a truck for sale. And old farm truck. It has a flat-bed trailer beside it. He took the truck and trailer on trade. I was thinking about buying it and starting a grass cutting business. You know, like a lawn service? Maybe have two men working on cutting grass, trimming shrubs, and cleaning yards. And they'd be working for the third man, the boss. I was thinking he could name the business after himself. Or whatever he wanted to call it. In a sense, it would be *his* business. He'd run it, he'd keep the profits, and he'd be the big boss man. All the man would have to do was pay me back for the truck, trailer, and lawn equipment. Say, oh I don't know," I hesitated, lowered my hand from my chin, and let Junior chew on what I had said.

"Maybe a year or two to pay it off," I shrugged.

"So you needs you a big boss man?" he asked.

I nodded my head as I lifted my hand to my chin again. As I rubbed my chin between my thumb and forefinger, Junior appeared to have a revelation.

"You needs you a problem solver, Mr. Toad. Sure nuff do. A boss man ain't gonna do it for ya. You needs you a problem solver, *and* a big boss man; just like a hog needs slop," he said as he rubbed his hands together and smiled.

"You got any ideas?" I shrugged.

"I don't have me an idea, Mr. Toad. I done solved you a problem," he grinned.

"Oh you did? How so?" I asked.

He reached down and grabbed the apple off of the prep table and took a huge bite. As he chewed the apple, he explained.

"I'll be that big boss man for ya, Mr. Toad. I'd do that for ya. I'd call the business *Junior's Lawn Service*."

I rubbed my cheeks in my hands and gazed his direction as if I were contemplating his offer.

"Damn, Junior. I never thought of that. Hell, you'd probably be able to make a damn sight more money doing that than working here. I know a guy who has a business with two men working for him, and he makes about four grand a week. Pays his help a grand a piece, and keeps two grand for himself."

"Whoooeeeee," he shouted.

He wiped his brow with the back of his hand, "Two grand a week? Lord have mercy."

"I could solve me some problems with that, Mr. Toad. I could buy the young uns some new clothes and all kinda stuff with two grand a week."

"What the fuck would I do about this damned kitchen, though?" I shrugged.

Junior rubbed his chin with is hand and stared up at the ceiling as if in deep thought, "Mr. Toad, anybody can take care of this old kitchen. Say little Franky, the boy who works on the weekends when I'm off work. He could sure nuff take this kitchen and make it shine. You'd need to get you a weekend man though."

I turned and walked toward the kitchen door, paused and turned around, "I can find *someone*; maybe one of the girls would step in for a while. You think you want this lawn business?"

"I sure nuff do, Mr. Toad. When would we start it?" he asked.

"Junior, *we* aren't starting anything. I'm going to buy all the stuff and get a man started. It's not *my* business. It's my *equipment*. Once it's paid for, the business and the equipment is the property of the owner. I'll need to set the company up with the city, register the business with the state, and list the new owner. Probably set up a Limited Liability Corporation. So, have we got a deal?" I asked as I extended my hand.

"Junior's Lawn Service. I likes me the sound of that," he said as he shook my hand.

"I like the sound of it too. I tell you what, let me take Sydney home, and we'll just go buy that equipment this afternoon. You and me. How's that?"

"I'd like that Mr. Toad. Now Miss Sydney, is she one of them, you know…" he paused and stared down at his feet.

As he looked up he narrowed his gaze, "Is she one of them women you uhhm. You hits? Is you hittin' that Miss Sydney, Mr. Toad?"

"Am I fucking her?" I chuckled.

"Yes sir," he nodded.

"No Junior, I'm not. She's just a girl I met a month or so ago. Kind of like you. She was down on her luck, and I gave her a job. She's digging herself out of a financial rut. Hopefully here pretty quick she'll be able to see a light at the end of the tunnel," I responded.

Junior reached for the rib, picked it up, and dropped it into the trash. As he wiped the prep table with a kitchen towel, he looked up and smiled, "I can see mine, Mr. Toad and she's as bright as the sun. You know something, Mr. Toad?"

"What's that, Junior?" I asked as I turned toward the kitchen.

"Well, you never smile unless you and me's a talkin', and then you can't stop. With your leather vest and that scruffy beard and your tattoos and such, you look like the devil himself ridin' that motorbike through town. For them what don't know you, you's an angry man who sure nuff shouldn't be crossed. Mean as a snake is what they say, you know. But when a fella gets to know you, and you let loose of that mean Marine look what's always on your face, you's a damn fine man. And you do kind things for folks who you don't even know. I just wanted to tell you that," he nodded.

"Thank you," I nodded as I grabbed the handle of the kitchen door.

I stood at the door, holding the handle and thinking of what Junior had said. He was probably right; I'm sure most who saw me through the course of a day considered me to be the devil. In public, I rarely showed emotion, unless a stern look was considered emotional. It was as if there were two of me; the Marine who was trying to duplicate the atrocities of war, and the thoughtful Catholic boy my parents raised. In a constant battle, the two fought for control of my soul. The Marine constantly seeking confirmation the violent acts and murder he committed during war were necessary and just; and the Catholic boy attempting to lend a helping hand and right the wrongs of his past. It seemed the Marine stood the clear victor. I guess I shouldn't have ever expected otherwise.

Once a Marine, always a Marine.

106

I pulled the door open and peered into the empty dining area. As soon as I saw Sydney, I realized I had totally forgotten to ask her about her brother. I stood and gazed at her admiringly as she told a story to Sarah and Kate. I continued to watch as she talked to the two girls, laughing and waving her arms as they listened intently. She was a beautiful woman and had a fantastic personality. For having very little she was extremely pleased and seemed content with what she did have. In some respects I became envious as I watched her, wishing I too could find the happiness she seemed to naturally possess. As the three girls began laughing at what appeared to be the end of a story Sydney had told, I recalled something my grandfather explained to me as a teenager.

Cambio, we all have a goal in life, an objective. If you surround yourself with people who share your passion and ambition; your desire will soon be at your fingertips. If you surround yourself with those who have different goals, yours will slowly become out of reach. Choose your friends wisely, Capisce?

As I stood and watched the girls continue to laugh, I decided spending more time getting to know Sydney just might be in my best interest.

SYDNEY

The sound of a motorcycle coming down the block caused me to jump from my seat and run to the window. After pulling the blinds slightly to the side and peeking outside, my suspicions and hope converged.

Shit.

I ran to the bathroom, grabbed my compact, and frantically began dabbing powder on my face. After a good dusting, I stood back and looked in the mirror. For a thirty second make-over, I looked pretty damned good. Except for my...

Hair.

Shit.

I pulled the hair tie from my hair and shook my head. A few seconds into teasing my hair with my fingers, and the doorbell rang. Eager to see Toad again after just having seen him three days prior, I took one more glance in the mirror and grinned.

Here goes nothing...

I tossed my compact into my makeup bag and threw it under the sink. After tip-toeing to the door, I turned, tiptoed into the kitchen, opened the cupboard, and rattled a few dishes around. As I began to close the cupboard door, the doorbell rang again.

"Coming," I shouted.

"Sorry, I was putting up the dishes," I said as I opened the door.

Expressionless, Toad stood on the porch and stared through the screen door. I leaned forward and pushed it open. As I held the door and slowly shifted my gaze upward, I noticed his cut was covered in blood and he wasn't wearing a shirt underneath it.

"You alright?" I asked as he stepped inside.

I knew better than to ask too much. His business as a Sinner was his business and the club's business, it certainly wasn't mine. Regardless, I was human, and so was he. The woman in me wanted to help him with whatever he needed, but the sensible side of me argued to leave it alone and keep my mouth shut. As always, the woman in me prevailed.

"Your cut's got a little blood on it. If you want to take it off, I'll clean it real quickly for you," I said as he walked to the table and sat down.

Without speaking, he stood, removed the cut, and held it in his hand. *Oh dear fucking God. I really wasn't ready for this.*

His body was that of a male underwear model. Without his cut, and standing shirtless, he looked like an Italian Abercrombie and Fitch model. Easily passing for ten years his junior, he could have told me he was in his early twenties and I sure would have believed him. Although I told myself not to, I couldn't help but stare at his abs as I reached for his cut. As I stood and gazed his direction, as if to make matters worse, he turned to his left. Revealing the Marine Corps Eagle, Globe, and Anchor tattoo, and several tattoos on his left forearm sealed the deal in the *Toad's sexy* department. Now gawking at his tattooed left side, his pronounced rip cage, and washboard abs, I knew I better speak or I'd forever look like a fool. As I swallowed heavily, my racing heart confirmed the lack of a male companion in my life, and just how well Toad checked all of the applicable boxes of my mental application for employment.

"Yeah, I uhhm. I'll just be right here in the kitchen where you can uhhm…"

Oh dear Lord don't turn away.

As he faced the window, I turned toward the kitchen and continued.

"…see me, I know you can't let me take this anywhere. No worries," I said over my shoulder as I walked into the kitchen.

Did he have a really pronounced chest? Killer pecs?

I quickly glanced in his direction. Now facing me and staring blankly at the table, I felt as if he was inviting me to take another look.

Yep, sure does.

I turned toward the kitchen sink and grinned, "Should just take me a few minutes. If you want to just stand there, I'll be done in a minute," I said cheerily as I reached into the cabinet.

After laying the cut flat on the counter, I realized most of the blood was on the lower left side. I poured vinegar over the bloodstain and allowed it to become soaked. Dabbing it with a clean kitchen towel removed the majority of the blood immediately. A second application removed all of the *red* stains I could see, but left discoloration on the leather. More than likely, this was as good as it was going to get. Somewhat distracted by my desire to clean the cut, I forgot he might still be standing beside the table behind me. I nonchalantly peered over my right shoulder.

Yep. Still there, still shirtless, and still looks ahhhmazing.

"Pretty tough stain, I may need to treat it with cornstarch. We'll have to wait for it to dry," I shrugged.

"I don't have to be anywhere, just wanted to hang out for a while," he mumbled.

After mixing cornstarch with water and making a cornstarch paste, I smeared it over the entire left lower side of the cut and carefully carried it to the table. Now standing with his arms crossed in front of his chest, he watched as I placed it flat on the table.

"After it dries, we can wipe that off of there. I think it'll be just fine. Happened a few times with my brother and some of his friends," I said as pulled a chair away from the table.

"You can sit," I said as I sat down.

He uncrossed his arms and sighed. The "V" shape in his lower abdomen that every man wants but select few ever obtain drew my eyes to it like a moth to a flame. I stared with my chin in my lap as it slowly disappeared below the table.

Or you could stand back up.

"I'd offer you a shirt if I had one that'd fit," I said, glad that everything I owned was much smaller than he possibly could wear.

"Normally keep some clean ones on the bike, but not today," he said flatly.

"So, you want something to drink?" I asked.

"I'm alright," he responded.

"So, you don't have an Ol' Lady?" as the words escaped my lips, I realized what I had said and wished I had worded it differently.

"Nope," he responded.

I nodded my head.

He turned to face me and rested his elbows on the table. After studying me for a long moment, he rested his chin in his hand and grinned.

"And you're single?" he breathed.

"Sure am," I said with a smile.

"How can that be? You're gorgeous, cool as fuck, and…" he paused and pressed his forearms onto the table as he leaned forward.

Officially melted.

As his gaze met mine, he grinned, "Well, you're just fun to be around."

Oh dear God.

"Well, I've been in a few shitty relationships. You know, guys beating on me and that type stuff. I told myself I'd never be in another relationship that wasn't what *I* wanted," I responded.

"What do you want?" he asked as he relaxed into the back of his chair.

As much as I wanted to tell him what I suspected he wanted to hear, I refused to do so. The complications of my past relationships needed to stay where they were, in my past. In my future, I needed to make sure whatever I decided to do, and whomever I decided to do it with was for all of the right reasons and with all of the best of expectations.

"Me? Well, I want a man who will treat me properly. I don't want flowers and some romantic courtship, but I want to be as close to an equal as I can be. I know I'm a woman, but I'm human, not a dog. And I want a guy I can be friends with, that's really important. And I guess especially after what I've been through, I don't want any rough stuff. I love sex more than most women, but I don't like being slapped around, beaten, choked, or having some asshole try and see how far he can shove his cock down my throat. I just want a conventional relationship with an unconventional man. If I can't get that, I'll settle for nothing," I stopped talking and waited for a reaction.

He leaned forward and rested his elbows on the table. As he lowered his chin into his hand, he smiled a soft smile, "You'll get it. You're too damned perfect to have to settle for anything less."

I stared blankly at his face, absorbing what he had said. An immeasurable amount of time passed. I may or may not have drooled on my hand and immediately came back down to earth to wipe it off.

"I hope so," I sighed.

He glanced over each shoulder, and began looking around the room. As his eyes became fixed on me, he began to speak again.

"Listen, I'm feeling pretty exhausted. I just, well I don't want to go home right now. You know? I uhhm…I was wanting to know if I could just hang out here…kind of relax. You mind if I uhhm…if I rest here for a bit?" he stammered.

I nervously glanced around the room, "Uhhm, no. Not at all. I don't have a couch or anything yet, but you can lie down on my bed if you want."

"You sure?' he asked as he stood.

I gazed up at his shirtless body and nodded my head, "Quite."

"Just for a bit," he sighed.

"As long as you need," I smiled as I began walking toward my bedroom.

After following me into the bedroom, he removed his boots and sat down on the bed. A quick survey of the room later, and he turned to me and smiled, "I like what you've done with this room. The paint looks great."

"Thank you," I grinned.

He lowered himself onto the bed and covered his eyes with his forearm. Although it wasn't much past mid-afternoon, within a matter of seconds, he was asleep.

In gazing down at him as he lay on the bed, I didn't see a biker or a shirtless Italian model. I saw a man who desperately needed rest, comfort, and no one to judge him for what he may have been involved in. I turned to the door and pulled it closed behind me.

After a few hours, I dusted the cornstarch from his cut. A light brushing and it looked as good as a ten year old leather cut ever could. Quietly, I tiptoed to the room and opened the door. Still asleep on the bed, it was apparent he was exhausted.

I softly placed the cut beside him, closed the door and cooked dinner. After opening the door and wafting the smell of my pasta primavera and baked chicken into the room for several minutes - to no avail - I decided he needed to continue sleeping.

After almost three hours had passed, I tiptoed to the room and opened the door. His light snoring confirmed what I had expected.

Two hours later, after putting up the dishes and cleaning everything in the house at least twice, I needed some rest myself. I tiptoed to the room, opened the door, and walked to the edge of the bed. After kicking my flats off to the side, I raised my legs onto the bed carefully, scooted in beside him, and relaxed. The warmth of his body and the light buzzing of his breathing provided a level of comfort I had forgotten even existed.

When I woke the next morning, he was gone.

I walked to into the living room, and immediately noticed a folded sheet of my stationary on the table. I reached down, picked it up and unfolded it. As I stared down at the perfect penmanship, I smiled and read what he had written.

Sydney,

Thanks for everything. And don't worry about finding your man, one day he'll find you.

Cambio

I folded the paper, hesitated, and unfolded it again. After re-reading it, I folded it and placed it on the table.

TAKING THE HEAT

I hope you're right, Cambio.
And I hope he's just like you.

TOAD

Otis took a drink from the bottle of beer, extended his arm, and stared at the label, "You know he doesn't act like it's a big deal, but I can see a huge difference in him. What the fuck is this shit, anyway?"

"I don't know, waitress recommended it while you were pissing. How much of it do you think is her, and how much is just that he's getting laid?" I shrugged as I studied the label on my beer bottle.

Otis tipped up the beer and took a long drink. As he lowered the bottle, he scrunched his nose and shook his head, "Don't order any more of these if I live long enough to piss again."

He stared at the bottle again, "Says *Founders Breakfast Stout*. I feel like I'm drinking mashed potatoes and fucking gravy. This is the thickest fucker I've ever tried to drink. Why'd you order this nasty shit?"

I choked down a swallow of the dark beer and shook my head at the taste, "Waitress recommended it."

Otis tipped up his bottle and finished the beer. As he slid the empty bottle to the end of the table, he rolled his eyes, "I swear, men do some dumb shit sometimes to impress women."

"I didn't do it to impress her," I said as I sniffed the mouth of the bottle.

"Smells like it tastes, doesn't it? Like shit. So tell me, would you have agreed on a bottle of black beer that said *breakfast* on it if some dude would have recommended it?" he asked as he waved in the waitress' direction.

I shrugged my shoulders, "I don't know."

"Well, *you* might not, but I sure as fuck do. You'd have told him to fuck off and ordered a couple of Budweiser's. Some chick asked you if you wanted to try it, or better yet," he paused and leaned his forearms onto the edge of the table.

"I'm going to guess it went something like this. She walks up and says, *What can I get you?* You don't want to sound like a basic biker so you respond, *Oh, hell I don't know. What have you got?* She names fifty different types of beer. You look up at her with a confused look. Not because you're trying to look cute, but because you ain't so much as heard of half the shit she names off. So you say*, what do you recommend?* How am I doing so far?"

"I'd say pretty good," I said as I slid my half full beer to the edge of the table.

"She responds, *I like the…*" he grabbed the empty bottle and turned the label to face him.

"*I like the Founders Stout.* And you respond, *Sounds good, bring us a couple.* Now she didn't tell you to try 'em because they're a crowd favorite or even that they taste good. She either did it because they're ten bucks a bottle and she wants to rack up a high tab, or because they only have two of them fuckers left in the cooler and they're getting rotten because no one will drink those nasty fuckers. Now let me ask you something, Toad. You ever had a bad Budweiser?" he leaned away from the table and slid to the end of the booth, waiting on my answer.

I shook my head, "I guess not."

"You guess not," he chuckled.

"Well, that's what we do for women, we drink beer that tastes like it came out of the ass of an elephant. It's instinctual behavior for a man to try and impress them. Drinking the shitty beer is the result."

I leaned back in the booth and stared down at my boots. As I shifted my gaze upward, I attempted to salvage my manhood, "I wasn't trying to impress her. I just agreed to try the beer."

"Keep telling yourself that," he chuckled.

"Where were we earlier?" he asked.

"Axton and Avery," I muttered as I turned toward the approaching waitress and grinned.

"Oh, yeah. How much of it's because of her and how much is because he's getting laid. I'd say part of it's her and part of it's the fact he's happy for the first time in his life. None of it's because he's getting laid. Slice don't give half a fuck about sex. Avery's a good damned woman. As far as Ol' Ladies go, she's as good as it gets," he paused and turned to face the waitress.

She smiled and cocked her head to the side, "Hey. You want two more Founders?"

Otis smiled and shook his head as he slid the two bottles to the edge of the table, "It was all I could do to choke the first one down and my buddy couldn't even finish his. How about a couple Bud's?"

"Bottle or draft?" she asked.

"Bottle," Otis nodded.

"Be right back," she smiled.

Otis shifted his gaze to meet mine and raised one eyebrow, "See?"

"What?" I asked.

"Well, I told her mine tasted like shit, and you couldn't finish yours. She didn't respond with *oh, wow I can't believe that, everyone loves them*, or *that's hard to believe*. She didn't say shit, because she knew they were nasty fuckers. Now, let's get back to what we were talking about, women. We all want a woman. I don't give a shit who you are. A man wants a woman in his life. Some of us don't want to admit it, and others keep 'em at bay like they're trying to preserve their feelings or keep from hurting 'em. Deep down inside we want one that suits us, Slice included. Hell, he'd been ten or fifteen years without a woman, and I ain't so sure, but I think he'd gone the same amount of time without even getting any pussy. That motherfucker *hated* women. Look at him now," he paused as the waitress walked up with the two bottles of beer.

"Here you go," she smiled as she placed the beers on the table.

"Appreciate it," Otis nodded.

As he slid a beer across the table he grinned, "Answer this. Don't look at her or turn around, just look at me and answer. What color is the waitress' fingernail polish?"

I shrugged, "Fuck I don't know."

"*Grey.* Eye color?" he asked.

"Got no idea," I responded as I grabbed the beer.

"*Green with brown specs.* I bet without turning around you don't even know her hair color," he said.

"Blonde," I responded.

"Good guess. *It's dark brown.* You know for a motherfucker who pays attention to everything around him, you sure as fuck aren't paying attention to her. Want to know why?" he asked as he raised the bottle of beer to his lips.

"Sure," I nodded as I took a drink.

"Right now *she* doesn't interest you beyond the normal instinct you have to try and impress her. Right now, you've got that cute little bitch, Sydney, on your mind," he chuckled.

"Bullshit," I sighed.

Otis slid to the back of his seat, "You're full of shit. For the first half hour we were here, you mentioned her four times."

"For fucks sake, I mentioned her once," I snapped.

Otis shook his head, released the bottle of beer from his grasp, and raised his fist in the air. As he spoke, he extended his index finger, "We no more than sat down and you said she made the best tea you've ever tasted."

He extended his middle finger, "Later, after we'd talked for fifteen minutes about whether or not beating a man's ass was a sin, you said she was a runner and asked if I thought she had a good body."

He extended his ring finger, "Then, right after we finished the first beer, that fucking apple cider bullshit you made me drink, you told me about Junior's rib, taking her to the bar, and that she had a great personality and was always happy. Then you started asking about Avery and Axton, and right before I went to piss…"

He extended his pinkie, "You said she was a natural on the back of your bike, and bragged on how well she rode back from Wichita and how well she rode to the restaurant."

"That was one long conversation not four separate ones," I shrugged.

"Again, tell yourself whatever you want to, brother. You know," he paused and situated himself in the back of the booth, against the wall.

"Here in the last week or so, something with you changed. I ain't trying to say it's Sydney, because it might not be. Maybe it was that trashy assed Sloan, I don't know. But *something* happened. Slice and I were talking about it yesterday. You know I asked you to come in here to have a few beers. I did it because I wanted to talk to you about this. As soon as we sat down, you started asking about Slice and his Ol' Lady.

How he'd changed and seemed happy…"

"Hold on, motherfucker," I grumbled.

Otis held his hand in the air, "*You* hold on. Let me finish what I'm trying to say."

I shifted my body lengthwise in the seat of the booth, facing the bar instead of facing Otis. As I stared blankly at the bar, I lifted my boots into the seat in front of me and leaned against the back of the booth.

"Whatever. Go ahead," I said as I grabbed my beer and relaxed into the seat.

"You know Toad, *normally* you'd be a hard motherfucker for someone to figure out. You fill your day with dumb shit to do. You don't really have anything you *have* to do, but you're all over the fucking place. Going here. Going there. You stay busy doing *nothing*. With the fellas you laugh and joke and you're an all-around good motherfucker to be around. But you have these mood swings. Slice and I always figured it was the war. When you get mad, you get *mad*. I've seen you beat a motherfucker's ass a damned sight more than it needed beat on more than one occasion. I'm the biggest motherfucker in the club, but who's been in the most fights in the last five years that you've been around?"

I looked over my left shoulder and raised my eyebrows as I tipped up my beer and took a sip. I knew he would tell me, but I lacked a little interest in hearing where the conversation was headed.

"*You*. Without a fucking doubt. You've probably been in ten or twelve fights in five years. Actual *fights*. Not bullshit or shoving a motherfucker, but fighting. Closest motherfucker to you, short of Slice, has probably been in one or two. I ain't callin' you out, I'm just saying you've normally got a lot of anger inside of you, brother. *Something*. And whatever it is, you *normally* run from it. Hell, even the women you

122

fuck with, you don't just fuck 'em. You choke 'em and slap 'em and tie 'em up. I know you ain't raping these bitches, but you're like a fucking sadist or something. I mean *really* brother, who wraps a bitches head in Saran Wrap and fucks her? I'm guessing it's a short fucking list," he paused and shook his head lightly.

He lifted his beer, took a long drink, and continued, "So again, *normally* you fight with yourself. You know; the entire good and evil thing. You always want to do what's right, what's justified, and what's good in the eyes of God in *your* opinion. Somehow, you justify your actions. And I guess what I'm saying is that here recently, something's changed, or it's damned sure *changing*. It's not that you're getting soft, but you're acting *different*. You gave Sydney the house. You said you bought Junior a truck, trailer, and lawn equipment. And as far as I know, you ain't fucked anyone since you took Sloan to Corn Dog's place; or at least you ain't said anything about it if you have," he hesitated and shrugged his shoulders slightly.

I shook my head and shifted my gaze to my boots. As I studied the laces, I began to feel uneasy. I took another sip of my beer. My eyes began to feel itchy. I blinked a few times and took another sip of beer. I didn't realize anyone could see a difference in me, but if they could, maybe it was…

I stared down at my boot laces, realizing I was roughly one breath away from snapping.

"I'll take that as a *no*. It just confirms what I was thinking and why I wanted to come here and talk. So anyway, the week or so you've been a little more concerned with what you're doing. You're being more of a do-gooder, asking questions about what people think, even arguing with Slice about a woman's place in a man's heart. So, did something happen? Is the war gettin' to you? Brother, if you need to take some time and go to the VA for therapy, or whatever it is, you know you can talk to me, Toad. It'll stay here," he motioned toward me with his hand and then pointed to himself.

I looked over my shoulder, shifted my gaze to meet his, and opened my mouth. As much as I wanted to speak, I knew if I did, I'd lose my composure. The entire thing just seemed childish. To talk to one of the fellas about it would make me seem weak, incapable, and unable to effectively act as their Sergeant at Arms and protect them.

I glanced down at my boots.

After a long moment of staring at my boots, I looked up and nodded my head once. I felt as if I needed to say *something*, but my throat told me otherwise. I swallowed heavily as I felt my eyes well with tears. I shifted my gaze slightly to the left.

"Don't matter what it is brother, we can get through this," Otis said.

I swallowed a lump the size of a golf ball and stared, "I uhhm. I was riding out by the lake. He'd been shot. Twice. Well, actually three times. I tried to save him. I really fucking tried. I uhhm. I did everything I could. It was…"

I paused and took a sip of beer. My eyes felt like they were on fire, but I knew better than to touch them. For Christ's sake, I was a grown man, and I knew I should be able to do this without losing control of myself. I gripped the cool bottle in my hands and continued.

I shook my head, "It was the other day, maybe a week or so ago, I don't know."

I hesitated and nodded my head repeatedly, knowing I was right. At the time, I dismissed it, but it had been eating on me ever since.

One fucking nibble at a time.

"What happened?" he asked.

Still staring down at my boots, I raised my beer and drained the last small sip from the bottle. My mouth felt as if I had swallowed a handful of sawdust. I looked up and nodded my head once. He asked, and I needed to be a man and tell him what happened. I gazed down at my boots, inhaled a choppy breath, and responded.

"It was a puppy. An innocent little fucking puppy," I said under my breath.

"What? A puppy?" he shrugged.

I nodded my head and attempted to swallow, but the dryness in my throat prevented it. I shifted my gaze toward Otis, opened my mouth to speak, and instead began to softly cry.

TOAD

One week earlier.

Nothing on this earth could compare to the freedom I felt while riding. If there was one thing people associated with living in the United States of America, it was freedom. The only time I felt free of all of life's constraints was when I was on the open road. Those who have never ridden would never know, and those who had would never find anything to replace it.

I rolled the throttle back and listened to the sound of the unrestrained exhaust bellow from the rear of the bike. As the warmth of the mid-summer sun beat down on my face, the unoccupied stretch of highway begged me to explore it. I unconsciously inhaled a breath, almost tasting the prairie hay the team of kids in the pasture on my right were picking up from the freshly cut meadow. As they neatly stacked the hay on a trailer, one of them looked my direction. I pulled in my clutch and revved my motor.

Future Sinner, no doubt.

As I came into a wide sweeping corner, I leaned the bike deep left, dragging to the toe of my boot on the pavement as the force of the aggressive turn pushed against me. A little more throttle, and out of the turn I shot, slightly faster than I had entered.

Fuck yes, this is living.

To my right I noticed a group of crows gathered on the side of the

127

road. Two or three were in the street, in my lane. As I downshifted and slowed to a safe speed, I noticed two down in the ditch. More than likely, I suspected a farmer or unsuspecting motorist had hit a deer, and the crows were picking at the flesh. As hitting a crow on a bike at 80 miles an hour would be the end of my riding career, I pulled in the clutch and revved the throttle to scare the birds from the side of the road. Although the noise seemed to shift their attention, it did little to scare them from whatever it was that had captured their interest. As I slowly passed, I stared down in the ditch out of curiosity.

I twisted the throttle slightly and began to speed up.

Was that a bloody dog?

I applied the brake, turned around, and pulled alongside the gathered crows. After kicking down the kickstand and shifting the bike in neutral, I stepped off and walked over to the side of the ditch. As the crows reluctantly fluttered a few yards away, I peered down into the ditch.

A small Pit Bull puppy attempted to lift his head. Exhausted, covered in blood, and clearly dying, he held his head an inch off the ground for a few seconds before collapsing. I hustled down into the deep ditch and stared down in disbelief at what I saw. Covered in dried blood and still bleeding, the poor puppy appeared to be close to death. As I carefully turned his body to inspect him, I noticed one bullet wound entered his shoulder and exited his upper back. Another bullet wound in his hind quarters appeared to not have an exit wound.

Fucking heartless cocksuckers.

His body, face, and legs were covered in old cuts and scars, undoubtedly from fighting. More than likely he had either lost a fight, and the owner was disappointed with his performance, or he wasn't as aggressive as the owner had hoped. Either way, someone had shot him twice and left him for dead.

"Hold on you little devil dog. I'll get you some help," I said.

I turned toward my bike. A quick recollection of what I had in my saddlebags turned up nothing to wrap him in. Frustrated and knowing time was of the essence; I quickly removed my cut and flipped it over my shoulder. After reaching down in the ditch and carefully picking up the pup, I ran across the highway to my bike.

Still holding the bleeding pup, I unlatched the left saddlebag and peered inside. A small tool kit was all that lay inside the bag. Cradling him in my arm, I grabbed my cut and wrapped the dog inside the leather vest.

"I'm wrapping you up in this cut, it'll keep you from going into shock. And although I don't know for sure, I'm thinking it's got special powers. Hold on, I'm going to get you to the vet. You'll be just fine. After he gets you stitched up, you can be this old Devil Dog's little devil pup," I said out loud as I lowered him into the enclosure.

I carefully placed the pup in the saddlebag and hopped on the bike. The closest competent veterinary office was in Wichita, almost fifteen miles away. I knew if the highway was as unpopulated at this short stretch, I could possibly be there in eight to ten minutes. I looked over my shoulder and into the bag. The pup blinked his eyes a few times and then they fell closed.

Devil looks after his own, little man. You're my little devil pup, and I'm a former Devil Dog. Hold on, 'cause I ain't going the speed limit.

Ten minutes or so of speeds in excess of 100 miles per hour, a few traffic signals I didn't stop for, and an all-out run down one of Wichita's major streets at 60 miles per hour, and I was in the parking lot at the vet's office. I kicked down the kickstand, reached into the bag, and cradled the puppy in my arms.

"I've got a puppy, he's got two gunshot wounds!" I shouted as I approached the receptionist's desk.

"Oh, uhhm. Give him here," the receptionist said as she held her arms outstretched.

I handed her the bloody pup. As she curled her arms to her chest, I realized I had just handed her my cut.

"I can't let you take that cut, hold on," I half-shouted as I pulled off my bloody shirt.

Standing shirtless, I reached toward her and lifted the pup from her arms. After removing him from my cut, I carefully wrapped him in my shirt. As I handed the whimpering puppy back to the startled girl, I forced a smile.

"I'll be right here," I said as I pointed toward the waiting area.

After filling out the necessary forms, waiting for thirty minutes with three angry caged cats, and answering two mid-twenties housewives' questions about the life of a biker, I began to wander through the office and look at dog collars and tags. A one inch wide camouflaged collar with a quick release fastener caught my eye.

"This is about the right size for him, isn't it?" I asked as I held it in the air for the receptionist to see.

She smiled and nodded her head.

"Does it snap apart like this to keep him from being choked?" I asked as I pulled the collar apart.

She nodded her head, "It's a safety collar. If they get hung up on something, it'll break loose, and keep them from choking."

We'll get you this one, I don't want you choking on anything.

I nodded my head once and looked around the rack for anything else which looked better. I wanted something that would fit the pup's aggressive stance and both of our personalities.

"Are you the gentlemen who brought in the Pit Bull Terrier mix?"

Holding the collar in my hand, I turned to face the voice. A man in his early forties was wearing a lab coat and holding a clipboard. His face was covered in hair and he smelled like chemicals.

"Sure was. How's he doing?" I nodded.

"I did everything I could for him. He didn't make it," he sighed, "I'm sorry."

I narrowed my gaze, "Little guy with two gunshot wounds?"

He nodded his head, "I'm sorry. One of the wounds was pretty invasive. His intestines and both kidneys were in pretty bad shape. He'd lost a lot of blood. I'm sorry."

"Motherfuckers," I grunted as I shook my head.

"Pardon me?" he said.

"Whoever shot that pup. I'd like to just…" I stared down at the floor and clenched my jaw.

"Did you find either of the slugs?" I asked as I looked up.

"Strange question. Actually he'd been shot at least three times, and yes. I recovered one of them," he responded.

"I want it. And I'll pay you for whatever you've done, don't worry about that," I said under my breath.

"I didn't doubt that. Hold on, let me see if I still have it," he said over his shoulder as he turned and walked away.

I slowly walked to the display area and hung the collar up on the rack. After a few minutes, the man in the lab coat walked from the double doors and into the hallway. With an outstretched hand he offered a small zip-lock bag containing a lead bullet. Although distorted, I could tell the caliber.

"Nine millimeter," I nodded as I studied the bag.

"Pardon me?"

"It's a nine millimeter slug. I know I never will, but I'd like to find the motherfucker who did this," I growled as I stuffed it into the front pocket of my jeans.

"Just between you and me, I hope you do. The punishment under the provision of the law is insufficient, in my opinion. And, for what it's worth, I'm truly sorry for your loss," he said.

"It was just some pup," I sighed.

As I looked down at the front of my blood soaked cut, I knew better.

TOAD

"No, it was just the straw that broke the camel's back. One more innocent life lost at the hand of evil. That, and the fact I couldn't do anything to save the poor fucker. Hell, I did all I could, and it wasn't enough. I'm just tired of it all," I complained.

"Seems strange," Otis paused and peered over both shoulders.

"You know, you cut that fucking child molester, and it didn't seem to bother you one lick. Now, some puppy dies, and you're shaken up pretty damned bad. Killing a human being is okay, but a dog dies and it rips you to shreds," Otis said under his breath.

"*The dog was innocent*," I growled.

Otis nodded his head and stared blankly.

"It was damned sure unnecessary for someone to shoot that pup. I said it then, and I'll say it again now…" I paused and looked over my shoulder.

It was mid-week in Wichita at eleven in the morning, and the bar was empty. I turned to face Otis, kicked my legs over the edge of the seat, and gripped the side of the table with my hands.

"That child molester *needed* to die. There wasn't anything evil about what we did to that son-of-a-bitch. Line up fifty motherfuckers like him, and I'll kill each and every one of 'em, and stand before God at the end of the day. Think about *this*; I know *you* don't have kids, but some of the fellas do. Imagine if one of the Sinners Ol' Ladies got a call from the cops, and they tell her that they have this child molestation case. They say they need her to come in and confirm or whatever. So she goes into the station house and they play a DVD for her. Has her son sucking fat boys cock and he shoots a load all over the kids face. Makes the kid jack him off…"

"Just stop, God damn it," Otis growled as he held his hands between us.

"I let you finish earlier, you let me finish. You brought it up," I grunted.

He nodded his head and waved toward the waitress.

"So, she watches and her kid jacks him off or whatever. They raid the house, arrest the guy, and the deal goes to trial; all the way to the jury. The jury finds him innocent, even though he's on the film with the kid. Some clerical error or whatever. They say they've got to let the guy off. The fat prick goes home and that's that," I paused and finished my beer.

"Now let's say she sees this fat child molesting cock sucker behind the laundrymat one night and she's got a knife or a pistol, or whatever. You trying to tell me she wouldn't do the same thing? Or better yet, what if the cops called her in and they showed her the film, and then said, *there the motherfucker is*, and they point him out in the interrogation room and hand her a knife. What's she gonna do?" I asked.

"She'd gut that fat bastard. Cut him from stem to stern," Otis breathed.

"You damned right she would. So comparing him to my puppy is a bad comparison," I said flatly.

"Point taken," Otis nodded.

"I'll tell you like I told Slice. I only do what I can justify. Might be bad in *your* mind, but in *mine* it's always justified. It may be contrary to law, society's belief, or the Bible, but in my mind it's the only answer. I'll never do what I believe to be evil or contrary to what I think God wants. If God didn't want me to kill that fat child molesting prick, he wouldn't have put him in front of me. It's no secret to God that I have the capacity to be one mean motherfucker. He knows it. I know it. I don't keep secrets with God, I make peace every night before bed."

"Well, for what it's worth, I'm sorry about the pup," Otis said.

"Appreciate it. I got the slug that killed him from the vet, and I'm going to find this prick," I said through my teeth.

"In case you don't know, Avery is working for a Federal attorney in Wichita as a legal secretary. He's some big deal. I don't remember his name, but he does Federal appeals, gun cases, and specializes in shit that includes firearms violations. Get this, one hundred percent of the cases he's taken to trial, he's won. One hundred fucking percent. So, if he agrees to take a case to trial, odds are you've got a pretty good case," Otis paused and leaned onto the edge of the table.

Half pissed off he offered this tidbit in the middle of the conversation, I responded in an irritated tone, "I'm not headed to federal court, but if I end up catching a case, I'll let you know. In case you forgot, we were talking about that fucking prick who shot my puppy."

"Well, I was *going* to make a point, but I got off fucking course. Just settle the fuck down Toad, and let me finish. So anyway, this guy's got connections in law enforcement, FBI, ATF, and so on and so forth. Well, Slice and Avery and I were talking about shell casings and bullets the other day, and this is really strange you mentioned this, but check this out," he leaned away from the table and took a drink of his beer.

"Everyone thinks they can trace a shell casing back to you, or trace a bullet. They can and they can't. Even if the gun's registered to you, they can't trace a casing or a bullet to your gun, unless they have the gun in their possession. There's no computer system in place to do it. They were trying to get a Federal database they could just plug the ballistic report into and *bam*, but the NRA threw a fit. So, they're fucked. *If* they get your gun, they can match it to a casing or bullet, but only if they have it. But here's the deal, or my point," he hesitated and leaned against the table again as he rubbed his hands together.

"When we were talking about it, Avery said the attorney turned down defending someone who was being tried on Federal charges of fighting dogs, primarily Pit Bulls. He said he didn't give a fuck if the guy was innocent or guilty, just being charged was enough for him to not want to take the case. *And*, it sounds like the guy was a local," Otis raised his hands in the air as if he'd completed an impossible task.

"Since when do the Fed's give a fuck about dogs?" I shrugged.

Otis shook his head, pushed himself away from the table, and tipped up his beer. As he placed the empty bottle onto the table, he leaned forward, "If you cross state lines, or if they can prove the dog has crossed state lines, it's a Federal case. But you're missing my point."

"This attorney might have the name of a local guy who fights dogs. He could be your guy, or he might know him," he said.

"Well, see what Slice's Ol' Lady can find out," I said.

"Two more?" the waitress asked.

"No thanks, but you can bring me the tab," Otis responded.

"Be right back," she said as she turned to walk away.

"Here," I said as I tossed a twenty dollar bill onto the table.

Otis pressed his fingers onto the bill and slid it across the table, "Keep it. You just bought a truck, trailer, and lawn equipment for Junior.

I'll get this one, you can get the next."

"Here you are," the waitress smiled as she handed Otis the tab.

Otis looked down at the tab, looked up at me, and grinned, "I fucking told ya."

"What?" I asked.

He turned the receipt around and shook it in the air, "Those two nasty assed beers. They were nine bucks a piece. When we go to Austin, you don't get to order the beers, you're too easily manipulated."

Maybe Otis was right and I was becoming easily manipulated and soft. For some reason, the puppy was definitely a turning point for me. The poor dog's death came at a time in my life when I either really needed it, or I really didn't.

I had yet to decide which one it was.

SYDNEY

After living for a considerable amount of time with nothing, I now looked at all life offered me and truly appreciated everything, being careful not to take even small things for granted. I learned in my time of misfortune that a friendly voice or a smile can be as valuable as anything else life has ever had to offer me.

"If you don't get another piece, Miss Sydney, I be likely to eat *all of it*," Junior grinned as he looked down at the remaining pizza.

"You go right ahead Junior, I'm full," I said as I pushed my chair away from the table slightly.

"Ever see you a pizza sandwich, Miss Sydney?" Junior asked.

I had an idea of what he planned, but I tilted my head slightly and narrowed my eyes, "No, I don't guess so."

He picked up a slice of pizza and laid it flat on the palm of his hand, "You takes you one like this, but he's got to be *cheese up*."

After removing another slice and holding it over the top of the first, he looked up and smiled, "And you lays you one down on top of it, but you got to go *cheese down* on the top slice."

"Now," he held the two pieces of pizza together, twisting the assembly back and forth, "you can eat it like a sandwich, and as long as you keep you a tight grip, nothin' falls on the floor. It's pizza, but it's a sandwich."

"That's a good idea,' I giggled.

Junior's hands were like everything else, huge. His fingers were as large as hotdogs, and his hands the size of small saucers. The size of a slice of pizza at the local pizza place was huge, but dwarfed by the size of Junior's hand. As he lifted the *pizza sandwich* to his mouth, he closed his eyes and moaned. After a few bites, he opened his eyes and lowered what little was left to his plate.

"You know the best thing about eatin' pizza sandwiches, Miss Sydney?" he asked as he wiped pizza sauce from the corner of his mouth with his finger.

"What's that, Junior?"

"You can eat a whole pie twice as fast. It gives you more time to do other things," he grinned.

"You don't like eating? Don't you enjoy it?" I asked.

He picked up the makeshift sandwich, took a few more bites, and as he finished chewing, responded, "When I was a young un, I used to eat and eat and eat. Momma says I wouldn't stop 'till my jaw got tired. I loved me some food when I was a boy. But now, I just eats to stay alive, Miss Sydney. If I still liked to eat like when I was a boy, I'd be a might bit bigger than I am now."

"I like to eat, I just don't eat very much," I grinned.

"You ain't much bigger'n a minute, Miss Sydney. But most white folk don't be quite as big as us black folks," he chuckled.

I shook my head and laughed. Talking to Junior was always a joy, regardless of what the subject was. It seemed most of the time when we talked, we talked about food or work. Now that he had another job, I hoped we would expand our conversations a little and get to know each other better. After he finished his pizza sandwich, he wiped his hands and took a drink of tea.

"I'll have to invite you over for some of my momma's cookin'. You'd eat like a little pig if you got a taste of some good southern food. My momma come up from Alabama. Her momma and grandmomma taught her how to cook just like the southern folk cooks. Ain't nothin' she can't cook, so she just cooks it all. You like macaroni and cheese, Miss Sydney?"

I grinned and nodded my head as I reached for my tea, "I suppose so. Yeah, I like macaroni and cheese."

He rubbed his palms together and grinned, "Well, my momma bakes it with crumbs on top. If you're lucky enough to get a corner piece, you can get some of that baked hard cheese; and whoooeeeee, that baked hard cheese is some good eatin'."

"It sounds good," I nodded.

He widened his eyes and shook his head from side-to-side, "Talkin' about it sure nuff ain't the same as having a helpin'. You know what a man ought to do, Miss Sydney?"

"What?" I responded.

"Make him a cookin' pan what has eight corners instead of four. And eight cornered pan. Then everyone could have 'em a corner piece. Cause if you ain't eatin' a corner piece, you ain't really eatin'," he said as he rubbed his hand against his stomach.

"Sure sounds like you enjoy your momma's cooking," I grinned.

"Sure nuff do. So, what's your mommas specialty? What's your momma's best food, Miss Sydney? The one you always have a hankerin' for?" he asked.

I knew at some point in time one of our conversations would have ended up heading in this direction. In time, they always do. The most difficult part for me was trying to be genuine while accepting all of the sympathy and sorrow when people expressed their condolences. I had learned in my short time on the earth that acting as if something was insignificant, in some respects, made it seem far less profound. Often I wished people would merely say *I'm sorry* instead of going on and on about my not having parents. After taking a shallow breath and exhaling I responded.

"Both of my parents passed away when I was really young. I never got to know them," I sighed as I studied my fingernails.

"I don't rightly know what to say Miss Sydney, other than I'm powerful sorry. What about your 'stended family? You got you some 'stended family, don't ya?"

I looked up from my fingernails, "It's okay. And what? My what family?"

He stretched his arms wide and smiled, "Your 'stended family. You're aunties and uncles and all of them."

"Oh, yeah. My *extended* family. I guess there's a few out there, but I don't know them. They didn't want us when we were little, so my big brother and I grew up in foster homes. I think it's crappy of them, so I haven't tried to get to know them, even now," I shrugged.

"Well, if'n you ain't got you a family, you can just go on and act like my momma's your momma. She likes her a big 'stended family," he grinned.

"It's okay, Junior," I said under my breath.

It's always nice to know when someone is sincere. So many times, people say things and you never really know if they're genuine or not in what they offer. Junior was sincere, and there was really no need to question him, his facial expressions confirmed it. As his eyes widened drastically, he reached for the last slice of pizza. Holding it in front of

142

his mouth, he smiled and continued.

"My little brothers and sisters ain't even my momma's babies. They're my aunties. She went off to the big house for smokin' that crack," he paused and took a bite of pizza.

"So is my brother. He's in prison," I chuckled.

My brother being in prison wasn't funny by any means, but the thought of all of it was, at least at this point. Junior's aunt in prison for crack, and his mother raising her children was admirable. Sometimes it seemed I couldn't catch a break, but regardless, I kept my chin up and was grateful for what life offered me.

"Prison makes me mad. For one man to lock another man up in a cage because he did something wrong. You know, when we was kids, my momma would slap our backside with a belt. That made us learn what to do and what *not* to do. She coulda locked us up in some cages, I suppose. But it shure nuff wasn't necessary. I don't think it's necessary for a man to lock another man in one of em, less maybe he killed somebody. Your brother didn't kill nobody, did he?"

I shook my head, "No, but they say he wanted to. A government agent asked him if he'd kill a member of..."

I hesitated and thought of how to word things. I wasn't ashamed of my brother's involvement in the motorcycle club, but I didn't want Junior to associate Toad's club with the actions or beliefs of my brother's club. I decided to simply call it a gang.

"...say, kind of like a rival gang. So, after discussing it for a few years, one night in the bar after several beers, he said he'd kill a member of the rival bunch if they were around. Or something like that."

He furrowed his brow and shook his head, "So the po-lice talked to him and fed him some beers till he said he would, then they put him in the big house just for *saying* it?"

I nodded my head, "Pretty much."

"Well, they ain't lookin' to keep him for long, is they?" he asked.

The thought of it made me want to cry. What he got and what he deserved were two totally different things. I wasn't one to complain, so I simply accepted it as what it was. I took a deep breath and exhaled. After a drink of tea, I shifted my gaze toward Junior and responded.

"They gave him life, Junior. He's in a federal prison in Kentucky. He doesn't ever get out."

Junior poked the remaining portion of pizza into his mouth. After chewing it and taking a drink of tea, he looked down at his shoes for a moment and closed his eyes. At the end of a lengthy awkward silence, he looked up.

"I said me a prayer for your brother, and for you, Miss Sydney. Sometimes tryin' to figure things out makes me want to just take off and scream real loud. Did I tell you 'bout the screamin' tree?"

I shook my head as I laughed, "No, you sure didn't."

"Well, I used to spend me some time out there when I was little. Now, I just goes out there once in a blue moon. She's a big tree north of town, by the river. She's old and mighty big and has branches reachin' for the sky," he hesitated and reached upward with both arms.

"One of her big bottom roots come up out of the ground and makes for a real nice chair. So, you can sit on that there root and scream all you want, and nobody hears ya, 'cause it's north of town. You go screamin' in town and folks think you's crazy, so it ain't a good idea. But screamin' makes me feel good sometimes, so I go's to my tree. It makes me a pretty good thinkin' tree too," he grinned.

I wasn't sure if I had ever screamed for nothing more than the sake of screaming. Something about it sounded fun. One day maybe I'd go to Junior's screaming tree and let out a lifetime of frustrations and anger.

"I'd like to see it sometime. I probably could use a good scream," I said.

"Well, as my momma always says," he hesitated and stood from his seat.

"There's no better time than right now. She says, *don't talk about it, be about it,*" he said as he turned his palms upward.

"I don't really have anything to scream about," I said.

"You can always scream about what you's happy about," Junior shrugged.

"Well, in that case, let's go," I smiled.

Because I'm about as happy as I've ever been.

SYDNEY

The screaming tree proved to be therapeutic. My yelling about the good things seemed like so much fun, I decided to scream about the bad things as well. After a few short bursts about my imprisoned brother, my parent's death, and my non-existent extended family, I was exhausted. After returning home I felt cleansed, relieved, and far less frustrated. Having a friend in general is always nice, but having one as genuine as Junior was a totally different type of blessing. For some reason, the majority of my friends since childhood had been male. I felt more comfortable with boys, and it never seemed I was in a competition with them for anything. With women, it was always a struggle for me. I always dismissed my reluctance to befriend women to lacking a father in my life and growing up with a brother as a best friend. Whatever the cause, I naturally migrated toward men for friendship and subconsciously avoided women.

After I sketched the final touches on the chalkboard, I leaned back and admired my work.

Not bad.

I stood, took a few steps back, and looked at the design for symmetry. Everything seemed pretty well placed. Even as a little girl, drawing and sketching had been an outlet for me. It seemed to provide a means of escaping reality back then, and now provided tremendous self-satisfaction. Although I hadn't done it for years, I purchased an old wood framed window from a local antique store, painted the frame, and painted the glass with chalkboard paint. After it dried, I used colored chalk and sketched a design on the board. Now I could hang my first piece of art on the walls proudly, knowing it was created with my hands and my mind. I blinked my eyes and took another step backward.

Happiness

is a friend

who doesn't judge

Each portion of script was encompassed in a banner, separated by various flowers and a leafy arrangement. The top banner was curved upward into the shape of a smile. It was perfect. I turned to walk to the utility room to get a screwdriver from the tools Toad had left, and was immediately startled by the doorbell. I hadn't heard a motorcycle, and from what I understood, Toad was going to Austin. I glanced down at my chalk covered sweats, grinned, and wiped my hands on my tee shirt. I quietly tiptoed to the door and pulled it open.

A woman holding a large cardboard box stood on the porch. Dressed in a vibrant blue dress, blue hat, and smiling from ear to ear, she spoke, "You must be Sydney. I'm Junior's momma, Shirley."

I grinned and opened the door, "Come in."

"Thank you, Baby. This darned weather can't decide whether to rain or just drizzle. Now grab this box if you can, it's killing my arms. I've got bad elbows from carrying all my babies around the house," she said as she extended her arms.

I reached out and took the box from her hands. The top was covered with cloth, so I wasn't able to see inside, but I assumed it was food of some sort. One easily identifiable smell was that of apple pie, one of my all-time favorites. As I moved aside, she stepped into the house and quickly took a look around the room.

She raised both hands to her mouth and screeched, "Oh Lord have mercy, you get robbed, Baby?"

"No, ma'am," I chuckled, "I just moved in. Well, kind of."

"Is this all of your belongings?" she asked as she motioned around the empty house.

I nodded my head, "Yes, ma'am, this is it. I'm grateful for what I *do* have, a roof over my head, and a bed to sleep in."

"Well bless your little heart. I do like your cute little table," she smiled as she pointed to the table Toad had left.

"Thank you. It's not mine, the landlord left it," I sighed.

She nodded her head toward the table, "Now put that box down on that table before it stretches your little arms out."

"Yes, ma'am," I grinned as I walked toward the table.

As I carefully placed the box on the table, she walked over and pulled a chair away from the table. After wiping the seat with her hand and inspecting her fingers for dust, she sat on the chair and grinned.

"Now let's have a us a seat, shall we? Like I said when I come in the door, my name's Shirley, but my friends will just call me Bee," she smiled.

"And I'm Sydney. Nobody calls me anything but that," I shrugged.

She smiled, removed the small towels from the box, folded them, and placed them on the table beside the box. One by one, she lifted the items from the box, placing them on the table carefully. As she did, she explained what they were.

"This is one of my apple pies. I won the spring contest down at the river with that exact pie. 1st place if I do say so myself. And this is sand hill plum jelly. Junior picked the plums, and I made it fresh last spring.

And this here's a jar of my pickled eggs. They're good for a snack or to eat with a sandwich, but you need to be mighty careful, Sydney. They'll make you pass gas," she paused and held the jar in the air.

I nodded my head and grinned.

"This is a jar of dill pickles, and this is a jar of sweet pickles. I don't mark the lids, but you can tell the difference because the dill pickles has a little red hot pepper inside, see it there?" she asked as she pointed to a very small red pepper in the side of the jar.

"Yes, ma'am, I see it," I nodded.

She pulled a Tupperware container from the box and placed it beside the pie, "This is my macaroni and cheese casserole. Kids cut all the corners out of it as quick as I took it out of the oven, so I couldn't get you a corner piece, but the middle's just as good. Now, Baby, you have to listen to me…"

I nodded my head and smiled, "I'm listening."

"Don't you dare take a bite of this casserole if it's cold. Promise me that," she said.

"I promise," I giggled.

"And when you heats this up, you can't do it in one of them microwaves; it'll ruin it. You've got to heat it in the *oven* at 350 degrees. Now be sure and pre-heat your oven, and about ten or twelve minutes is plenty. Now don't dare heat it in my Tupperware, put it in a casserole dish or a metal cake pan. It's the only way to get it back to right. Understand?" she asked.

I nodded my head eagerly, "Yes ma'am."

"Oh Lordy, you don't have you any dishes, do you?" she asked.

"Yes, ma'am. I have dishes and silverware. I'm just a little short on furniture," I chuckled.

As she carefully placed each item back in the box, she began to speak, "Now Junior tells me your momma died when you was a baby. And your daddy too. I'm downright sorry that happened, Baby. I know I can't ever replace your momma, but I can sure be here for you when you need me. A little girl needs to have her a momma to talk to. When you grow up, you'll understand. Now how old are you, Baby? About eighteen?"

"No, ma'am, I'm not eighteen, that's funny. I'm uhhm, I'm thirty. Well, I'll be thirty on October 1st. And yes, my parents both passed when I was young."

"Well, just because you're a grown woman don't mean you can't use a little lovin'. Like I said, if you ever need me you just give me a call or come on by. My phone number is in the bottom of the box. I wrote it down with my recipe for the casserole. Now I've got to get out of this hard little chair. My hind end is a killin' me," she said as she stood from the chair.

I grinned and stood from my chair, "I appreciate all of the food, and just I love apple pie. From what Junior said, I'll love it all. As soon as I'm finished with them, I'll bring all your dishes back to you."

"Whenever you're done. Oh my, now did you make that? That's cute," she said as she pointed to the chalkboard leaning against the wall.

"Yes, ma'am, I just finished it," I said as I tilted my head toward the wall.

"*Happiness is a friend who doesn't judge*. Oh, Baby, that's precious. Happiness is a friend who doesn't judge, amen to that," she said as she raised her hand to her mouth.

"I like it. I made it after Junior took me to his secret tree."

"When he was a little boy, well now let me tell you, Junior was never *little* but when he was a *boy*, if I couldn't find him I always knew where he'd be. Out at that darned tree sittin' and thinkin'. Junior's a thinker for sure. And Junior sure don't judge. No, Baby, he sure don't. I raised him different than that. I can tell you had good upbringing, you're respectful and polite, and you don't judge either. Cute little white girl bein' friends with Junior. We don't see that too much, especially in this small little town. Junior's boss is a blessing too," she said as she clasped her hands together.

"He saved me from the mess I was in, that's for sure. He put me up in this house, gave me a job, and asked for nothing in return."

"I love what that man has done for Junior, I just don't like his name. *Toad*. Now you know a toad is the warted frog, the one that'll put warts on your fingers if you touch him. You know that don't ya?' she asked.

I grinned and nodded my head even though I knew it wasn't necessarily true, "It's short for his last name. *Todelli*, I think."

"Well, I knew it was something like that. But yes, he's a good man. He's proof you can't judge. Townfolks call all those boys names; the ones on the motorbikes. Ain't never been nothin' but friendly to me. This little old town is like a step back in time. I guess it's both good and bad. Now I better get to gettin', I've got some errands to run," she said as she turned toward the door.

"Thank you again," I said as she turned around.

"Don't even mention it, Baby, and you let me know what you think about the pie," she said as I opened the door.

"I sure will. Bye, Bee," I grinned as she stepped onto the porch.

She raised her hand and waved as she cautiously stepped off the porch. I watched as she walked out to the street and got into her car. After she pulled away, I closed the door and turned toward the table.

The smell of apple pie filled the house. I closed my eyes and took a deep breath, wishing I was at the old tree again.

To scream about the good things.

TOAD

The ride out of Wichita was a reminder of what being a biker was all about. Although it wasn't raining when we left, Oklahoma produced a horrendous thunderstorm. Now riding through one of the hardest rainstorms I had ever seen, the drops felt like needles pressing into my skin. Riding without a helmet might not be the most sensible thing a man could do, but for me it was another way for me to thumb my nose at society, rules and regulations. As Slice, Otis, Biscuit and I cut a path through the wet stretch of highway I could see a hint of sunshine off in the distance.

Regardless of the ninety degree summer temperatures, the fact I was soaked from head to toe and not wearing any more than a tee shirt, my cut, jeans, and boots left me feeling uncomfortable. I began thinking of the day I met Sydney, her wrinkled blouse, and how cute she looked otherwise. Lost in thoughts of her kind nature, good attitude, and smart mouth, the next thirty miles passed in what seemed like a matter of minutes.

Finally, sunshine.

Slice released his left grip and pointed at his gas tank. I nodded my head and pointed down at my gas tank. Biscuit, riding to my left, looked down at his fuel gauge and grinned. As the warmth of the summer sun began to suck the moisture from the highway, we took the next exit and pulled into a gas station.

"Glad that shit's over. Hell of a storm," Slice said as he pumped gas into his tank and looked off to the north.

"Raindrops felt like fucking razors," I said.

"Try riding this motherfucker with no windshield and fucking ape hangers," Slice grunted, "the only thing to stop that shit is my face."

My motorcycle was equipped with a fairing, windshield, cruise control, and a CD player. The rain, although not eliminated, was diverted by the small windshield. My head, clearly above the windshield, caught road debris, rain, and bugs no differently than anyone else's, but it was fractionally less direct.

"Not interested. I'll keep this bagger," I nodded.

"Fucking raining like a cow pissin' on a flat rock," Biscuit chuckled, "I'm going inside, need to get some Red Bull in me, I'm dryin' out."

Biscuit drank Red Bull energy drinks by the case. He kept a refrigerator in his home stocked with them, and drank roughly eight or ten a day. We all assumed they helped with his sharp wit and fast mouth, but we had no means of comparison because he was *always* drinking them. As Slice followed Biscuit inside the gas station, I turned toward Otis.

As I took off my cut and hung it on the handlebars, I spoke over my shoulder, "I'm thinking when we get back to town I'm going to see if Sydney wants to go out. I'm tired of following her around wondering if she'll say yes or no."

He scrunched his nose and narrowed his eyes, "Go out?"

"Mmmmhmmm," I said as I pulled off my wet tee shirt.

"Like *out*? You're going to go on a fucking date?" he chuckled.

As I leaned over and unlatched my saddlebag, I responded, "I can't tell you the last time I took a chick somewhere. Maybe I'll see if she wants to go eat or something."

Otis crossed his arms and cocked his head to the side, "A date? That's funny as fuck, brother."

"Now I'm funny as fuck. Thanks, O," I said as I pulled a clean tee shirt from the saddlebag.

"Nothing wrong with it, hell I hope everything works out. You've been talking about her for a month and a half. It's just funny, seems like just the other day you were Saran Wrapping Sloan into a ball and butt fucking her and now you want to ask little Miss Innocent on a fucking *date*," he said.

"Who's going on a date?" Biscuit grunted as he took a sip from his can of Red Bull.

Oh Jesus, here we go…

Otis continued to gaze my direction, raised his eyebrows and waited.

I pulled the tee shirt over my head and grabbed my cut from the handlebars. As I slipped my arms through the cut, I responded, "I was telling Brother Otis I was going to ask Sydney out when we got back."

"The girl with the stinky twat from the bank? Well isn't that cute," Biscuit sighed.

"She doesn't have a stinky twat," I snapped.

"You smelled it? I'm just going off what she told us. She said if you were gonna tap that shit you needed a warm washrag and soap. Sounds like a stinky twat to me," Biscuit shrugged.

"Sinners don't fuck girls with rotten pussies. We fuck princesses," Slice chuckled, "Who's fucking a nasty bitch?"

"Toad's gonna fuck the girl from the bank with the stinky pussy. He's gonna ask her on a date as soon as we get home," Biscuit said as he finished the can of Red Bull.

Axton knelt down and pulled his dipstick, checking his oil level. As he wiped the dipstick and pushed it back into the engine case, he peered over his shoulder, "Girl from the bank's got a stinker does she? Hell, I saw her at your barbeque joint the other night; she *looked* like she was clean. She didn't wait on me, so it'd be hard to say for sure, but I didn't smell anything. Guess a man can never tell."

Biscuit hooked his thumbs into his front pockets and tilted his head toward Slice, "Her rotten twat ain't the topic of *this* discussion, Slice. Topic's *this*, Toad's going to ask her on a fucking date. You ever seen Toad on a date?"

Slice stood and crossed his arms. After studying Biscuit for a short moment, he turned to face me, "You going on a date with one of your employees? That's probably not the best plan a man can come up with, but I'm pleased in your progress, Toad."

"Stinky twat girl's gonna be fuckin' the boss man," Biscuit chuckled.

Otis, as always, was the only one not commenting. Generally, Otis kept his mouth shut during situations like this. He didn't want to encourage Biscuit, and as long as *someone* was speaking, Biscuit would continue. If no one else spoke, he'd persist as long as everyone would listen. Personally, I was done listening.

"I'm going to piss," I sighed.

"If the next stop's Wichita Falls, I better take a piss too," Otis agreed.

As we walked into the gas station, Otis didn't say a word. I could always count on him to provide useful feedback on a matter I was willing to discuss, and maintain silence when I wasn't willing to speak. Other than Axton, there wasn't another member of the Sinners who was as solid and caring as Otis.

Second guessing myself wasn't something I did often, but as I walked out of the bathroom and through displays of snacks, I began to wonder if asking Sydney out was a good idea. While I stumbled along the dingy tile floor thinking, Otis stepped from behind an aisle and extended his arm.

"Here," he said as he handed me a box.

I looked down at the pink box. *Massengill Country Flowers Disposable Douche.*

"You might need it," Otis chuckled.

I tossed the box into the display of corn nuts and sunflower seeds, "You know I was just thinking how much I appreciated you *not* acting like an asshole earlier. Good lookin' out, Otis."

"I thought it was funny. You want to know what's funnier?" Otis said as he slapped me on the back.

I shook my head and opened the door, "What's that?"

As Otis walked through the door, he turned and looked over his shoulder, "That this shit-hole gas station carries douches."

"Maybe there's a plague of twat funk down here. Hell, we are in Oklahoma," I chuckled as I walked out to the bikes.

"Enough said," Otis said under his breath.

"You ready to hit the road, lover boy? Or you want to text your girlfriend and tell her you're alright before we go?" Biscuit growled as he lowered himself into the seat of his bike.

"No, I already sent her a text, while I was taking a shit," I responded.

"Let's roll," Axton said as he started his bike.

Spending a week with Biscuit after his finding out about my interest in Sydney could prove to be irritating. I reached for the hand controls and flipped the ignition on. As the engine started, I grinned at the sound of the high performance cams. The engine had a definite *don't fuck with me* rumble to it now.

"Race to the entrance on the highway?" Otis hollered.

I nodded my head as I pulled my sunglasses down from my brow, "I thought you'd never ask."

Slice and Biscuit followed as Otis and I pulled our bikes onto the road leading to the highway. After pulling his bike to the side, Biscuit stepped off and stood in front of us with his hands up. After Otis and I both acknowledging our state of readiness, Biscuit dropped his hands.

I released the clutch and twisted the throttle to its limit. After shifting through three gears, I was fifteen feet ahead of Otis and traveling 80 miles per hour. As I slowed down to enter the highway, I began to wonder if Otis *allowed* me to win, or if I did so because my bike was truly faster.

Either way, it was exactly what I needed when I needed it.

SYDNEY

Every time I had moved into a new home or apartment, I felt out of place for a period of time; almost like an imposter. Waking up and realizing I was in an unfamiliar place made me feel uneasy. Dishes in a different cupboard, the dresser in an odd location, or a new route home from work acted as a reminder I was in a new location. The uneasy feeling lingered for various lengths of time, but inevitably a day would come when I felt like it was truly *my* home, and I belonged there.

Today was that day.

"No, I don't ride, but I'm going to take the course and learn," she responded.

"Some more tea?" I asked as I stood.

"Sure," she responded as she lifted her glass.

I carried our glasses to the kitchen and filled them with ice and tea. Avery had been visiting for almost an hour, and as much as I disliked females, I couldn't help but like her. She was a no nonsense woman, and seemed to have no issues whatsoever with speaking her mind. After meeting in the restaurant, she explained she was the Ol' Lady of the President of the Selected Sinners. Discussions of my brother being a biker followed, and I later shared with her how I was renting a house from Toad. We immediately hit it off, and I invited her to come over, talk, and get to know each other better.

"Here you go," I said as I slid the glass of tea across the table and sat down.

"I really like that, you made it?" she asked as she tilted her head toward the chalkboard.

"I sure did. I got an old window, painted it with chalkboard paint, and just scribbled on it," I responded.

"Well, I like it. You've got talent. And you know, a friend who doesn't judge is like an impossibility to find," she sighed.

"They're rare, that's for sure," I grinned.

"You know, I had this friend, Sloan. Well, I guess I still have her. We went to college together. We were best friends. And when I started seeing Axton, she became kind of jealous. She started hitting on him, and walking around the house half naked hoping he'd come over. When he and I started seeing each other seriously, she became *more* jealous. Then, it was almost like she became obsessed with finding a Sinner to fuck just to compete with me. I guess it's not really judging, but jealousy. You ought to make another that says *happiness is a friend who doesn't get jealous*," she giggled.

I nodded my head as I took a drink. As I swallowed the tea and placed the glass on the table, I shook my head slightly, "*That* is why I don't have many female friends."

"I'm not big on people who are dishonest; male or female. And jealousy seems like dishonesty to me. It just causes people to act differently, and sooner or later, someone is doing something shady," she said.

"I never thought of it that way, but you're right. So did your friend, Sloan, ever find her Sinner," I asked.

"No, not really. She hung around Toad for a while, but she irritated him, so he told her to kick rocks," she said.

Strangely, the thought of Avery's friend being with Toad made me feel uneasy. In some respects, I suppose I felt jealous, no differently than what she and I had been discussing. I had no right to feel the way I did, but I felt it nonetheless. After a short pause to collect my feelings and come to terms with the fact I may be more attracted to Toad than I wanted to admit, I smiled and spoke.

"*Kick rocks*. My brother says that a lot in the letters he writes me. I don't know if it's a prison saying or a biker saying, but he sure says it a lot," I nodded.

"I picked it up from these guys. Did your brother do time?" she asked.

"Doing time now and forever, he's doing life," I said flatly.

"Life? Oh wow. I'm sorry," she said.

"It's okay. It's just kind of frustrating. If he actually did something, I'd probably accept it more. He was in a club, like I told you earlier, and there was this ATF agent," I paused and reached for my tea.

As I twisted my tea glass in a circle, I continued, "This ATF agent infiltrated the club. He acted like a biker, grew a two foot long beard, shaved his head, got tattoos, and really looked the part. He started hanging around, and then became a Prospect. After he was patched into the club, he began asking about a rival club and what they'd do if they encountered anyone from the other club in their territory. This went on for two years. One night in a bar, after he was half drunk, my brother said he would kill them if he saw them. The sad thing is my brother didn't *offer* to kill them; he was kind of *coerced* to say it. The ATF agent kept asking him *would you kill them, would you kill them, would you kill them?*"

"Eventually, my brother said *yes*."

She sat up in her seat and pushed her tea aside, "Holy crap. They set his ass up. Like a reverse sting."

"Exactly," I sighed.

It was always nice to have someone share my opinion about my brother's lack of involvement in the *crime* he committed. It acted as confirmation he didn't deserve the punishment he received, and provided me reassurance I didn't feel the way I felt simply because he was my brother. Later, it always seemed to make me feel a little more saddened by the fact what happened *actually happened*.

Avery's eyes filled with excitement, "Sounds like a classic case of entrapment to me. I don't know how RICO plays in with entrapment, I'll have to look. I hate to ask, but I kind of have to, did your brother ever kill anyone before this ATF agent approached him?"

"No, you might have misunderstood. He didn't kill anyone. Not before, during, or after. He's never killed anyone," I explained as I stared at the ring of moisture my glass was leaving on the table.

"As far as you know, had the club ever been to trial at any other point in time for murder or conspiracy to commit?" she asked excitedly.

I looked up from my glass of tea, "You sound like an attorney. And I don't know if they had ever been in that kind of trouble before, why?"

She quickly stood from her chair and raised her hands to her face. As she rubbed her temples and stared toward the chalkboard, I began to wonder why she was asking all of the questions. After a long silence, she looked down and spoke.

"Sorry, no I'm not an attorney. I majored in Criminal Justice, love law, hate cops, and now work for an attorney who specializes in Federal Appeals. I was trying to think of a case we studied in college. It was an entrapment case. I can't think of it now, but it starts with an S. Fucking hell," she said as she began to pace the floor.

Sometimes it took me a minute to realize exactly what Avery had said. She talked a hundred miles an hour, and often it seemed I had to wait a moment and really think of what she was saying after she was done saying it. It was pretty obvious she was intelligent and her mind worked as fast as she spoke.

I stood from my chair, "So what's the case say, whatever it is?"

"Well, the *law* says this. The defendant, your brother in this case, must be predisposed to commit the crime charged in the indictment prior to being approached by government agents," she blurted.

"Okay, what does that mean?" I asked.

As she continued to pace the floor, she responded, "Okay, listen carefully. If I was an ATF agent, and I wanted to arrest a killer without having him actually kill someone, I'd have to do it in *this order*. First, prove he was a killer. Second, approach him. Third, get him to admit he was planning to kill again. If the first step isn't met, and it must be met *first*, the law says the ATF agent can never approach the man. Entrapment is against the law. And, entrapment is when a government agent coerces or induces a person who otherwise lacked the predisposition to commit the crime to commit a crime. So, if he hadn't killed anyone before or wasn't advertising the fact he wanted to, they couldn't as a matter of law ever approach him."

"I think I'm still lost," I admitted.

"Okay, how about *this*. It's against the law for the ATF to ask your brother if he wanted to kill someone if they can't prove he was *already* a killer, and they knew that fact before they ever walked up to him and said *hi*," she blurted.

"Oh wow. Really?" I asked

"Really," she immediately responded.

"Did he appeal the conviction?" she asked.

I shook my head, "No."

"Did his attorney mention entrapment or try to introduce it as a defense?" she asked.

"No," I responded.

"You sure?" she asked as she raised her hands to her mouth.

"Positive, I sat through the entire trial," I responded.

"Did he have a public defender? A free attorney provided by the government?" she asked.

I nodded my head, "Yes, he sure did. I hate to say it, but the guy was a lazy fat prick."

"Fuck yes! Might be an Ineffective Assistance of Counsel claim right there. It's enough to get our foot in the door, anyway," she shouted.

"I really hate to get my hopes up. He can't afford an attorney, and I know I can't either," I shrugged.

She stopped pacing and turned to face me, "I'll talk to my boss. He may take the case for the exposure alone. If he won't, fuck it. I'll do this motherfucker myself."

"But you said you weren't an attorney," I said.

"I'm not. But if we have to we'll file the shit *pro se*. One way or another, we'll get something filed and see if we can get a new trial," she said as she clapped her hands.

"So you could actually do this yourself?" I asked.

She nodded her head, "Hell, anyone *can* do it, but you don't want some dumb ass doing it. It has to be someone who knows their shit. It's called *pro se*. It's Latin, it means *on one's own behalf.* Because you only get one shot, and you must reference *good law* in your legal motions, you don't want to make a mistake."

"Sounds complicated and time consuming," I said.

"It is, and it's right up my alley. I'll get copies of all of the court records and start reading as soon as I get them. I'll keep you posted on what I find. I'll need his name and the case number if possible," she said as she walked toward me.

"I'll get it all gathered up and let you know. Now that I've finally got a phone, I can do things like that," I grinned.

As she opened her arms and stood in front of me, I was surprised. I barely knew her, and she was offering to do something like this. I doubted it would really make any kind of a difference, but it sure seemed like she was going to try. Hugging an almost stranger seemed awkward, but considering the circumstances, I opened my arms and embraced her.

"Okay, I'm going to go get started reviewing law," she said as she released me.

"It's ten o'clock at night," I chuckled.

"I've got inferiority issues. I need to do shit like this to prove to myself that I'm not worthless," she responded.

Avery's visit made me feel great. She was genuine, intelligent, full of energy, absolutely gorgeous, and not a typical female. It was almost as if she was a man trapped in the body of a woman. So far she was proving herself to be a great person, and if things continued the way they were, I could see myself becoming very good friends with her.

"You're not worthless," I smiled.

"We're about to find out," she responded as she walked to the door.

I held my hand to my chest and grinned, "I already have. I enjoyed this. Thanks for coming over."

"Well, my man's out of town, and I need something to do anyway.

Maybe I'll see you again tomorrow," she said.

"I'd like that," I smiled.

After she drove away, I closed the door and turned toward the table. The chalkboard on the wall behind the table was becoming more applicable as the days passed. For Avery to volunteer to do what she was going to do without knowing me, my brother, or the Hell's Fury club, she was truly a person who didn't judge.

I picked up the glasses of tea, dumped them in the sink, and got ready for bed. As I lay in bed staring at the ceiling, I realized since the day I met Toad, my life had slowly began to fall into place. The silly chalkboard I had made could really be applied to all of the people I had met through Toad.

Biscuit and Otis were both willing to hand me money upon learning of my being homeless. Toad, without a doubt was nonjudgmental. Junior, his mother, and Avery were the same. Still staring at the ceiling, I closed my eyes and did something I hadn't done since I was a very small girl.

Thank you, Lord, for introducing me to my new friends. Please keep them from harm. In your name I ask these things, amen.

TOAD

Axton slid his arm through his cut, began walking toward the bathroom, and glanced over his shoulder, "I think I cut my fucking ear shaving. What did you fuckers decide? Are you going downtown or are you going to just wait in the lot?"

Axton and I had stayed in the adjoining room, and Otis and Biscuit had stayed in the other. After a good night's sleep and a shower, we were ready to go to the meeting and get our day of relaxation in Austin started. The temperatures in excess of 100 degrees were perfect for riding and enjoying the sun. Additionally, Austin was a place for everyone, bikers included. The cities motto was *Keep Austin Weird.*

"Doesn't make good sense to go downtown if the meeting's only going to be thirty minutes or so, we can wait outside," I responded.

Axton had explained that the meeting was to include only one spokesperson from each club. The existing clubs in the area would meet with the spokespersons from the new club, and after finding out the potential new club's anticipated membership, intent, and claimed territory would vote on whether or not the club posed a threat or would be allowed to assemble in the territory requested. The fact the club asked for a meeting spoke highly of the founders of the club, as many MC's start up every day without so much as understanding the proper protocol.

Starting a club and wearing colors with rockers claiming territory without the permission of existing clubs is a sure fire way to get killed. Texas was not only a Bandido state, it was *the* Bandido state. 1%er clubs in Texas were rarely given the right to even fly a rocker claiming the state as their own. The Bandidos refused to give permission. Being established in 1966, they were the original Texas 1% group. A great club with equally great men, but they had no interest in sharing the claim to their state. A non 1% club would have no problems starting up, though. At least this club was starting out on the right foot. After a short meeting, we, as well as all other clubs in attendance, would know their intent or interest in territorial claim. .

"Whatever you fellas want to do," Axton sighed as he walked out of the bathroom holding his ear.

"I don't know that it's a good idea for you to be running across town alone. I'd feel more comfortable with the four of us. One Sinner is an easier target than four," I responded as I looked toward Otis.

"I agree with the Sergeant at Arms. Fuck, last one of these I went to in Wichita lasted about twenty minutes, shouldn't be a big deal. We'll sit in the parking lot, out of sight so we don't *intimidate anyone*," Otis chuckled.

"All you got to do is show up, Otis and you intimidate people. Point taken, Toad. We'll roll out there, I'll go in the meeting, and when it's over we'll all go out and you fellas can have some beers. Hell, maybe some of the other clubs will want to go," Axton said as he removed the bloody tissue from his ear.

"I'm going to go into this deal looking like an idiot who doesn't even know how to fucking shave," Axton said as he wiped his finger along the bottom of his ear.

"These are the richest, snottiest, brattiest little bitches I ever seen, but

I can't stop watchin' this shit," Biscuit said as he stared at the television.

"You're the only motherfucker I know who doesn't have a television, Biscuit. What the fuck are you watching?" Axton asked.

"What is it, Otis?" Biscuit asked as he continued to stare at the T.V.

"*Keeping up with the Kardashians*, he's been watching it for three hours," Otis laughed.

"This is some good shit. One of 'em just dropped a $75,000 earring in the ocean, and she's throwin' a fit. Who wears $75,000 earrings anyway?" he asked.

"Shit, I bet that bitch wipes her ass with $75,000 toilet paper," I chuckled.

"Big basketball player boyfriend just found it. Ain't that some shit? You know they found that sum bitch when they was on a commercial. He probably handed it to that big dumb prick and told him to claim he found it when the commercial was off. God damn, these girls are hot," Biscuit howled.

"You do realize that they edit this shit, right?" Otis asked.

"What do you mean?" Biscuit shrugged.

"Nevermind," Otis sighed.

"Alright. Jesus fucking Christ, enough about the Kardashians. Good God, men. I feel like I'm in a room of high school girls. Let's roll. My ear can air dry. It's already 105 degrees in this God forsaken place," Axton growled.

"Rollin'," Otis said as he pointed to the door.

Biscuit, still standing with his eyes glued on the television, held his finger in the air, "Gimme just a minute."

Frustrated with Biscuit, Axton shoved the hotel room door open and burst out into the parking lot, "I swear, I wonder if you motherfuckers don't just do shit to piss me off."

He hopped on his bike and immediately started it. After the engine warmed, he began revving the motor, blowing the loud exhaust against the building.

"Poor fucker doesn't have a T.V. at home," Otis yelled.

I nodded my head as I started my bike. Within a couple of minutes of coming outside, we were all revving our motors loudly. It sounded like a bunch of children had been given control of the throttle of our bikes. As the deafening sound of our exhaust echoed against the wall of the brick building, Biscuit came through the door.

"Sorry fellas. Had to see how it ended," he yelled as he hopped on his bike.

"It *doesn't*," Otis laughed as he released his throttle, "That one you're watching is a few years old."

"I don't even want to know how you know that," Axton hollered over his shoulder.

"Meeting is at some warehouse two miles south of here. Two abreast, and maintain distance, who's up here with me?" Axton hollered.

I raised my left hand. Axton nodded his head, released his clutch, and slowly began to move forward. As we rolled out of the parking lot and onto the access road which ran parallel with the highway, the sound of the bikes echoed against the concrete structure supporting the elevated highway. Being in the club provided a sense of brotherhood, but something about riding in a group always provided me with a feeling of brotherhood *and* power. As we merged into traffic, our positioning and ease of riding with each other reminded me of Marines marching. When the Sinners rode in groups, we were always synchronized.

After a few miles, Axton's left arm shot upward, indicating a right turn. As we exited the highway, it was immediately apparent which building we were going to. A few hundred feet from the intersection was a metal building with a small concrete parking lot out front. Twenty bikes perfectly positioned in the small lot stood as proof the riders were in tune with club practices. Axton tossed his head in the direction of the building. I nodded my head in affirmation as I pointed toward the building.

As we pulled into the lot, we situated our bikes at the end of the row of motorcycles already parked. A quick check of time by Axton indicated the meeting was probably underway or close to it. Now even more frustrated, Axton stepped from his bike and turned toward Biscuit.

"You and that fucking Kardashians shit," Axton growled.

"Can't help it boss, that girl turns my fuckin' crank. I'd like to fuck her until she couldn't even walk," Biscuit said.

Axton shook his head and turned to face his bike.

"Don't imagine Kanye West would appreciate that," Otis chuckled.

Biscuit turned toward Otis and shrugged his shoulders, "Who the fuck's Kanye West?"

"Alright, you three can stay out here and talk about rappers and millionaires, I'm going in. Don't be dicking around out here making a bunch of noise or racing up and down the street like a bunch of fucking kids. Just stand here and enjoy this weather. I'll be back in thirty minutes or so," Axton said as he looked at his ear in the rearview mirror of his bike.

"Got it, boss," Otis nodded.

"I'll keep it civil," I said flatly.

"Do that," Axton said as he turned and walked toward the door.

Biscuit stepped toward Otis and me, pushed his thumbs into his front pockets, and grinned, "So, when we were headed toward Temple and that truck kicked that fuckin' rock up and hit my windshield, it got me to thinkin'. What's the biggest thing you ever had to dodge on the road? And I don't mean some deer on the side of the highway that startled you. I mean you had to take the ditch or hit the shoulder or the other lane or somethin'? Biggest object or whatever?"

"You all know my story. When we were headed to Sturgis in 2006. On that two lane highway when a truck in the other lane lost half a tire. I was riding sweep, and keeping my distance, and this motherfucker lost a tire. I watched that fucker roll toward me thinking it was going to miss me. Next thing I know, boom! I hit that motherfucker, blew out a front tire, and rode on the rim for a half mile before I got stopped. Damn near shit my pants," Otis responded.

"Don't count. I said dodge. You didn't dodge shit, brother. You *hit* it. What have ya missed?" Biscuit snapped.

As Otis stood and thought, I stared blankly across the street. The building where we were parked was in what appeared to be a residential area. The adjoining streets were filled with small poorly taken care of homes. A street perpendicular to the street in front of the building intersected a few feet beyond the far side of the lot the building was on. Close to the intersection of the two streets, a man sat in an old Ford Taurus. An intermittent puff of smoke indicated the car was running. The manner in which he was positioned in the seat indicated he was either half asleep or he didn't want to be seen.

"Guess it would have to be a dog. Had one run out in front of me chasing a cat or squirrel or something. Motherfucker got in my lane, stopped, and just fucking stared at me. Hell, I was east of Wichita, coming in for a poker run. We stared at each other like we were both in a trance. At the last minute, it was pretty obvious he was either too stupid to move, or stubborn as fuck. I took the other lane and missed him by about five feet," Otis said.

"That's a boring as fuck close call. What about the Toad man? Whatcha got Toad," Biscuit asked.

I shifted my gaze from the car to Biscuit. Although the car and the occupant made me uncomfortable, I didn't dare say it. Spending many years in Iraq, I learned to study people, their patterns of behavior, and their body language. Seeing someone nervously walking toward a car in Iraq typically indicated the vehicle was loaded with a bomb or the person was in route to plant an Improvised Explosive Device. How a person held their arms as they walked or what they were wearing may indicate they were hiding a weapon. In previous wars, our troops were fighting a force of resistance who were in uniform, and clearly identified as the opponent. Encountering a person in civilian clothes provided our soldiers and Marines with comfort the person was in fact a civilian, and not a threat. In Iraq and Afghanistan, the opponent was incapable of being labeled a civilian or a threat by their dress alone. Anyone, at any time, could be a threat. As a result, we learned to identify a threat based solely on their behavior.

Upon returning from the war and becoming a Prospect for the Sinners, I repeatedly made verbal note of anyone who made me uncomfortable. The constant replies of *you're not at war anymore, Toad, no one's out to get ya* caused me to stop revealing my thoughts. My nervous attention to detail, however, never ceased.

Biscuit's fast talking brought me back to a conscious state of awareness, "Where'd you wander off to, motherfucker?"

"Huh?" I responded as I attempted to focus my eyes on Otis.

"Over here," Biscuit said as he snapped his fingers.

"You alright brother? You go back to Afghanistan for a minute?" Biscuit chuckled.

"No, I was…I was just thinking," I responded.

Biscuit looked down at his feet as he kicked a rock from the concrete lot toward the street, "About stinky twat?"

"She doesn't have a stinking fucking twat, and no. Just, I don't know, thinking. Why the fuck are you fucking with me?" I snapped.

He looked up with widened eyes, "Whoa. Settle down, killer. Did ya get enough sleep last night? Maybe you need to take a little nap."

"Fuck off, I'm fine," I snapped.

"Damn, take it easy. We was talkin' about dodgin' shit in the road. What's your best?" he asked.

I glanced toward the car. The occupant was still slumped in the seat. After a few seconds, a puff of smoke from the exhaust provided proof the car was still running. After staring blankly for some time, I shifted my gaze to Biscuit.

"A wheelbarrow," I responded.

"No shit?" he asked.

"Yep," I nodded.

"Already heard this, it's a good one. Tell him, Toad," Otis chuckled.

"Well, I was on the highway headed up to Newton. I'm behind this guy in a truck. The highway's a two-lane at that point, headed north on 35. So, I'm behind this prick, and there's a string of cars on my left, and cars behind me for a mile. It's rush hour, if Wichita has one. It was like 5:15, just after everyone's getting out of work," I paused and glanced toward the car.

As I shifted my gaze to the fellas, I continued, "So I'm behind this fucker, and his tailgate on the truck is down, and the back is full of construction shit: tools, shovels, a tool box, and this fucking wheelbarrow. I'm behind him about twenty feet, following pretty close, and I'm studying this wheelbarrow. It's bouncing up and down, and I'm thinking *is this motherfucker tied down?*"

"So I study it, and I watch it wobble around for a few miles. Now you know how when you see something like that you try and decide if it's a threat or not?" I asked.

Biscuit reached into his saddlebag, "Red Bull anyone?"

I shook my head. As Biscuit took a drink, he nodded his head eagerly, "I sure as fuck do. I pay attention to all that shit. Hell, Brother, you gotta keep your eyes peeled."

"Okay, so we hit this expansion joint or whatever, and this fucking wheelbarrow flies out of the back of his truck. Now I'm tooling along about 80 miles a fucking hour, and this motherfucker comes out and right toward me. Fucker'd have killed me if I didn't react," I shrugged.

Biscuit's eyes widened as he took another sip of Red Bull, "So?"

"Well, I grabbed a handful of brake and laid on the back brake, car behind me damn near hit me. Let off the brakes and immediately swerved right, into the fucking narrow part that has the drunk bumps on it. Came to a complete stop and collected my thoughts," I hesitated, knowing there was more to the story, and Otis had heard it a few times.

Biscuit waved his free hand in my direction, "Holy shit, that's a good one. Better'n mine, for sure."

"Tell him the rest," Otis laughed.

"There's more?' Biscuit asked.

I glanced toward the car. The man sat up in the seat slightly, looked our direction momentarily, and lowered himself back down into the seat.

I glanced toward Otis and considered saying something about the car.

"Uhhm, yeah. When I pulled off the side of the road, the fucking wheelbarrow immediately smacks the car behind me in the front, he hits his brakes, and the fucking thing flips over the top of his car and lands in the windshield of the car behind him. The fucker with the wheelbarrow in the windshield hits the car in *front* of him; which was the guy behind me. I sat and watched this shit like it wasn't even real. After about thirty seconds, there's a ten car pile up, one of which has a fucking wheelbarrow stuck in his windshield."

"Jesus jumped up Christ. Did ya run down the cocksucker in the truck?" he asked.

"No, I stayed and helped out with the accidents. Filled out police reports, and bullshit like that. But they caught the guy," I nodded.

"Serves the dumb fuck right," Biscuit said as he stomped his boot on the empty can, smashing it flat.

"Tell him how they caught him," Otis said.

I looked at Otis and rolled my eyes.

Otis slapped Biscuit on the shoulder and began to tell his version of the story, "Ol' Toad here knows the tag number. After all that bullshit, car wrecks, and such, the cop asks if anyone got the plate number of the truck. Hell, it's been an hour after the shit goes down. Toad says yeah, I got it memorized; it's BR549 or whatever the fuck it was. Fucking guy pays attention to all kinds of stupid details, but this time it paid off."

"He's a nervous acting fucker sometimes, that's for sure. Yeah, I notice shit too, motherfucker, I been noticing you starin' at that car across the street since we got here. What the fuck's wrong with you today?" Biscuit asked.

"Nothing's *wrong*. Fucker just makes me nervous. We've been here about twenty minutes, and the fucker's been sitting over there waiting," I snapped.

"Yeah, parked cars freak me out too," Biscuit laughed.

"Fuck you, Biscuit. I'd rather have my shit wired tight then get blindsided," I hissed.

Biscuit carried the smashed can to his bike and dropped it into the saddlebag. As he glanced up, he continued, "Yeah, Austin is full of ISIS and Al Qaeda."

Fuck you, motherfucker. You wouldn't make it ten minutes in combat.

I turned to face Otis. As I shook my head and lifted my shoulders slightly; the sound of people coming out of the building shifted my focus to the door. Several men walked out, got on their bikes, and left. Others lingered, standing by their bikes talking. As Axton walked out talking to a man dressed in cargo shorts and a wife beater, I laughed to myself at his choice of attire. He looked like a big, bald, musclebound weight lifter wearing tennis shoes. Knowing he either had to walk here or ride one of the bikes parked, I assumed he must have rode one of the bikes. More than likely, considering the fact he wasn't wearing a cut, he was one of the potential members of the new club. .

What a fucking idiot.

"Couple of these fellas are going to roll with us to the bar. Said we ought to go to the Red Shed Tavern," Axton turned to face the big idiot as he finished speaking.

The big bald man nodded his head as he walked in our direction beside Axton. I stared down at his shoes and shook my head in disbelief. As he approached, he pulled his right hand from the pocket of his shorts.

You better not even try, you wannabe motherfucker.

Although most people don't realize it, there's an unwritten rule regarding shaking a 1%er's hand. Most outsiders perceived the standoffish nature as arrogance, but in reality it was more a precautionary measure and a means of not affiliating ourselves with someone who didn't *measure up.* If an outsider ever approached a 1%er and introduced himself with an outstretched hand, most would be met with a blank stare. Not many 1%er's would be willing to shake the hand of a man they didn't know. If another 1%er introduced that person, however, it would act as a reassurance of the outsider being a stand-up guy and confirmation he was worthy of a formal introduction. At that point, if the fellow 1%er didn't shake the hand of the outsider, it would be disrespectful to the man introducing him. I wasn't in any way willing to shake the hand of this oversized bald headed motherfucker covered in a combination of garage and free world tattoos.

As I pressed my palms into my armpits and crossed my arms over my chest, I noticed a few more men walk from the building. One, in particular, immediately caught my attention. I shifted my gaze from the big bald idiot toward the door.

Can't be…

You're dead.

I blinked my eyes in disbelief. As Axton and the oversized bald-headed fool stopped in front of the three of us, I stepped around Axton without speaking and stared toward the two men standing by the door. Seeing one of the two men caused me to immediately feel a flood of indescribable emotion.

The man, dressed in jeans, desert boots, and a white tee-shirt, stood talking to another man who wasn't wearing a cut. The man he spoke with was wearing an oversized black hoodie and looked nervous. I wiped my eyes, shook my head, and stared. This was impossible. As I stood filled with skepticism and stared, the man gazed my direction. As our eyes met, the look on his face confirmed my suspicion.

But you died...

TOAD

After the explosion of a roadside bomb severely injured several Marines in our small convoy, myself included, we were removed from what was left of our Humvees, and the more seriously wounded were treated by a Corpsman while waiting on a medevac chopper. The entire area immediately took tremendous fire from insurgents in the small village, primarily from the rooftops of surrounding buildings. As every one of the vehicles in the convoy was damaged, all we could do was wait.

Wait and hope.

A highly decorated Staff Sergeant who was in our convoy took a large piece of shrapnel to the hip, and was bleeding profusely. Refusing treatment, and with only one useful leg, he drug himself to a position of cover, propped himself against the rear of an abandoned car, and began returning fire. I attributed my having survived for the amount of time it took to be medevaced out to his bravery and courage. As I was literally being carried to the chopper, I watched in horror while he was shot twice as he attempted to crawl away from the cover of the car. I later learned upon returning to my battalion that he had died while being treated for his wounds.

Now, I stood in sheer disbelief as I either stared at his twin, or was simply losing my mind.

It can't be…

"Staff Sergeant Jacob!" I yelled.

The man immediately straightened his posture and turned to face me. For a long moment, he stood and gazed my direction. As he slowly walked away from the man in the hoodie, his mouth began to curl into a smile.

"Sergeant Todelli? The fucking Toad? Holy shit, Brother, I thought you were dead," he exclaimed as he approached.

"Fuck, I got medevaced out, treated, handed a Purple Star, and went right fucking back. But I watched you get killed," I said as I stretched my arms outward.

"Holy shit, I thought you *died* from that wound. I was out damned near six months with mine, but far from dead. Longest six months of my fucking life. Had to beg those bastards to send me back; when I got to battalion they said you were dead," he said.

"Far from it," I sighed.

"The medevac chopper flew out, and I laid in the fucking street returning fire until a Corpsman drug me behind that building. Cocksucking sniper shot me twice, but your chopper hadn't made it out yet. Hell, I had to stay and make sure my Marines got out of there safely," he said as he wrapped his arms around me and slapped me on the back.

"*Ready for anything, counting on nothing*," I said, reciting the motto of the 2/7 Marines.

"Isn't that the truth. Damn, it's good to see you," he said as he leaned back and studied me from head to toe.

"Good to be seen," I said, "And fuck it's good to know you're alive."

My heart felt like it was going to beat out of my chest. Full of emotion, adrenaline, and memories of the battle, I looked down at my hands. Shaking almost uncontrollably, I was filled with the excitement of being reunited with a Marine who I was certain was dead. Not only was he a 2/7 Marine and a true brother, he was someone I perceived as a modern day hero; a man who risked his life in an effort to save the lives of many others who were in much better condition to fight than he was, including myself. On many occasions and many nights, I recalled the battle in Haditha and his heroism. I also attributed my having lived through that particular day of combat to his act of selflessness. I lived my post-war life filled with the deepest feelings of regret; knowing I could never repay him for saving my life. Standing before him now, I began to wonder how much of my PTSD, and more particularly, what portion of my Survivor's Guilt could be attributed to my *belief* that he gave his life in exchange for mine on that memorable day.

As I gazed upward, I noticed all of the men gathered in a circle around the few bikes which remained parked. The man in the shorts and the man in the hoodie stood by Otis. Axton stared in the mirror of his bike as he pressed his index finger against his ear. As Axton glanced in my direction, he grinned.

"I'm guessing you two fuckers don't need an introduction?" he growled.

"Not at all," I chuckled, "So what the fuck are you doing *here*?"

"Trying to start a new chapter for our club. Just trying to make sure we don't step on any toes," he responded.

"One percent club?" I asked.

"I'm not a one percenter, no. We don't claim territory, and we don't have any hustle. We just ride and have a deep brotherhood. It's a nationwide group of firefighters, military, and friends of. We can talk about it at the bar. Damn it's good to see you. Let me introduce you to the soon to be Vice President and Sergeant at Arms. Two of the best motherfuckers to ever grace this earth," he hesitated and held out his right arm.

As the big bald headed man in the tennis shoes approached, Staff Sergeant Jacob patted him on the shoulder.

"Big bastard here is Mike Ripton, but just call him Ripp. Ripp, this is Toad, a Marine brother of mine. Toad, this is the one and only Ripp," he nodded.

I looked at the man dressed in cargo shorts and a wife beater. As I held out my hand, I chuckled, "Nice to meet you. Do you ride in those fucking tennis shoes?"

"It's a pleasure to meet ya, but these ain't tennis shoes, Brother. They're fuckin' Chuck's," he said as he lifted his leg, grabbed his foot, and held it at chest height. "And fuck, yes, I ride in 'em. Hell, I even keep 'em on when I fuck."

God damn, that big son-of-a-bitch is limber.

"Ripp's going to be the SAA. And this fella here," he paused and pointed toward the man in the hoodie.

Holy fucking shit.

"You're Shane fucking Dekkar," I shouted.

He rolled his shoulders, extended his hand, and smiled, "Sure am. Pleasure to meet you, Sir. And call me Dekk."

"You've got to be fucking shittin' me. You've got the Heavyweight Champion of the fucking World as your Vice President?" I chuckled, "Otis, did you see this?"

"Sure as fuck did. Already met the man while you were zoned out," Otis nodded.

"Pleasure to meet you Mr. Dekkar, call me Toad. And that fight a while back, against Brock? Best fucking fight I've ever seen. We all watched it in our clubhouse. Son-of-a-bitch that was a good fight," I said excitedly as I shook his hand.

"Thank you, Sir, I appreciate it. He was a tough opponent," he grinned.

Humble prick.

As we all stood between the motorcycles and the building, I stepped away from the men and turned to face Staff Sergeant Jacob. Otis, Biscuit, Ripp, Shane Dekkar, and Staff Sergeant Jacob stood to my right behind our bikes. The bikes they were riding were several feet away, closer to the door. Axton stood to my immediate right, beside his bike and in front of the rest of the men, still fucking with his ear. With all of the men facing me except Axton, I proudly raised my hands.

"Fellas, I want you to meet Staff Sergeant Jacob. Known by his Marine brethren as *The A-Train*, because when he's coming, not a fucking thing can stop him," I shouted as I raised my hands in the air and pointed toward Staff Sergeant Jacob.

"Well, if all you fuckers are done swapping spit and hugging each other, maybe we should head out to the bar," Axton growled as he continued to study his ear in the mirror.

Out of the corner of my eye, I noticed the Ford Taurus from across the street slowly rolling into the narrow parking lot through the entrance on my far right.

"Axton, my two o'clock," I said under my breath.

Axton lifted his blood soaked finger from his ear and stared at it. The car was slowly approaching behind him. As the Taurus began to speed toward our position, Staff Sergeant Jacob instinctively turned to face the car.

"Axton, *behind you*," I said through my teeth as the car began to approach more rapidly.

Everyone turned around except Axton, who continued to fuck with his ear. Standing to my right, Staff Sergeant Jacob narrowed his gaze as he studied the driver. As he made eye contact, he bent his knees slightly and raised his hands as if preparing to fight. I didn't like what I was seeing. I glanced toward the car. The driver slowly raised a pistol into sight.

"Remember me, motherfucker?" the driver said as he raised the weapon and pointed it in the direction of Axton and A-Train.

As the muzzle of the pistol tilted slightly, I realized he was going to fire the weapon. I instinctively jumped between the car window and where Axton and A-Train stood.

The deafening sound of the weapon being fired filled the air, immediately followed by a crushing pain in my chest. A burning feeling slowly washed over my entire upper body. Incapable of standing, and certain I was knocking on death's door, I collapsed into Staff Sergeant Jacob's arms.

As the noise of screaming and screeching tires became faint and indistinct, I heard the dull sound of a motorcycle start and speed away. Slowly, everything around me started to fade into a faint, fuzzy black and white. I began to feel as if I was being forced down through a tunnel of water, and to survive I needed to swim to a surface far from my reach. Paralyzed from moving a single limb, I continued to sink deeper and deeper. I realized all I could do was attempt to speak.

I'm coming to see you, Nonno. I'll be there real soon.

"God damn it, Sergeant, hold on. Open those eyes for me, Todelli. Talk to me…" a muffled voice said, "Get a fucking ambulance; we don't have a way to get him out of here!"

I opened my eyes and stared blankly at Staff Sergeant Jacob. Regardless of my desire to do so, I couldn't seem to force myself to talk. Eventually, as my eyes fell closed, the words began to roll from my dry tongue.

"We're…you and me…we're…" the blood vibrated in my lungs as I attempted to speak.

"Hold on Sergeant Todelli. Medevac's en route. You hear that chopper, brother? It's almost here," the voice said.

As much as I realized I was dying, I felt I needed to say it. It was crucial to my recovery from a life I had lived for almost a decade; running from the fact I survived while others had lost their lives. I dug deep within my being and fought against the pain in my chest.

The blood filling my lungs gurgled as I struggled to force the words from my lips.

Forgive me Lord, for I have sinned. I pray that you may give me the strength to speak one last time.

Cradled in his arms, I stared upward and attempted to focus on Staff Sergeant Jacob's eyes. Although I knew what I *wanted* to say, forcing the words from my lungs required more strength than I was capable of gathering. Channeling every bit of energy I could muster, and pushing against the pressure building in my lungs, I heard myself begin to produce audible sounds.

"We're…even," I eventually muttered.

And slowly everything turned to black.

SYDNEY

Living is a combination of choice and chance. The path our life travels upon is by our own choosing. Similar to playing poker, life is a complex game which requires decisions on our part; the *choice*. The *chance* comes after we make the decision, as we wait for life to deal us a card from the deck; each one potentially having a varying effect on the outcome or end result. We make a choice and reserve hope the chance we have taken is the one which might make all of the difference we had hoped for. Sometimes, the change we see from the card we were dealt is not what we expected, but something we are forced to accept.

"Unexpected visitors are like gifts," I grinned as I opened the door.

Upon taking a good look at her, it was obvious; Avery was very upset and had apparently been crying. Her eyeliner was smeared all over her face, and her hands appeared to be shaking. Someone I would have expected to be stable at *all* times, I wondered what had happened to make her feel the way she felt. She stepped into the room and immediately placed her hands on my shoulders. After inhaling a choppy breath, she began to cry as she attempted to exhale.

I slid my arm behind her back and began walking toward the table. After lowering her into a chair, I sat down beside her and reached for a napkin.

"What happened?" I asked.

She continued to sob.

"You want something to drink?" I asked as I handed her the napkin.

As she dabbed the tears from her eyes, she slowly began to regain her composure. Her breathing improved from every breath faltering to steady shallow breathing. Knowing women tend to overreact to almost everything, I eagerly waited for her to reach a point where she could explain what had happened. I suspected more than likely Axton had done something in Austin she didn't totally agree with.

"Whenever you're ready, I'm here to listen," I whispered as I reached for her hand.

She nodded her head and took a shallow breath.

"I'm just going to *say it really fast*. I'm afraid if I try to explain, I'll lose it," she said under her breath.

Avery spoke faster than I could possibly listen, so to have her *say it really fast* would be pretty much normal for her. A few seconds after she said whatever it was she had to say, I'd process it and respond appropriately.

I nodded my head as I clutched her hand in mine, "Okay. Just say it."

"Toad was shot he's barely alive with collapsed lungs and they're operating on him now it's really bad and he saved Axton's life by jumping in front of the bullet...I think I need to throw up," she blurted.

Toad was shot and he was dying. I fought against the bile rising in my throat. I reached for the napkins, picked one up, and held it in front of my face. One of the kindest men I ever met had made a choice, and taken a chance. For whatever reason, the card he was dealt wasn't what he had hoped for. My mind fought for answers. I quickly came to the realization maybe it *was* what he had hoped for. Knowing his knack for performing selfless acts and his willingness to help others, the choice he made and the chance he took probably produced an outcome he was prepared for and totally expected.

"How far is Austin?" I asked.

"Ten hours," she blubbered.

Strangely, I hadn't cried. Maybe the severity of everything hadn't sunk in yet. Quite possibly, I was in a mild state of shock, and unaware of the depth of my inner feelings. Either way, I was oddly comfortable and relatively stable. I began to wonder if Toad meant as much to me as I tried to tell myself he did.

I stood from the chair and walked toward the kitchen, "I'm going to call in to work and see if I can take a few days off. I'm going to go down there and see him."

"Can we..."

"Can we go...together?" she stood from her chair and wiped eyeliner across her face with the napkin.

I nodded my head as I dialed Sarah's number.

"You'll have to drive, I'm a wreck," she sighed as she tossed the wet napkin on the table.

"Let me see if I can get off work," I sighed.

"I already took off work, my stuff's in the car. We can take it, but you'll have to drive," she said.

As Sarah answered the phone I nodded my head, "Sarah, this is Sydney. I've got an emergency out of town, and I need to take off for a few days. Can you and Kate pick up my shifts?"

"I'll be fine. No, maybe three or four, I'll keep you posted," I said.

"Thank you. You too," I said as I hung up.

"It's all set. Let me grab a few things. We'll need to stop at two places before we go," I said over my shoulder.

As I walked to the bathroom, a rush of emotion washed over me.

After I gathered my makeup and essentials from the shower, I braced myself against the sink. A quick glance in the mirror revealed the reflection of a scared little girl, fearful for the loss of yet another loved one. Holding the edge of the sink for stability, I stared blankly into the mirror and tried to accept what Avery had said.

Toad had been shot and he was dying.

My lips began to quiver. My hands started shaking. Eventually my legs finally gave way, and I collapsed onto the floor.

I grasped my knees in my hands and pulled my thighs against my chest. Without thinking, I began to hum an unknown tune as I pulled against my knees with my hands. As I rocked back and forth on the floor, the humming eventually turned to tears. Slowly, the crying became more intense. In no time, I was a blubbering mess.

As I felt an arm wrap around my shoulder, I tilted my head to the side. Avery sat down beside me, released my shoulder, and clasped her hands around her knees. My entire life, I grieved alone. I never had anyone to comfort me, assist me, or help me understand why I felt the way I felt. Now, as I began to feel helpless, incapable, and as if I was cheated out of the best man to ever enter my life, someone was right beside me through it all. As we both rocked back and forth on the bathroom floor, humming and crying; I glanced at Avery and realized two things.

For the first time in my adult life, I was not alone.

And girls *can* be the best of friends.

SYDNEY

We tend to find comfort while embracing whatever it is we place faith in. The presence of faith provides reassurance, and with it comes comfort. As true faith isn't something we simply obtain by want or wish, those of us who possess very little faith must first find a place of comfort and hope that faith soon follows.

"Before you go, Miss Sydney," Junior paused and wiped his eyes.

"You ever felt pain this deep? Before now?' he asked.

I considered what he had asked. I knew my answer ought to be a simple one, but I was quite shocked by what I felt my response *should* be, considering how I felt. As if he *knew* how much pain I was in, he stood and waited for me to respond.

"It seems weird saying it, but I don't think so. I really don't. At least not that I can remember," I responded.

"Me neither. And, it's because Mr. Toad has touched our lives with a hand more kind than we ever expected anyone to. He's a very special man, Miss Sydney, he sure nuff is. My momma says this," he wiped his eyes with the tips of his fingers and inhaled a deep breath.

Junior rubbed his hands on the thighs of his pants and gazed upward. As if he was reading from a banner in the sky, he recited his mother's words of wisdom, "God uses our deepest pain as the first stepping stone to our greatest reward."

"Holy cow, that's good. I like that," I said.

"I likes it too. Now you go on and tell Mr. Toad when he wakes up that I'd come on down there and see him, but I gots to stay here and make him proud," he grinned.

"I'll be sure and tell him," I breathed.

"Give me a hug, then you and Miss Avery better get to getting'," he said as he stretched his arms outward.

As he held me in his arms, I realized I wouldn't have ever met Junior if it wasn't for Toad. Grateful for having both Avery and Junior in my life, I gazed in the window of the car at her as I hugged Junior.

"Alright, we better go. It's a ten hour drive, and we won't be there until tomorrow morning the way we're going," I sighed.

"Drive safe," he said.

I nodded my head, "I will. And I'll tell him what you said."

As Junior turned and walked toward the lawn mower, I reached for the door handle. After a short hesitation and reflection of his mother's opinion regarding the pain I was feeling, I opened the car door and sat down in the seat.

"Just one more place," I said as I pulled the door closed.

Avery turned to face me and nodded her head. She looked like warmed over death. As I started the car, I closed my eyes and hoped she could obtain a little satisfaction from our last stop. If nothing else, I knew it would provide me enough strength to make the trip without falling apart.

I reached for the gear shift and pulled the car into gear. As I released the brake and pulled forward, I nervously gripped the gear shift lever in my hand. As Avery clasped her hand over mine, I turned to her and smiled.

As she smiled in return, I came to realize whatever happened, we could get through this.

Together.

SYDNEY

I stood on the root of the tree and stared up past the branches and into the sky. The longer I gazed off into the sea of blue, the more relaxed I became. I released the trunk, crossed my arms, and took a deep breath.

"Don't…" I screamed at the top of my lungs.

I took another shallow breath and bellowed toward the sky, "You… Dare!"

I sat down on the tree's large root and closed my eyes. As much as I felt I *could* say, I decided those three words summed up my feelings. I opened my eyes and stood.

"Is that it?" Avery asked.

"Yep, that's all I've got to say," I shrugged, "You?"

As I stepped from the tree's root and turned toward the car, Avery walked past me and climbed onto the base of the tree. I stopped and gazed her direction. After wiping her eyes and tossing her hair over her shoulder, she cupped her hands to her mouth and tilted her head rearward.

"What she said!" she screamed.

As we walked toward the car together, I began to feel as if she was the sister I never had; but always wanted. Regardless of the outcome, if we continued to lean on each other, we'd be twice as strong as if we were alone.

"I think he'll be alright," Avery sighed.

Without speaking, I turned to face her and raised my eyebrows.

"Devil looks after his own," she shrugged.

For that moment in time, I wondered just who it was who had possession of Cambio Todelli's soul. Regardless of the outcome, and even if he fully recovered, I realized I may never know the answer.

SYDNEY

"The bullet impacted his left clavicle, causing a group III fracture on the medial third. It then took a downward path and in doing so, grazed the top of the left lung. The resulting collapsed lung was treated by releasing the pressure in the chest cavity, allowing the lung to expand. Although the tear in the tissue of the lung was small, we weren't pleased with his immediate recovery from the pneumothorax, or collapsed lung. After consultation with several of the doctors, a chemical pleurodesis was performed. This procedure introduces chemicals through a chest drain, and is typically an extremely painful one. The chemicals cause irritation between the parietal and visceral layers of the pleura; which closes off the space between them and prevents further fluid from accumulating. In a sense, we're attempting to force the hole in his lung to heal from a result of the chemical irritation."

"I see, so a broken collarbone and a collapsed lung. Is it typical for a patient with these types of injuries to be comatose?" I asked.

"I've learned in my many years of practice that nothing is typical," the doctor sighed.

"Having said that, to provide you with an answer, I'll offer this," the doctor paused and glanced down at his clipboard.

"Sometimes our mind, body, or spirit needs a well-deserved rest. Everyone reacts differently to the same exposures or injuries. Am I surprised in his condition? Yes, and no. I would say a more accurate answer will be able to be given within a few days. He's a former Marine, and from what his friends have shared, he's a true fighter. Let's allow him to continue to fight, and see what changes we see in the next few days," he said as he picked his clipboard up from the desk.

"Anything more?' he asked.

I looked up from the floor and shook my head, "No, Sir. Thank you for taking the time to explain."

He nodded his head and turned away. The smell of the sterile hospital reminded me of the nurse's station at the orphanage. As uncomfortable as the facility made me feel, I turned toward the corridor and began walking down the hallway and toward Toad's room. After what seemed like an eternity, I finally stood outside his room. I stared at the number on the wall beside the door.

724.

Unlike other hospital rooms I had been in, the room's wall facing the hallway was glass. Curtains were partially drawn across the glass wall, but the open door allowed me to see inside. Otis, Avery, and who I assumed was Axton stood beside the bed. The nurse explained three people were the maximum amount of visitor's allowed, and although their policy included only family as approved visitors, they had and would make an exception for Toad and his *family*.

I drew a shallow breath and walked through the door.

Immediately Otis turned to face me, "Hey Syd, I'm glad you could make it."

"Me too," I whispered as he reached out and gave me a hug.

Something about Otis was extremely comforting. As big as he was, and as intimidating as most probably perceived him, I saw right through the façade and into a heart of gold. As he held me against his side with one arm, I exhaled and leaned against him, pressing my face into his side.

As Avery turned to face me, so did the man beside her. The name on his cut and the *President* patch revealed he was in fact who I suspected.

"Avery and I will go on down, she needs to get something to eat. I'm glad you're here, Sydney. I appreciate you coming with Avery," Axton nodded.

It was immediately apparent why he was the president of the club. His mere presence and the fact he looked mean even when he smiled would deter the earth's toughest men, causing them to think twice before crossing him. A few days growth of beard did little to hide his well sculpted face and natural good looks. His eyes and aura advised me to keep my distance.

With her arm around Axton's waist, Avery nodded her head as they walked past. I smiled at Axton and patted her on the back as they stepped around Otis and me. After they exited the room, I released Otis, walked toward the bed, and looked down at a man who appeared to be dead or awfully close to it. With tubes in his chest, throat, and each arm, he appeared to be more mechanical than human. After a few seconds of studying him, I turned toward Otis.

"So what happened?" I whispered.

"Well," he paused and began rubbing his temples.

"We uhhm, we went to this meeting…he told you what that was about, didn't he?"

I nodded my head.

He lowered his hands and gazed down at my feet as he began to speak, "So we were all out in front of the building standing by our bikes and waiting on Axton to come out. Toad spent the entire fucking time we were out there staring across the street at some car. Biscuit starts giving him shit, calling him paranoid for worrying about whatever this guy in the car was doing; but there was something about this car and the guy in it that made him uncomfortable. I don't know if you know it or not, but the man has some kind of sixth sense about shit going down."

Although Otis had yet to make eye contact, I nodded my head as I continued to listen.

"So, we're all just standing and talking, and Axton and some other fellas come walking out. It ends up one of these local fellas of this new Austin chapter is an old Marine friend of Toad's. So when he walks out of the building and Toad see's this guy, he all but loses control. Ends up this guy saved Toad's life in some epic battle in Iraq, and all these years Toad thought he was dead. After Toad gets introduced to everyone else, he turns and makes an announcement to the fellas on who this guy is," he hesitated and took a few steps to his left.

"So Toad's standing *here*," he pointed down at his feet.

"And we're all standing about where you are, kind of in a line by our bikes. And all of a sudden the car from across the street pulls in the fucking parking lot. Hell, I didn't notice it, but I heard Toad. He's starts saying shit to Axton, trying to...trying to uhhm...he was trying to get him to move...you know...move out of the way," he paused and shook his head as his voice began to convey his emotion.

He shifted his gaze up from the floor and looked around the room for a moment. As his eyes met mine, he continued, "You know, it uhhm, it all makes sense now, but all this shit went down pretty fucking quick, Syd. And at the time..."

He raised his hands to his head again, and began to almost frantically rub his temples, "At the time I wasn't really paying fucking attention.

I don't know, it was hot and I was ready to get the fuck out of there."

As I stood in the uncomfortable silence and waited for him to continue, the sound of the monitor beeping became more and more prominent.

"Okay, so this car pulls up, and uhhm....he pulls up, and Toad's trying to warn Axe...he's saying shit to Axe, and I uhhm. I'm standing there and it's all slow motion. Like slowly coming into focus, fuck I don't know how to describe it. So the fucking guy pulls...he uhhm, he pulls out a..."

Seeing Otis in this condition did me no good whatsoever. For the entire 10 hour drive to Texas, I reserved hope Toad wasn't really as bad as Avery had indicated. Now seeing Otis, and having him in an emotional state where he was almost incapable of speaking made me realize just how delicate of a situation this actually was. I stared down at his boots as I waited for him to continue.

"Okay. So he pulls out a piece, you know, a pistol, and points the motherfucker out the window..."

"Oh my God," I interrupted.

"Yeah. You got it. So Toad's trying to warn Slice and his Marine buddy, A-Train. And this prick says *hey motherfucker, remember me?* So it's still slow motion like. And I watched him....I uhhm watched... so Toad see's the piece, and he jumps between the gun and Axton and the A-Train fella, and then there's this explosion..."

I felt as if I was going to vomit. Hearing him say it made everything seem all too real. I realized I was crying. Without speaking I reached for my cheeks and wiped the tears with my index fingers. Eventually Otis continued with the most gut wrenching part of the story.

"So it ends up the guy....he uhhm...he and the Marine had a beef a while back, but no one realized this was the guy until it was too fucking late."

As he finished speaking, I realized my mouth was covered with my hands. I moved my hands to my side, turned toward Toad, and exhaled a breath I had no doubt been holding for the entire conversation.

"And the guy? Did they catch him?" I asked over my shoulder.

"Well, one of the fellas with this Marine buddy of Toad's was some big mean bald headed son-of-a-bitch. He boxes and street fights for a living; the cat's name's Ripp. So this Ripp fucker hops on his bike and shoots out chasing after this bastard before we even know what the fuck's going on. Hell we're all in shock and trying to keep Toad from… you know…from bleeding…from uhhm bleeding to death…" he paused and wiped the sweat from his brow.

"Okay, so we find out later this crazy fucking Ripp chases the guy down until he gets caught in Austin's afternoon traffic. When he does, Ripp dumps his bike on the highway, jumps off, and busts this guy's window out with the butt of his fucking pocket knife. Then, he pulls this fucker out and beats on him till the cops get there. Only reason Ripp doesn't get shot, is because this dumb fuck tossed his piece out on the highway."

"But they've got him?" I asked.

"What's left of him. Apparently Ripp didn't do him any good. Cops were up here earlier taking statements. Said the guy's a career criminal. Some guy on the highway saw him toss the piece, and they've got it. So they said he'll probably get life in prison in *this* state, Texas doesn't fuck around. Anyway, the cop said he actually saw this guy and he looked like he'd been in a head on collision with a train."

"Holy shit, this is just crazy. So Toad got shot on purpose? He literally jumped in front of the gun to save his Marine friend?" I shrugged.

Otis nodded his head as he rubbed his temples, "There's uuhm, there's more."

As he began to speak, his blank stare warned me of the significance of what he was about to say. When he continued, my eyes became unfocused as I listened to his voice.

"So, we're waiting on the ambulance, and Toad's uhhm, he's uhhm...he's sinking fast, Syd. He's uhhm...he's going in and out of consciousness. Fucking A-Train's holding him in his arms, telling him a chopper is on the way. *Medevac's en route* he tells him. Fucking medevac's en route. So Toad opens his eyes and looks up at the Marine, you know, the one who saved his life in Iraq, and he...he uhhm...he opens them again, and we're all standing there...knowing he's fucking dying, Syd. We uhhm, we could *see* it. We could...we could *hear* it. His...oh fuck...his lungs...they were full of blood...and he's trying to just say *something*. The motherfucker," he hesitated, lifted his hands to his face, and wiped his eyes.

"He was trying to talk. And he's uhhm gurgling. And he keeps trying. And he finally opens his eyes again and he uhhm..."

"He uhhm, he opens his eyes and looks at A-Train and says...*we're even...*"

I couldn't face Otis. Not in his condition. As big and as tough as he was, he'd reached his limit in telling me his version of what happened. Out of the corner of my eye, I saw him turn to face the door. I turned toward Toad and began to cry. His heroic act, and the statement he made to his Marine friend, at least in *my* opinion, summed up just exactly who Cambio Todelli was. A man long since removed from war who continued to fight his own inner battles with what he believed was good, what was evil, and where specifically he should stand. To me his choices were clear. He stood precisely where *he* believed he should; in between evil and the unsuspecting or innocent recipient.

"Can I uhhm. Would you give me a minute, you know, alone with him?" I asked as I stared down at the bed.

"Sure, Cafeteria's on the uhhm, it's on the first floor. Take this elevator down, go left then left again, can't miss it. I'll head down there. We'll all wait for you," he said as he gripped my shoulder softly with his hand.

I glanced around the empty room and wiped the tears from my face. After moving to the left side of the bed, I gazed down at Toad. I cupped my hands around his. I rubbed my hands softly along his palm and fingers, attempted to warm his cold fingertips as I began to whisper.

"My entire life I wanted one thing and one thing only, to have a family; but all I ever had was a brother. My brother was taken from me, leaving me nothing. I met you, and as strange as it may seem, you offered me a family. You, Junior, Junior's mother, the girls at your restaurant, Avery, and even Otis. All of these people are in my life because of you. I've never been happier than I was yesterday. Not that I can remember. And today, I'm in more pain than I have ever felt."

I stood, looked around the room, leaned over, and rested my face beside his. I placed my hand on his shoulder, and my mouth against his ear.

"I need you to do something for me, Cambio," I whispered into his ear.

"Not for you, *for me*. I need you *here*. Here in my life. Your time here is not done. Not even close. I need you to come back, Cambio. Not for you, for me, *Capisce*?" I breathed as I nervously patted his shoulder.

I didn't speak Italian, but I knew one word; the same one everyone else did from watching any mafia movie. I thought it might make him comfortable hearing something in his native dialect.

I stood and wiped the tears from my eyes. Looking at him lying in the bed was difficult. Filled with tubes and covered in a mass of wires, he appeared weak. Nothing could be further from the truth. Cambio Todelli laid before me as a war hero, a hero to his friends, his brothers, and a hero to me. Without hesitation, he had forfeited his life to save the life or lives of his brothers. Regardless of his rugged exterior and tough façade, he was truly an unselfish man, always willing to give. Feeling as if I had done all I could do, I leaned down and kissed his forehead. After lingering for a long moment, I raised my head and gazed down at his face.

Much to my surprise, his cheek twitched.

Then it twitched again.

And slowly, his eyes opened.

SYDNEY

Whatever we are currently feeling will naturally be compared to feelings we've had in the past. Our previous feelings are used as a baseline or means of comparison. As we live life, we experience more, and inevitably *feel* throughout the process. Based on what experiences life offers, and what we feel as a result of this exposure, our baseline is constantly moving. The most pain and the greatest joy I had ever felt was a result of having met Cambio Todelli, and both feelings were felt in the same day, within a few minutes of one another. The severity of the pain felt caused the joy I was now feeling to be that much sweeter.

"Oh my God," I gasped.

I raised my shaking hands to my face. Past my quivering lips I began to try to explain, "Okay, oh God. They've got your arms tied down, so you can't move. And there's a tube down your throat, so you can't talk."

"Uhhm. Let's see. Uhhm. Can you hear me? Blink your eyes if you can hear me," I babbled.

He blinked once.

I almost peed my pants.

"Okay, once for yes, twice for no. Do you know where you are?" I blurted.

After a short pause, he blinked twice.

"Do you remember what happened?"

He blinked twice.

"Do you know who you are?"

He blinked once.

"Do you know who I am?"

He blinked once.

Thank God.

My mind was racing, and my thoughts were all jumbled. I realized I needed to call for a doctor, and let all of the fellas know he was awake, but I deeply desired at least a few seconds alone with him. I wanted to be the one who told him what happened. I wanted to be the first person he actually spoke to, even if it was in a manner that was unconventional. For this particular moment, I was selfish, and I needed to be alone with him.

"You were at a meeting, and a man pulled up in a car with a gun. He had a beef with a former Marine friend of yours. He pulled the gun, and you dove in front of it. He uhhm, he shot you. But you saved the life of your Marine friend, and probably Axton too," I softly sobbed.

He stared at me for a considerable amount of time, and eventually blinked his eyes once.

"I should probably get a doctor," I blubbered as I wiped the tears from my cheeks.

He blinked twice.

"Uhhm, everyone's downstairs in the cafeteria. You want me to call them up here?" I whispered.

He blinked twice.

"Okay…uhhm."

I stood nervously and considered what to say. Instead of speaking legibly and intelligently I simply began babbling, "I know this might sound weird or creepy, but I hope not. I realize you've only been gone for two days, and I don't really see you every day anyway, but knowing you were actually gone, like *out of town* gone, I uhhm. I've missed you. Like a lot."

He blinked once.

He must be delirious.

"You missed me too?" I asked as I pointed to my chest.

He blinked once.

How quickly things change. I now had a *new* best feeling I had ever felt. And I was feeling it now, as I stood and admired one of the most interesting men I had ever met. Without speaking, and full of emotion, I stepped to the edge of the bed, leaned over, and kissed his forehead. As I slowly stood, I gazed into his eyes.

And he blinked once.

TOAD

As we all must have *something* to believe in, it comes as no surprise that the majority of people on this earth believe in a God of their choosing. And, as humans, at some point in time we develop doubt. An event or situation in our life which we feel is beyond acceptable for a higher power to place before us causes us to question his very existence.

I no longer wonder, I *know*.

For an immeasurable amount of time, in a place words can't accurately describe, I existed. In his presence, and under his care, I remained until I was released back through the tunnel onto earth.

There was no fear, no feelings, no time, and no material existence.

Not certain if I would ever describe it as a *spiritual* existence, I felt strangely comfortable. *I* was there. Not a spirit, apparition, or ghost, but *me*. When I returned, I returned with knowledge and an understanding that I had either lived a life acceptable to God or he was far more forgiving than I would have ever imagined.

"How's the pain today?" A-Train asked.

"Unbearable, but I'll manage," I breathed.

"Well, the doc said it's a pretty painful recovery."

"He's sure as fuck right, this is awful," I sighed.

"Be a lot better if you'd take your pain medication," he chuckled.

I shook my head and sat up in the recliner as I ratcheted the back into a more erect position, "I'm not getting strung out on that shit. It's been

215

two weeks, I don't need it. I'll be fine."

"Well, only you know how much pain you can stand. If you need it, I've got it in the kitchen," he said as he placed a bowl of oatmeal and some ham on the table beside the chair.

I looked down at the plate and nodded my head, "Appreciate it."

"Eat that shit. The fellas will be over here before long, maybe we can sit out on the back deck and enjoy the sun for a while before it gets too damned hot," he said as he walked toward the large glass doors that opened onto the back deck.

As he parted the blinds, the sun filled the room. I turned toward the windows and shook my head, "It's too fucking early for all that light, Brother. Damn."

"The sun's up. Anyone sleeps past sunrise is either a lazy motherfucker or a criminal. Get up and eat your chow," he grunted.

Leaving me in A-Train's care was probably the best choice the fellas could have made. Without a doubt, he wouldn't cut me any slack, would make sure I ate properly, slept plenty, and didn't get depressed about my slow recovery. To be honest, I knew I would never become depressed. I did, however, look forward to the arrival of the upcoming weekend. If for some reason it *didn't* happen, I may slowly sink into a mild state of aggravation. Not having my phone left me without a means of communicating with all of the people who were important to me. Knowing Sydney was scheduled to spend the weekend with me kept me sane, at least for now.

"So, what day is it," I asked as I reached for the oatmeal.

"It's fucking Friday. Yesterday was Thursday, remember? You sure you don't have mild brain damage?" he said over his shoulder as he walked into the kitchen.

"I couldn't remember, I was hoping it was, though," I said as I spooned the oatmeal into my mouth.

"Slow down, you're eating that shit like a starving hostage. You know it doesn't matter when you get done with it, Sydney won't be here until late tonight," he chuckled as he sat down on the couch.

"I know, I just need to eat and get showered before the fellas get here. I can't believe you three live next to each other," I said as I placed the empty bowl on the table and grabbed a piece of ham.

"Dekk's as good of a fella as any Marine you'll ever know. Hell, after he got his first big paycheck, he built a new fucking gym and these three houses. Crazy fucker donated the money to build a school too, right behind us. It'll be a while before his son's ready for school, but when he is, it'll be right there," he said as he pointed toward the back deck.

As I bit into the ham, I heard the lock on the front door turn. Surprised, I turned to face the door. It opened, revealing Ripp, a drop-dead gorgeous brunette, and a little girl. After the door was wide open, and they were inside the house, Ripp turned around and knocked on the door.

"Time to wake the fuck up," he hollered.

"Michael Allen Ripton," the brunette snapped as she nodded her head toward the little girl.

"He never knocks," A-Train shrugged as he stood from the couch.

"Toad, this is my wife Vee, and my little girl Jessie," Ripp said as he slowly walked into the house with the little girl holding his hand.

"Nice to meet you," I said as I stood.

I wiped my hand against my sweats and began walking her direction. As she gripped my hand and shook it, she nodded her head and smiled.

"Pleasure's mine. And thank you for your service. After getting to know A-Train, I'm a softie for a Marine. I'm just glad you're finally out of the hospital," she grinned.

"So am I," I agreed, "And if it wasn't for your husband here, the guy who shot me would still be running around shooting people."

"Oh, believe me," she chuckled, "Pulling that guy out of the car and beating the crap out of him was nothing…"

"Why do you say that?" I asked.

"Believe me, he's done far worse," she laughed.

"Mind if I tell him?" A-Train asked.

"Not at all," Vee responded.

I lowered myself into the recliner and grabbed my half-eaten piece of ham. As I relaxed into the chair, Ripp sat down beside A-Train and sighed.

"You see, you and Ripp are a lot alike," A-Train paused and exchanged glances between Ripp and I.

"What I've learned about Toad since he's been here is that you two are damned near twins," A-Train chuckled.

"How you figure, bro?" Ripp shrugged as he propped his right sneaker onto his left thigh.

"Well, Toad's lived his life as a whore, just like you. He's spent his life fucking women and has never been in a relationship with one. Swears he doesn't mistreat them, because they sign on for his sexual punishment when he gives them some long stretched out speech about how he's only fucking them, and never going to actually love them," A-Train paused and glanced my direction.

I rolled my eyes.

"Sound familiar?" A-Train asked as he glanced toward Ripp.

"I'm taking her onto the deck," Vee sighed as she picked up the little girl.

"Ain't no shame in fuckin' bitches. I spent a long time fuckin' a whole bunch of 'em," Ripp grinned.

"But when I met Vee, it was all over," he sighed.

"That's not *exactly* what I was going to tell him," A-Train interrupted.

Ripp's face contorted and he threw his hands in the air, "What the fuck was you gonna tell him?"

A-Train stood and walked to the loveseat across from the couch. As he sat down, he responded, "I was going to tell him about your court battle. You know, how you had a life changing experience, and after it, how you recovered."

Ripp shook his head and pointed at me, "He got fucking shot, dude. I just had some asshole pull a gun on me."

I took the last bite of my ham and waited anxiously for the story.

"Let's hear it," I breathed as I relaxed into the recliner.

"Well, this is kind of personal, and I know it goes without saying, but this stays here," A-Train explained as he leaned forward on the couch.

"Did you forget who the fuck you're talking to?" I snapped.

"Just had to say it, Brother," A-Train responded.

"My girlfriend, Katie, is Ripp's sister. She got raped a while back," he hesitated and took a shallow breath.

"Damn, I'm sorry did…" I began.

He raised his hand in the air, "Just let me finish."

I nodded my head and swallowed heavily. To me, the thought of someone raping a woman wasn't much different than what the child molester did to the children. I'd line up every rapist and do the same thing to them I did to the child molester. There was no place on the earth I lived in for anyone who did those types of things to women and children. Frustrated at the thought of A-Train's girlfriend and Ripps' sister being raped, I sat quietly and waited for the rest of the story.

"So this was before she and I were seeing each other seriously. Ripp finds out what happened, and he takes off in his car damned near like he did the day you got shot. Hell, we had no idea what was going on, because although Katie told *him*, she hadn't told anyone else. Ripp goes to this guy's house, and knocks on the door. At this point, he's got it in his mind he was going to toss this asshole in the trunk and haul him to the police station," A-Train paused and turned toward Ripp.

"Let me tell it, bro," Ripp said as he moved his shoe from his thigh, rested his elbows on his knees, and leaned forward.

A-Train nodded his head, "Fine, tell it."

"So there's the version I told in court," Ripp paused and looked around the room, "and the *real* version. This is the real version."

"This fuck-bubble raped my sister. We're all at Sunday dinner at my folk's house, and she gets upset and jumps up from the table in tears. I went to see what was wrong, and she told me what this guy did to her. I hopped in my car and hauled ass to this fucker's house. You see, I knew this fuck-tard because he used to date her. When I knock on the door, he opens it with a fuckin' Glock in his hand. And, because he thinks he's got ol' Ripp right where he wants him, he admits to raping her and a few other girls. Now I don't know all this whappitty-whap gun snatchin' shit you Marines know, but I been in a fight or two," he paused, flexed his biceps, and kissed each one independently.

"So I hauled off and hit this fuck-nugget with a right cross to his forearm. The pistol falls to the floor, and I get this asshole in a choke hold and start choking him out. Now, although I was *originally* goin' to take this piece of shit to the police station, at this point, takin' him *anywhere* is the furthest thing from my mind. I squeeze a little harder, and a little harder," he hesitated and stood from his seat.

"And *snap!* I break this prick's neck like a twig," he said as he turned his palms up and widened his eyes.

"You broke his neck? You fucking killed him?" I asked as I sat up in my seat.

He raised his eyebrows and nodded his head, "Deader'n a fuckin' mackerel. Right there on his porch. So I sat down beside him, pulled my phone out of my shorts, and called Vee. I said, *you better get ready, 'cause we're headed to court. I just killed a motherfucker.*"

Somewhat dumbfounded, I shook my head.

"Vee's a heartless bitch, so I knew everything was gonna be fine. So, they arrest me and charge me with murder. And when we go to court, she makes fools of these bastards, and I get found *not guilty*. She's the best fucking attorney in the great state of Texas," he grinned.

"Wait, she's an attorney?" I asked as I tilted my head toward the deck.

"Sure as fuck is. Damned fine one too," Ripp nodded.

A-Train stood from his seat, "Alright, so my point was going to be this…"

"I realize I don't know what you've been up to since I saw you last, but there's no one, and I do mean *no one* who was more of a whore than Ripp. And now? He's found the woman of his dreams, and he's happier than ever. You have any regrets, Ripp?" A-Train asked as he gazed Ripp's direction.

"Fuck no, dude. You know that," Ripp said as he sat down.

"So, there's nothing to be afraid of. If you want to get to know this girl, get to know her. And if you're afraid of being in a relationship, don't be. If it's meant to be, it'll be, and if it's not, it won't," A-Train turned up his palms and waited for me to respond.

As I attempted to sit up in my chair, a sharp pain shot from my shoulder through my neck. My broken clavicle continued to remind me it was going to be a long time before I would be able to ride again; yet another fear in my list of many.

"Let's say she feels the same way I do, but I don't even know if that's the case. Let's just say it is. Well, I'm afraid I'm going to fuck it up. I've never done this, and hell I hate to say it, but I might not even be able to perform. I'm telling you, my head's a wreck, Brother. For the last five years or so, I couldn't even get my cock hard unless I was tying some bitch up or choking her. Being in a *real* relationship might not *ever* work," I explained.

Ripp slapped his hand against his knee, and turned my direction, "Bro, tell me about it. I couldn't even get it up if I wasn't getting' rough with a bitch. My cock wasn't interested if there wasn't some really good shit goin' on. Now? Shit, it's weird, but now I'm good to go. I think it's all about when you get comfortable with someone. I'm comfortable with Vee, so it's all good."

"Let's just say I've had the same concerns. I think you'll find just about every combat Marine has. I don't have them any longer, and I'll leave it at that," A-Train said.

"I don't know, I hate to think about going after this chick, getting up to the plate, and I don't even have a fucking bat to swing," I groaned as I leaned forward in the chair.

A-Train laughed as he picked up the plate from the table beside me, "Well, I can tell you this for sure. Damned near every man on this earth sooner or later settles down with a woman. It doesn't make you less of a man to let a woman into your life *or* heart. Your fears are valid, but I'm afraid they're probably a little inaccurate. If I were to guess, I'd say you're afraid of *change*. Don't be. Regardless of what your one percenter brothers tell you, having a woman in your life doesn't make you a pussy. Two of the meanest, toughest motherfuckers to ever grace this earth are Dekk and Ripp, and they're both married with kids. And ol' Ripp here *still* gets in a fist fight damned near every time he swallows a couple beers."

"True story," Ripp chuckled.

"Did settling down with Vee change who you are?" I asked.

Ripp stood, shook his head and walked to the kitchen. After grabbing a beer from the refrigerator, he opened it, took a drink, and walked back to his seat.

"Let me ask you a question, Bro," he said.

"Alright," I responded as I attempted to get comfortable.

"If you go out in the country and find a wolf, bring it home, and feed it Purina Dog Chow, will it turn into a good pet?" he asked.

"I doubt it," I responded.

He shook his head and tilted the bottle of beer my direction, "It sure won't."

He tipped up the bottle and drank about half the beer in one gulp. As he wiped his mouth with the back of his hand he continued, "I'll tell you why. Because no matter what you do with that wolf, he'll always be a wolf; and you can't ever change that. We are who we are, Bro. You'll always be you. Adding a woman to your life just means there's going to be someone there by your side to enjoy watching you be yourself."

I sat and gazed at Ripp. A matter of weeks before, I had judged him based on his clothing, choice of shoes, and bold in-your-face presence. Hell, until A-Train introduced him, I wasn't even willing to give him the satisfaction of having me shake his hand. Now that I had taken some time to get to know him, it was apparent he was as solid of a man as any of my brothers in the club. Although he had a different approach than most, the advice he provided seemed to make perfect sense.

I just needed to determine if Sydney was as interested in getting to know the *real* me as I was in having her do so.

SYDNEY

I've heard many people say *when you're at the bottom, there's nowhere to go but up*. I suppose there's some truth to that statement, but it isn't necessarily *always* accurate. Some can simply stay at the bottom and never recover, wallowing in the depression, pity and angst associated with being where they are. Having been at the bottom, and now hovering somewhere near the top, I was able to look down and realize the distance I had traveled was remarkable. Keeping my vision clear enough to continue to accurately see the pit from which I so desperately dug myself from was of the utmost importance. It remained a constant reminder of what *could* be.

I stared into my glass of wine, took a sip, and tilted the glass in my hand as I watched the wine shift from side-to-side, "So why did you sign the name *Cambio*?"

"You know, to my brothers in the club, I'm *Toad*. Hell, half of them probably don't even know my actual name. I'm good with that. I don't really care if *anyone* in that little town knows my name, but I have one and I like it; I was named after my grandfather. I guess there comes a point in time when we all need to take a step back and become who we *really* are for just a minute…"

As he paused, his finger pressed against the glass of wine, moving it from in front of my face to the side. My focus immediately shifted from the glass of wine to his face. He grinned, gripped the glass in his fingers, and pushed it down onto the table.

"I think I wanted you to see me as Cambio, at least while you were reading what I wrote," he said as he released the glass of wine.

I nodded my head lightly and lifted the glass without thinking, glancing at it as I did. His hand immediately pressed against the stem, pushing it back into place. I shifted my gaze toward him and grinned.

"Got it, glass stays on the table," I said with a grin.

"The glass needs to stay where it doesn't obstruct your face. I don't care what you do with it; I'm tired of trying to look *through* it. I want to look at *you,* I waited all week for this," he said as he leaned forward.

I pushed the glass of wine to the side, pressed my forearms against the edge of the table, and leaned forward, "Well, I liked it. I liked that you signed your actual name, and not *Toad*. I think that was the turning point for me, when I read that. I read it several times, wondering exactly what you meant. We're a funny breed."

He leaned into his chair and winced from the apparent pain in his shoulder, "I don't even know if I've known who I actually was until all of this happened. I know who I used to be, but I'm not real sure of just who the fuck I've been for the last ten years. That war fucked me up a lot more than I ever thought it did. I've been wandering around since I got home feeling guilty for having lived through it. I've been running from place to place and person to person trying to make up for something I didn't need to make up for. I don't guess it really matters, but I'm not sure if it was finding out Staff Sergeant Jacob was actually alive, or the fact I took that bullet, but one of those two things gave me a huge relief. All of that guilt I've been living with is gone."

As much as I felt sorry for him, or anyone else who was exposed to the violence and death associated with fighting in a war, I was intrigued by the complexities of it all. The human mind's capacity, or lack thereof, to process events or feelings attached to something as simple and natural as living. Cambio had spent almost a decade feeling guilty for living through the war. Now, after having learned that a fellow Marine who he assumed had died actually had lived, his guilt faded into nothing. I knew one thing if I knew nothing else; the *new* Cambio was a man I had great interest in being with. Although he acted *differently* toward me now, and had officially asked me out on a future date, I wondered what he wanted, expected, and hoped for. No differently than I expect any other woman would be, I wanted more definition to what it was we were doing, and what to expect in the future. For fear of scaring him away, I treaded lightly and hoped he would simply provide the answers as I muddled through our conversations. Well, either that or just kiss me.

He gazed beyond me, and his eyes became distant. After a moment, he began to speak softly, "Back to what we were talking about earlier, I never told you, but I had uhhm. I was riding out by the lake and there was this puppy in the ditch. Crows were all gathered around him, and I slowed down to keep from hitting them. I saw him out of the corner of my eye, and stopped. He'd been shot several times, but he was still alive. He looked like someone had used him for fighting. I loaded him up, hauled ass to Wichita, and took him to the vet. I picked out a collar for the little guy, and waited for them to get him stitched up and ready to come home. When the vet came out and told me he didn't make it, I lost it. Something in me snapped. I do think there's a point where death is a necessary evil, and it always will be, but someone killing a puppy was different. When I got out to my bike, I realized my blood covered shirt was still in the vet, and my cut was covered in blood. I didn't come to your house to get cleaned up, I came there for...well, I came there for…"

A puppy. The blood on his cut was from a puppy.

As my eyes began to well with tears, I leaned forward and reached for the center of the table. He gazed down at the table and raised his hand from his lap. Slowly, his hand moved across the table until it met mine, encompassed my fingers, and provided me with a comfort only he could provide.

"Comfort," he sighed, "I came there for comfort."

It seemed odd. Although I had just made the chalkboard about passing judgement, when he arrived on that particular day, I made assumptions about the blood on his cut, and how it probably got there. My suspicions about the origin of the blood were solely based on who he was and what I suspected he was involved in. For even the most caring of souls, not passing judgement is often difficult. Relieved to find out what had *actually* happened, but now feeling sorrow toward him for entirely new reasons, I held his hand and fought not to cry.

"So as soon as I can ride out of here, you're going to do that? Go out with me?" he asked as he squeezed my hand.

I glanced up from the table and nodded my head like a child who'd been asked if he wanted a second helping of ice cream, "Yes. Yes, I am. Will. Absolutely."

"How much longer?" I asked.

"I don't know," he said as he released my hand, "My lung is down to a dull steady pain. My shoulder's a different story. It hurts to lift my arm, shower, cough, damn near any quick movement kills me. I can't even hold it out in front of me, I damned sure can't ride home."

"What about riding home in my car, and maybe taking your bike home on a trailer?" I said under my breath as I reached for my wine.

228

"Not going to happen. Only time that bike'll be on a trailer is if it's broke down. If I can't ride, I'll just go down and do a swan dive off of that bridge downtown and end it all. Sorry," he growled.

"Just a suggestion. So why aren't you wearing your sling?"

"I don't fucking like it," he snapped.

"Might speed things up," I shrugged.

"I look like a pussy when I wear it," he said as he positioned his left arm across his chest, mimicking the position of the sling.

I guess I shouldn't expect a biker, Marine, and the Sergeant at Arms of a Motorcycle Club to act any differently. He was his own person, and he had his pride, whether I agreed with his decisions or not. Being my selfish self, I was ready to start this *going on a date* thing just as soon as we were able. Coming down to Austin on a weekend every other week left me for the time in between doing nothing but counting the minutes until I hopped in my car and held my breath for another ten hour drive. It all seemed too good to be true, and I wanted to take the next step.

"You could stay here," he said under his breath.

I glanced around the large concrete deck and down at the swimming pool. As much as I'd love to stay with three overly wealthy and extremely gracious boxer/bikers while I waited for him to recover from his broken collar bone, I couldn't. I desperately needed to work and earn the money to pay rent and provide what little furnishings I needed for my new home.

I shook my head and laughed lightly, "I can't, I have to work, you know that."

He grinned and raised his index finger in the air, "I'm the boss, I'll give you time off with pay. A vacation."

I shook my head, "I can't accept that. It's a handout, and it wouldn't be fair to the other girls. Just get better as soon as you can, and we'll go from there."

"Sorry to interrupt, but I wanted to introduce you to my wife," a voice said from behind me.

As Cambio stood from his seat, I pushed my chair from the table and turned toward the voice. A very attractive man wearing a hoodie was standing with an adorable blonde woman at his side. As he brushed the hood from his head, he wrapped his arm over her shoulder and playfully pulled her into his chest. As he did, she pushed against him with her hands, leaned back, and slapped his shoulder with her hand.

"Stop it Shane, quit goofing around. Hi, I'm Kace, Shane's wife. He's the idiot wearing the hoodie in this heat," she laughed as she slapped his back.

"It's like his security blanket. I got him to quit wearing it for almost a year, and now that all these new people are around, he's back to his old tricks," she said as she held her hand out.

I wiped my hand on my shorts and shook her hand. After studying the man in the hoodie, I remembered seeing him at the hospital with the big bald guy. The visit to the hospital had become nothing more than a big blur for me, but I was fairly certain he was the same person.

"Nice to meet you, Kace. You're adorable, and I love that dress," I said as I shook her hand.

"Thanks, I like it. Vee and I were shopping, sorry but I didn't know when you were going to get here, so I didn't rush home. Vee and I shop a lot to get away from these three oversized children. Don't ever marry a boxer or a Marine, they're like big kids. Hi Toad, how's the shoulder," she said without taking a breath.

Toad cleared his throat as she finished speaking, "Just a little sore, and what? Did you forget I was a Marine?"

She pressed her hands into her hips, glanced at Shane, and turned toward Toad, "Nope."

I like this girl, she's spunky.

She twisted her shoulder my direction and smiled, "Who else came with you?"

I stood admiring Kace's shoes. As she spoke, I quickly looked up and alternated glances between her and Cambio, "Just me. Otis is going to ride down tomorrow. Oh, and I almost forgot, Otis is bringing your phone."

Cambio rolled his eyes and nodded his head. I grinned, shrugged, and shifted my gaze to Kace.

She was roughly five feet tall, blonde, and absolutely gorgeous. Outfitted in a tangerine summer dress and sandals with leather straps that tied around her ankles, she was dressed the way I *used* to dress and hoped to one day dress again. One day when I could afford it.

"And I think we met at the hospital when I came down, the day he uhhm. The day he uhhm, the day he woke up," I muttered as I held my hand toward Shane.

He nodded his head and smiled, revealing very prominent dimples, "We did, nice to see you again, ma'am."

Ma'am? Must be a proper southern boy.

"Do you mind if we sit?" Kace asked.

"Not at all, hell it's *your* house," Toad chuckled as he sat down.

I turned, glanced toward the house, and down at the pool below, "Oh, this is *your* place? I love it. The pool, the deck, the house, it's beautiful. We just walked over from A-Train's, I didn't know which one of you owned this one."

Simultaneously, Shane and Kace pulled chairs away from the table and sat side-by-side. As Kace sat, she flipped her hair over her shoulder, picked up my glass of wine, sniffed it, and began babbling as she carefully placed it in front of me.

"Thanks. Shane makes a lot of money from beating people up. Isn't that funny? He punches people in the face and they give him sacks of money for doing it. He bought this after he won the championship. Ripp and A-Train, the other two idiots, live on each side of us, and we're in the middle. Is that Mascato? I want a glass," Kace blurted as she waved her hand toward the house.

"It is, I brought it from A-Train's," I chuckled, "I can get you one."

She tilted her head toward Shane, but continued to gaze my direction, "No, you stay here, I like talking to you."

She turned to face Shane and stared.

Shane stood from his seat and motioned toward Cambio and me, "I'll get it, Kace. You need anything else?"

We both shook our heads. As Shane pulled the hood over his head and began walking toward A-Trains house, I turned toward Kace and grinned.

"I don't always treat him like this, but he's in trouble," she said flatly.

I raised my eyebrows and responded in a somewhat sarcastic tone, "Oh *really*?"

"Yep. I was pregnant and he hopped on his bike and disappeared for a few months. Rode around the country beating up people in bars while I was home alone wondering where he was. Didn't call, didn't text, nothing. He was just beating up random people trying to decide if he should come home or not. A-Train found him down by Mexico somewhere and made him come back. He didn't tell me *that* part at first, I thought he came home on his own. I just found out the other day, after *this* happened," she responded.

"Oh wow, how long ago was that?" I asked, clearly seeing she was far from pregnant.

"I don't know. It was with our first, maybe a little more than a year ago," she responded flatly.

Surprised she had produced *any* children and looked the way she did, I quickly responded, "You've had children?"

She shook her head and bit her lower lip slightly. As she released her lip, and cleared her throat, she shook her head lightly, "No just one. We lost the second one. She was a little girl. There were complications."

"I'm so sorry," I breathed.

"It was God's will, not ours," she responded as she gazed downward.

After a few seconds of silence, and me feeling like an absolute idiot, she glanced up and immediately continued with her playful behavior. She glanced toward Cambio, shook her head, and focused on me.

"You see, no matter how big or tough they are, they need us more than we need them, don't let anybody tell you different. And don't let anyone be mean to you, either. I was in a bad relationship with a guy who'd rather punch me than love me, and Shane helped me understand just how wrong it all was. I finally smacked him with a cast-iron skillet after he knocked this tooth out," she chuckled as she tapped her tooth with her index finger.

"Even though Shane helped me get out of the relationship, it doesn't mean I owe him anything. I just explained all of that so you'd know what type of person he is. Anyway, men act like they're tough and all that stuff, and maybe they are. But it doesn't mean they're in charge *all the time*, or that they're entitled to anything more than we are. Sometimes we just have to take charge and remind them it's a two-way street, you know, that we're not doormats. That's what I did with Shane," she paused and turned toward Cambio.

It was becoming immediately apparent not only was Kace full of spunk and a little bit of attitude, she was also a very courageous, understanding, and brave woman.

"And don't you dare ever mistreat her, Toad. Do you hear me?" she squealed.

My head swiveled his direction.

"I won't," he responded.

I turned to face Kace, anxious to see if there was more.

"You're going to be good to her aren't you?" she snapped back.

My head ratcheted his direction.

"Yes, I am," he immediately responded.

My gaze quickly shifted back to Kace.

"And you're never going to pull some shit like Shane did, running off on that bike and leaving her, no matter how bad things get, are you?" she huffed.

I glanced toward Cambio.

He shook his head and grinned, "Sure won't."

She tossed her head my direction, "See?"

"That's why I like Toad. He's nice. Well, that and he lets me cut his hair," she grinned.

I turned to face Toad, smiled, and shrugged my shoulders.

He raised his right hand to his well-manicured Marine haircut, "I uhhm, I can't do it, my shoulder kills me when I try to reach the back of my head, no matter which hand I use."

Kace turned toward me and placed her hand on my shoulder, "I got some clippers at Walgreens. I've been cutting it every four days, he's kinda *needy*."

"So how long have you two been seeing each other," Kace blurted as Shane sat down with a bottle of wine.

Before I could even think to answer, Cambio cleared his throat and responded, "Two weeks."

Huh?

We're seeing each other?

"Two weeks? Two weeks ago is when you were in the hospital, dork," Kace responded as she reached for the wine glass.

She tilted her head my direction, "You're all he talks about by the way."

I gazed at him and waited, hoping he had more to say. I couldn't hear enough about what he was thinking about me.

About us.

"Yeah, two weeks," he responded, "We started the day she whispered in my ear and woke me up."

And just like that, a girl I didn't know provided the answer to a question I had yet to ask, but longed to hear the answer to.

And from that moment on, as hard as I tried, I could no longer see the pit from which I had so desperately dug myself from.

Because I was floating in the clouds.

TOAD

The two weeks Sydney had been away were filled with thoughts of her arrival, boyish anticipation of seeing her again, looking forward to spending time talking to her, and finding out just exactly what she was willing to accept from me regarding any advancements I may wish to make into her life.

Her presence didn't make it difficult for me to proceed along my previously calculated path of slow steps, soft talk, and winning her heart; it seemed to have made it impossible. I was now under what I would personally describe as a full-scale attack, and she was providing minimal resistance to my approach.

I couldn't accept that I had simply been shot, hospitalized, and was now in recovery; my beliefs were more complex. Convinced I had been shot, died, and was now resurrected, I viewed life, my existence, and Sydney much differently. In clear contrast to my former way of thinking, I no longer felt guilty for my presence on earth.

I was now truly grateful to be alive.

Lying flat on my back, I stared up at the ceiling and spoke, "You know, my parents named me after my grandfather, right?"

"Yes, you told me that," she responded.

I tilted my head her direction slightly, "Do you know what it means?"

She raised her eyebrows and opened her mouth slightly. After a few seconds of silence, she breathed her response, "No, I guess not."

"*Change*. Cambio means *change* in Italian," as I finished speaking I shifted my gaze to the ceiling again.

"I didn't just get shot. I'm going to tell you what I think happened and you can believe me, I don't know…*consider* it…or think I'm crazy and go in the other room. I uhhm, but I'm going to tell you anyway," I said.

"I won't think your nuts," she said under her breath.

"Hold that thought," I responded.

"Some people get tossed in prison and they look at whatever it is they've done and make a decision to change. They decide if they don't, they're going to continue to repeat their behaviors and end up right back in there. That's what the system hopes for, making the criminal *think*, and causing them to change into a law abiding citizen as a result. I guess you could call the experience of going to prison, for this particular person, an eye-opener," I paused and tilted my head her direction.

She blinked her eyes as she nodded her head slightly. To relieve the pain in my shoulder, I shifted my eyes back to the ceiling.

"So I'm sure some people get shot, end up in the hospital, and make a conscious decision to change their life afterward. You know, just like the guy in prison. Make sense so far?" I asked.

"Makes perfect sense," she responded.

"Okay, well that's *not* what happened to me. I got shot, went to the hospital, and at some point in time, I died. I know I did. I was dead, Sydney. And I came back from that place, and now I'm a different person. I didn't decide this, it just happened. I guess I need to back up, I'm not different, I see *life* differently. It's hard to explain," I shifted my eyes her direction and waited for a response.

She had moved from resting her head in her hand and looking my

238

direction to lying beside me and staring at the ceiling.

""What was it like, being dead?" she asked in an almost eerie monotone voice.

I stared up at the ceiling and spoke as if recollecting a scene from a movie, "My reply is probably what you'd expect me to say. *Strange. Hard to explain.* I don't know, *difficult to think about.* It seems like a dream, but it wasn't. I was weightless, but the experience was heavy. I felt like there was weight on me or with me at all times. I wasn't a ghost or spirit, it was really *me*."

"You know I have to ask, where'd you end up in your opinion? Heaven or hell?' she asked.

"Heaven as far as *I'm* concerned. I mean it was peaceful. Not chaotic, like I think hell would be; and my grandfather was there, but he wasn't sick. He was the way he used to be before he got sick, still old, but really full of energy and he seemed to be having fun," I said.

"Did you talk to him? I mean in the experience?" she asked.

"No, he was out of reach. Just close enough I could see him, but not so close I could touch him. You know," I paused and tilted my head her direction.

"It's weird. It's like an entire lifetime of time passed in the 24 hours that I was in the coma. It's just weird."

She rolled her head to the side and grinned slightly, "I suppose so."

"You believe me?" I asked.

"Uh huh, I do," she breathed.

"I just don't want you to think I got shot, ended up scared of dying, and decided to try and become someone I'm not going to be able to be. If anything, I'm *not* afraid to die, not now. And this wasn't something I decided. *It happened* and *I'm different.*"

"I believe you," she said as she rested her elbow on the bed and her cheek against her palm.

"So you still going to ride in the club?" she asked.

I shifted my body her direction until the pain reminded me to stop, "Fuck yes, I am. It might have changed me, but it didn't change me into a *twat*. Jesus. I guess along with the change, it made me want to *live* life instead of just *existing*."

"I was just asking," she said with a laugh, "And you weren't just existing, believe me."

"Well, whatever I was doing, I've decided I want more out of life," I said as I shifted my gaze to the ceiling.

"Starting when?' she asked.

"Now. Starting *now*. I want to kiss you," as soon as I heard the words escape my lips, I wished they hadn't.

It wasn't that I didn't want to kiss her, because I did. Although my *mind* was obviously ready, I feared *I* wasn't. Not yet. Before I had a chance to retract what I had said, apologize, or claim some type of mental incompetence, she sat up on the bed, leaned over me, and pressed her lips softly against mine.

Prior to the kiss, I couldn't for the life of me recall the last time I actually kissed a woman. As our tongues fought for possession of the space our combined mouths created, I knew one thing for certain.

I'd never forget this kiss.

And I didn't want it to end.

As the weight of her upper body shifted on top of my chest, she lifted herself by pressing her hands into the bed. Her breasts now lightly brushing against my chest as she straddled my torso, I pulled my lips away for a much needed breath.

As I attempted to focus on her face, I brushed her hair from her face, and over her shoulder.

"I just needed to take a breath. My lung…"

"Oh, I'm sorry. Maybe we should stop," she sighed.

"No. No, we don't need to stop, I just needed to…to take a breather. You might want to shift your weight a little lower. Move your hips down on my hips, and keep your little butt off my stomach. It'll be less painful. You were sitting on me. Just lay on me," I groaned.

As she shifted her weight and repositioned herself, she lowered her mouth to meet mine. As we began to kiss again, my mind filled with emotions I never knew existed. Feeling as if I wanted to cry, laugh, and scream for joy at the same time, I continued to kiss her eagerly. As I felt her weight against my hips, I realized, much to my surprise, my cock was steadily rising against my very low resistance sweat pants. I felt like I was in high school again.

Well, that's a first.

Somewhat embarrassed and hoping I could convince it to recede - at least for a while - I attempted to think of anything *but* Sydney. As she continued to be the aggressor, kissing me passionately, I realized my attempts were not only feeble, but quite unsuccessful. When our lips finally parted for another much needed breath, she lifted her weight from my chest completely.

Now sitting on my upper thighs with her arms dangling at her sides, she gazed into my eyes and grinned.

"We're together, right?"

Somewhat confused, and still reeling from a whirlwind of emotions, I pressed my elbows into the bed until my shoulders lifted slightly from the comforter, "Say again?"

"You and me? We're together, right?" she said as she began to fumble nervously with the bottom of her tee shirt.

"Oh, yeah. Absolutely," I nodded.

"No one else?" she said under her breath.

"No. Hell no, I want you to know…"

She leaned forward and pressed her index finger against my lips, "Shhh. That's all I needed to know. Lean back."

She lifted her shirt over her head, unclasped her bra, and tossed both on the floor beside the bed. As my cock continued to test the tensile strength of the cotton fabric of my sweats, I watched as she gripped the waistband and pulled them to my thighs. As my cock popped out of the sweats and stood at full attention, she shifted her eyes from my face to my cock, and back.

"Wow," she gasped.

"That's all I've got. Wow," she chuckled as she reached down and gripped the shaft in her hand.

She slid her body along my legs until her boobs were pressing against my knees, and her blonde hair was draped over my hips. I could feel her warm breath against the tip of my pre-cum covered cock as she spoke.

"I'm far from a virgin, and I'm not even going to act like this is the first cock I've ever sucked, but I can tell you this," she paused and licked the tip of my twitching cock.

"If you grab my head and try to force it down my throat, it'll be the last," she gripped my cock in her hand tightly and slapped it against her lips as she waited for my response.

Incapable of doing much other than staring, I blinked my eyes, considered speaking, and nodded my head once instead.

"Agreed?" she asked as she slapped it against her lips again.

I moistened my lips, opened my mouth, and listened as the word *absolutely* puffed from my lungs.

She tossed her hair over her shoulder, licked the pre-cum from the tip, and slowly began to slide her full lips along the swollen shaft. As if witnessing a miracle, I watched as she worked her mouth up and down the shaft half a dozen times.

I attempted to lean forward and reach for her perfectly sculpted breasts. As the pain in my shoulder reminded me of what I'd been through, I fought against it and pressed my elbows into the bed, leaning up into an almost seated position. I slowly slid my hands along my thighs, not wanting to confuse her in any way regarding my intent. As my hands cupped her breasts and my fingers fumbled with her nipples, my breathing immediately changed.

Surprised, sickened by my lack of performance, and beyond embarrassed that I was reaching climax in a matter of seconds, I considered lifting her head away from my cock. Instead, I released her breasts and pressed my hands firmly into the comforter.

As the sound of my heavy breathing filled the room, I closed my eyes and arched my back slightly. In tune completely with where my mind, body, and sexual state of arousal was, Sydney began to stroke and suck my cock simultaneously. I closed my eyes as I felt every muscle in my body constrict. My fingers dug into the comforter as I held my breath, attempting unsuccessfully to prolong the experience.

I opened my eyes and stared as she lifted her mouth from the tip of my throbbing cock, stroked it twice, and smiled a smile of complete and utter satisfaction as she watched a geyser of cum erupt all over my thighs and sweats.

"Holy..."

"Fucking…"

"Shit…" I breathed as I released the comforter from my grasp.

She gazed into my eyes and smiled, "Sorry. I just, uhhm, I wanted to watch you, you know…cum. I wanted to see it, knowing it was me that did that for you."

"Holy shit." I sighed, "Sorry I didn't last longer. I got kind of excited."

"Me too," she chuckled as she leaned over and rolled off the edge of the bed.

As I watched her tip-toe shirtless to the bathroom, realized just how delicate, sweet, and utterly adorable she actually was. It didn't in any way change my perception of her, or my opinion of who she was or where we were hopefully going. It did, however, cause me to mentally place her in a category where no one else had ever been placed.

As Sydney walked from the bathroom with a washrag, I closed my eyes and allowed her to slowly seep into the void in my heart the war had long since left. As she leaned over the bed and kissed my lips lightly, I felt her continue to fill the vacant space. I opened my eyes and admired her beautiful face as our lips parted. For a lingering moment, she silently hovered over me; gazing into my eyes, and smiling the entire time.

I closed my eyes and grinned.

I had breathed life into Sydney when I saved her from herself at the bank. In turn, she had breathed life into me in the hospital; the day she whispered in my ear. Both of us acted not for reward or recognition, but out of a natural desire to be kind. One we certainly always possessed, but rarely exhibited toward others.

"You know," she said as she wiped the warm cloth over my hips and thighs, "If you have two broken cars, or two broken toys, you can take the two broken objects and make one working one? Like use the pieces from one to fix the other?"

She paused and held the washcloth in her hand as she waited on my response. Having no idea what point she was trying to make, I smiled and nodded my head.

"Yeah," I nodded.

"Well," she paused and wiped the clean side of the washcloth along my sweats, "As individuals, we're both broken. I think together, maybe we'll make a complete, unbroken *us*."

"Let's just take a shower together," I sighed as I painfully watched her attempt to clean up the mess I had made.

She carefully climbed off of me and stood on the floor beside the bed.

Knowing I had been broken beyond repair for almost a decade, I considered what she had said, and wondered if there was any validity to her statement. Quite possibly, I decided, jointly we could become a couple who was able to be together what we were incapable of being independently. Combined, it would stand to reason we would be at least twice what we were as individuals.

"It makes sense. You know, what you said a second ago," I paused and raised my hand to my chin.

"Unbreak me, Sydney," I said as I stood.

She stopped walking, turned, and looked over her shoulder. After an awkward pause, she smiled.

"Let me," she said over her shoulder.

As she held her pose and waited for me to respond, I admired her every feature. Slowly, I felt her fill what little void remained; completely.

"I am," I said under my breath.

As simple as it sounded and as complex as it seemed, I knew she was slowly doing just that.

Unbreaking me.

SYDNEY

Life has never provided me anything without taking something in return. If I ran in an effort to stay in shape, my joints became overworked and eventually turned weak and fragile. If I lay in the sun to obtain a glowing tan, my skin would eventually develop premature wrinkles, and appear worn beyond my years. If I worked excessively to earn money to purchase the finer things life offered, I would miss out on all of the life I could have lived while I was working. There are no free rides, there is no such thing as a free lunch, and with everything comes a price. Life, in my opinion, comes down to whether or not you're willing to pay for what it is you wish to obtain.

Is the give worth the get?

I had spent my life convinced I had paid in advance for something I had yet to receive. As much as I gave in my early years, and as little as I collected in return, I believed one day life would simply provide me my reward.

I had no idea Cambio Todelli would be my reward.

The smell of fresh coffee woke us both, and after a few minutes of whispering and kissing, we opted to get out of bed. The voices in the other room acted as a reminder that I wasn't the only one who was here to see Cambio. It appeared at some point in time through the night Otis had shown up as well. Reluctantly I rolled off of the bed, brushed my teeth, and considered brushing my hair and getting dressed. I settled for twisting my hair into a messy bun and wearing sweats.

"I like your hair like that," he said as I walked out of the bathroom.

"Seriously? Do you know what this is called?' I laughed as I raised my hand to the back of my hair.

He shook his head, "Nope."

"It's called a *messy bun*; because it's a mess and a bun at the same time. It's like a quick fix," I said.

"Well, I like it; it shows your face and all of your jaw. I like it. You've got a good face." he grinned.

"Thanks. You've got a good face too. I'll make a personal note to wear my hair up as much as possible," I said as I reached for the door and waited for his approval to open it.

He stood silently and gazed my direction. After a long moment, he grinned.

"You know, I want to take you to see my grandfather. Not *him*, you know, *his grave*. It'll have to be after I get a little better, it's a long ride."

"Oh wow. I'd love that. Where is he buried?" I asked.

"Philadelphia," he breathed.

"I though you went to see him all the time? You ride to Philly to see him?" I asked, shocked at the distance he was traveling to go to the gravesite.

"Yeah, it's about 2,700 miles round trip. My folks live up there too. Maybe we'll stop and see them. It'll be a nice trip. I haven't seen them in a bit, but maybe we'll talk about that later," he said as he slowly approached.

No differently than any other woman, I wanted definition to our relationship. In some respects feeling as if I had thrust myself into something I hadn't prepared for, I wondered if he was as devoted as I was to what it was we were doing. His actions as well as his words were proving he was as invested in this as I was. I stood, holding the door handle, and simply grinned at the thought of going to Philadelphia with him.

"I'm ready if you are," he sighed.

I turned toward the door and pulled against the handle. As soon as I pulled the door open, I immediately jumped back. Startled by the fact Otis stood directly in front of the door, I screeched.

"Oh my God!" I shouted.

"Holy shit! You scared me to death," I said under my breath.

"Morning, Syd," Otis grinned.

"What the fuck you doing, Brother Otis? Standing there with your ear against the door? Hell, we're brothers, I'm not keeping secrets in here. You wanna know something, just ask," Cambio chuckled as he ducked under my arm and walked past.

"You scared the shit out of me," I said as I pushed against him with both hands.

Playfully, he stumbled rearward as if my pushing knocked him off balance. At probably close to 300 pounds of solid muscle, ten of me couldn't budge Otis on a good day.

"Well, I guess it's nice knowing there's no secrets," Otis said as he continued to stumble toward the kitchen, "I was just coming to tell you two lovebirds that breakfast is ready. Coffee too."

"We smelled the coffee," Cambio said as he walked toward the kitchen.

"Brought your phone, and the battery's all charged up. Phone, watch, your ring, wallet, knife, boots, and that bracelet thing you wear; they're all there in the kitchen. Sorry about that, but when they showed up, they just cut your clothes off and tossed the shit everywhere. Shit they cut your jeans in half. They'd have sliced your cut in two if we let them," he paused and started laughing out loud.

"What about my cut?" Cambio grunted, "Where's my fucking cut?"

"Slice has it in the shop, locked up. He said you can get it when you get home. Maybe he's using it like an incentive," Otis shrugged.

"Cocksucker. He expects me to ride home naked? Well, at least I can call him now," Cambio hissed.

"You know, it's a damned good thing there wasn't a girl paramedic in that bunch. That big fucking paramedic fireman guy sliced off your pants and there you were, covered in blood and all commando and shit. Your poor shriveled half-dead cock was just flopping in the breeze," Otis laughed.

"Yep. Good thing there wasn't. Cock's officially off limits," he said flatly.

Otis shrugged his shoulders as he alternated glances between Cambio and me, "What the fuck's that mean?"

"It's hers now," he said over his shoulder as he grabbed the coffee pot.

Mine?

Otis playfully nodded his head. As he tilted his head my direction, he grinned and gave me the *thumbs up*. I smiled in return and raised my thumb in the air.

"Appreciate it," Cambio said as he set the two cups of coffee at the bar and glanced down at his belongings.

The house we were in belonged to Cambio's Marine friend, A-Train. The main body of the house was very large, and tastefully decorated with furniture and miscellaneous large photographs of nature and landscape.

The living room was open to the kitchen, only separated by a long island that served as a bar and eating area.

"How you feeling?" Otis asked as he sat down on the bar stool.

"Better, just sore. Lung feels, fuck I don't know how to describe it," he paused and shook his head, "Like it's working overtime. I sure as fuck know it's there."

"Shoulder?" Otis asked.

"Feels like I got shot," he responded flatly.

"Probably ought to be wearing a sling or something, huh?" Otis shrugged.

"Probably ought to get some business of your own, Brother Otis. I'll be fine," Cambio snapped.

Otis shook his head and picked up his cup of coffee, "You want to ride out of here before winter, you need to be wearing that fucking sling."

"Cream? Sugar?" Cambio asked as he walked toward the stove.

"The invisible man speaks again. Guess no comment on the sling remark, huh?" Otis said.

I stared at Cambio. He returned the stare as if waiting on *my* response instead of commenting on what Otis had said about his failure to wear the sling. After a minor staring session, I decided he wasn't going to respond to Otis.

I blinked my eyes, "Black's fine."

He turned toward the other counter and removed a spoon from the drawer.

"Where's A-Train?" Cambio asked over his shoulder.

"He just left, went over at the boxer's house to watch the kid. Boxer had to run to the gym, and his wife had a hair appointment or something.

251

Said he watches that kid as much as they do," Otis responded.

"A-Train said to make sure you ate something, so I made some scrambled eggs. Couldn't find any bacon, so there's some ham there," Otis said as he tilted his head toward the stove.

"I'll eat in a minute," Cambio responded as he grabbed the cream.

"I didn't cook that shit for *my* health, eat it now, before it gets cold," Otis growled.

Seeing Cambio and Otis together was much different than seeing my brother and his biker friends before he went to prison. Although they all call each other *brother*, it's rare to see any of them truly act like brothers would act. These two were the clear exception. Bickering like a couple of brothers, it was nice to see Otis truly cared about Cambio as much as he did. The little time we had spent together in the hospital proved he was as considerate and as kind as any person I had ever met, if not more. Although I would never tell him, he seemed to me to be like a big teddy bear.

Well, a big teddy bear with a scowl on his face most of the time.

"While you're plating up the eggs for you and your girl, I've got a quick question," Otis said as he sipped his coffee.

"Fine, I'll eat now," Cambio responded as he slid a cup of coffee across the bar, "Hungry?"

I nodded my head. Cambio walked to the stove and pulled the lid from the skillet and looked inside.

I pulled out a stool and sat down beside Otis. Otis glanced in my direction and winked as Cambio began to spoon eggs on two plates. I did my best to wink back.

"So, the day in the bank," he paused and alternated glances between Cambio and me.

Cambio turned and looked over his shoulder, "Yeah, what about it."

"Well, being we decided you aren't keeping any secrets, Syd here was with the guy that robbed the bank, wasn't she?" he asked.

I raised the coffee cup to my mouth and took a permanent drink as I waited for Cambio to respond.

"Sure was," Cambio responded.

"I knew it. I fucking *knew* it," Otis said as he slapped the countertop with his hand.

"All you had to do was ask," Cambio sighed as he turned and carried the plates to the bar.

"Well, you know how I roll. It's none of my fucking business. But being she's the owner of your cock," he paused, turned my direction, and winked.

"I figured she's around for the long haul. So, I thought I'd ask. Now, second question; You a thief, Sydney?" Otis chuckled.

I lowered my coffee cup onto the bar and shook my head, "Not even close. I met the guy the night before, outside the bar where my car was parked. He thought I was coming out of the bar, but honestly I was getting ready to go to bed. He had a nice car, and was hitting on me, so I went with him. I basically used him for a shower, and to save you from wondering…"

"I didn't do anything with him. The next morning he drove to the bank on his way to take me back to my car. I had no idea what he was doing. Seriously," I explained.

"That's all I need to know," he said as he patted my shoulder.

"So, when's the wedding?" Otis asked without an ounce of emotion.

"Fuck you, O," Cambio chuckled.

Otis took a shallow breath, sighed, and glanced in my direction.

After studying me for a moment, he turned to face Cambio.

"Well, as far as I'm concerned, a man's Ol' Lady is an extension of the club. You know how I feel. And you know I'm only tight with a few of the fellas; you and Axe, to be truthful. Now Avery? There ain't a better bitch on this earth than that girl. She's solid as fuck, and I'll leave it at that. This one?" he paused and tilted his head in my direction.

"I like this little bitch a lot. I really do. But if she was prone to robbing a motherfucker or stealin' shit, I needed to know. You know, keep my shit under lock and key," he chuckled.

"But if you're finally layin' claim to her, and she's not a thief, I guess I'll welcome her to the family," he said as he reached over and patted my shoulder again.

"For what it's worth, I never thought you were a thief," Otis said as he took a sip of coffee.

"She's solid," Cambio said under his breath as he nodded his head my direction.

As I was filling with emotion, and feeling as if I was making quick progress toward being accepted by the men who mattered most, I smiled and nodded my head. I lifted my coffee cup and took a small sip, attempting to act like it was just another day in the life of Sydney. Truthfully, I was on cloud nine. Being referred to as *solid* by a biker was the highest form of affirmation I could ever receive.

"Axton says Avery said she sent you a text and you need to read it," Cambio said as he looked up from his phone.

I looked down at my plate, and realized I hadn't begun to eat.

"My phone's in my purse. I'll look as soon as I'm done eating," I responded.

"Huh, that's weird. Got a text from the vet. Wants me to call him.

Can't remember now if I paid that girl before I stomped out of that place," he said as he continued to mess with his phone and eat ham at the same time.

He stopped eating, and raised the phone to his ear. As I began to eat my almost cold eggs, Cambio began pacing through living room and talking on his phone. I turned toward Otis and grinned.

"Thanks for making breakfast," I said, "It's really good."

With his coffee cup dangling from his index finger at the height of his chin, he turned toward me, raised his thumb in the air, and smiled. There was something about Otis that was completely comforting. He had an almost magical presence that only became apparent after being around him for a while. I suspected I was no different than most people, and at least initially was very intimidated by his size and stature. After I was able to relax around him, I realized he was not only much different than every other *biker* I had met, but truly unlike *anyone* I had ever met. He was the type of man I'd never get sick of being around, and always looked forward to seeing.

"Holy shit! Devil looks after his own. Hot fucking damn!" Cambio howled.

"What's going on?" Otis said as he spun his bar stool around.

Cambio walked in my direction as he began to respond.

"That was the vet on the phone. That pup had some chip in his neck. He gave me the name of the fucker and his address," he paused, placed his hands on either side of my face, and kissed me lightly on the lips.

As our lips parted, he gazed into my eyes and then kissed me lightly again. He turned to face Otis as he tossed his phone onto the bar.

"He said some states require vet's to turn in someone they suspect is abusing animals, and some states don't. Well, Kansas does. He said he struggled with telling me who this guy was, and finally decided he'd rather live knowing the guy got what he deserved than live wondering if he'd continue to abuse animals after getting his wrist slapped by the court. He made me promise not to kill him. Can you fucking believe it? Must be living right," he said as he slapped his hand against the bar.

"Give me the fucker's address, I'll have it all taken care of by the time you get home," Otis said flatly.

"Shoulder's feeling better already," Cambio responded as walked to the other side of the bar and began shoveling eggs into his mouth.

"You told me in the hospital you were a changed man," Otis chuckled.

"You said you saw the light," he raised his hands in the air, spread his fingers and began waving his hands back and forth, "I don't want you ruining that, Brother."

Cambio dropped his fork onto the plate, "I'll tell you just like I told her. I haven't got one fucking doubt that I died and was resurrected. Believe me or don't, I don't give a rat's ass. And when I died, I went to some place that sure wasn't like hell. Confirms my life's been lived in accordance to what the man wants to see."

He extended his index finger and pointed it upward, "I might be changed, and in some fucking respects I might be different, but I'm still a fucking Sinner."

Otis nodded his head once, "Good to know."

On the previous night, when Cambio explained everything about being a changed man and seeing the world and its offerings through different eyes, part of me was elated while another part was somewhat disappointed. I don't know whether or not it was a result of growing up around my brother, or from lacking a father figure, but the male bravado-macho-tough guy types had always appealed to me. In thinking of Cambio being a softer, more passive biker, I was slightly dissatisfied. I felt as if I was forfeiting part of what made him attractive to me. Having him continue to be the hard, tough, take no shit person he had always been, yet continue to be sweet to me would be the best of both worlds. I guess now that he had cleared things up, I would no longer be left to wonder just who it was I was falling in love with. Being a Selected Sinner was one thing, being a *sinner* was another. Clearly Cambio intended to be both. In my opinion it was exactly where he belonged.

I looked up from my plate and nodded my head, "Amen."

SYDNEY

Being *honest* and being *open* are two totally different things, and they're worlds apart. Although I have always perceived myself as being brutally honest, I've never been a person who I would consider to be open. Volunteering information about myself, my past, or my life's experiences isn't something I have ever been comfortable with.

After spending the day at Shane and Kace's pool sunbathing and swimming, Cambio and I had taken a shower, and were relaxing on the bed. The fact I had not been open with Cambio about my past was beginning to bother me, and I was seeing my lack of willingness to have previously volunteered any and all things about myself as dishonesty.

I rolled onto my side and rested my cheek on the palm of my hand, "I need to tell you some things about me. About my past."

He tilted his head my direction and grinned, "I don't care about your past. I mean I do, but not about past relationships or anything. I really don't."

"It's not that," I sighed.

He rolled onto his side and rested his head against the pillow, "Okay, let's hear it."

"It's a bunch, so let me finish, okay?" I asked.

He blinked his eyes and nodded his head once.

"I told you about my brother, but I didn't tell you *everything*. My parents, they were killed when I was a baby. Well, my father killed my mother and then killed himself. I was three. I lived in an orphanage on and off until I was a little older, and then we were placed in foster care. The foster family we lived with wasn't a really good one, but it was all the family I have really ever known. He was a preacher and she was a housewife. They had their own children, and they had other foster children too. The uhhm, the older kids mistreated the girls. You know, they messed with us, sexually," I took a shallow breath and tried to decide what to say next, not feeling comfortable just yet about revealing the fact I was repeatedly raped as a little girl.

"I'm sorry about your parents. And I'm sorry about your foster family. People can be so inconsiderate sometimes," he placed his hand under my chin, lifted it slightly, and continued, "I'm sure growing up without a family was tough. Just know that, well, know that I'm here for you. I know it sounds cheesy, but I am. I'll do the best I can to make up for everything you've missed out on."

I grinned as I pressed my cheek against his hand, "Thanks, I know you will. And yeah, it's still tough, you know not having a family. No Christmas, no Thanksgiving, no birthdays, I hate it. Jack was all I had, and with him gone, well, I guess I've just got you. I'm just glad you have a family."

He released my cheek from his hand, rolled onto his back, and stared at the ceiling, "Well, I guess I should tell you something about me. I *have* parents; real good parents to be honest. I've been back from the war for almost 5 years, and I've seen them once; right after I got home. Haven't seen them since."

"Oh wow. Can I ask why?"

"You know, all this time, I kind of wondered. I told myself for a long time I was just busy. I knew better, though. I haven't been home for a holiday, nothing. Hell, I quit even answering their phone calls. I'd ride up to see my grandfather, and sometimes I'd ride by their house, but I wouldn't stop. Guilt, I suppose. I mean if you want to be specific," he glanced my direction and immediately shifted his eyes back up to the ceiling.

"Yeah, I'd guess it'd be the guilt," he said under his breath.

"About what?" I asked, confused as to what specifically he'd be guilty about.

He stared at the ceiling and continued to speak in a monotone voice, "The war, killing, living through it all, fuck the list goes on and on. You know, I was medically discharged from the Marines, because of the PTSD. They said I was too fucking crazy to continue to fight. Too crazy to be a Marine, kind of funny when you think about it. That's probably the biggest thing, the fact I was discharged. So maybe it was guilt and a little embarrassment."

"But you were honorably discharged, weren't you?"

"Yeah, sure was. Complete with commendations and medals. But my father's era doesn't understand. Maybe that's why I talk to my grandfather, because he doesn't argue with me about it."

"Have you tried talking to your father about it?"

"Nope. I'm thinking maybe I will now, though," he tilted his head to the side and stared.

"Here's an interesting statistic about PTSD, veterans, and their mental health. 22 Veterans a day commit suicide. That's one every 65 minutes, all day, every day, 365 days a year. It's fucking sad. I didn't want to be another statistic, so I dealt with my PTSD the best I knew how. I surrounded myself with people who didn't ask questions, and tried to be nice to the people I liked and mean to the ones I didn't. I went to my mental health at the Veterans Administration when I needed to, and I figured I'd skate through life doing what I was doing. Now that all this has happened, and with you mentioning family and all, it all seems wrong."

"So they don't even know about…about you being shot?" I asked.

He licked his lips and stared blankly, "Nope."

I sat up on the bed and gazed down at him, "You probably should."

He turned his head and gazed up into my eyes. After lifting his hands in the air, he reached for me as he spread his fingers wide. Naturally, I reached for his hands and interlocked my fingers in his.

"I will. And you're going with me when I do. We'll ride up there as soon as I can stand the pain," he responded, "Okay?"

I nodded my head, "Okay."

The thought of meeting his parents was terrifying and exciting both. I realized part of why he may want me to accompany him was for comfort and probably to keep his parents from being too harsh regarding his extended absence. No matter what his reasoning was, it excited me to meet them, and to make another step in the direction of being in a permanent relationship with him. As he pulled me down on top of him, I realized just how much I enjoyed simply being in his company.

"I uhhm. I really like you," I said as I landed against his chest.

I really like you?

Seriously, Sydney?

Did you just say that? Out loud?

I sounded like a complete juvenile. For a grown woman to tell a grown man she *really liked him* was probably one of the most meaningless and utterly ridiculous statements that could have been conjured up. Before I could give any explanation for my childish behavior, he wrapped his arms around me, pressed his cheek against mine, and rested his mouth against my ear.

"I passed that stage a long fucking time ago," he breathed into my ear.

I exhaled and relaxed into his arms. Exhausted from spending the day in the sun, and completely relaxed by the comfort he provided me, I quickly fell into a state of bliss as he continued to breathe into my ear and hold me against him.

I closed my eyes and thought of where I'd came from, what I had accomplished, and just where I may be going. I wondered if he might be doing the same, and if so, what he felt the future may hold for us.

And slowly, I fell asleep in the arms of the man I was deeply in love with, but obviously too afraid to tell.

SYDNEY

I pulled my mouth from his cock, licked the tip, and continued to stroke it with my right hand. I reached down with my left hand and slid my middle finger along my pussy and held it in the air for him to see. Although *I* needed no confirmation, my glistening finger provided it. I was completely soaked. As my heart began to race even more, I shifted my gaze from my finger up and into his eyes.

"You make me so wet. Just stand there. Don't move," I breathed as I stood from my knees.

He stood with his back to the wall, and gripped his rigid cock in his hand.

"You might have to bend your knees a little, but I'll do all the work," I said eagerly as I bent over in front of him and rested my hands on my thighs.

As I attempted to back up into the tip of his cock, his hands gripped my hips and guided me in for a perfect landing. Although I knew the thirty minutes of kissing, a half-assed blowjob, and my wandering mind had me beyond ready from a *lubrication* standpoint, the size of his massive cock and the fact my pussy was absolutely tiny left me wondering just what complications we might encounter from a *physical* standpoint. No matter what they may be, I was willing to try and work through them. I eagerly reached between my legs and guided the tip of his cock against my dripping pussy lips. As the tip began to penetrate me, I opened my mouth and groaned.

"Oh God. Take…it…slow," I gasped.

Without responding, he slowly slid his cock from inside me. What little relief I felt was immediately followed by disappointment. I wanted it back inside me. Before I had a chance to release my lower lip and speak, he slowly began to slide it in. I bit into my lip a little more and rolled my eyes back so far it hurt.

Although every woman who enjoys sex wishes for her man to be well endowed, we all have our limits. Although no one in their right mind wants a man with a dick the size of a Vienna sausage, one the size of a baseball bat is even more useless. The best, I suppose, would be to have a man with the largest possible cock that would *eventually* fit, and slowly work it into place.

Cambio's cock was the size of my wrist, and without a doubt, had a few inches that would never see any action inside of me, regardless of our efforts. As I rocked back and forth on my heels, slowly working my ass closer and closer to his hips, he began to moan. I continued to bite my lip, breathe through my nose, and refused to forfeit the fight.

"Holy fuck you're tight," he groaned.

I might have a tight pussy, but unless he was fucking a Hippopotamus, his cock would completely fill any pussy he attempted to shove it into. As I finally found a rhythm that seemed to work, I felt myself relax slightly. Things were beginning to come together. I released my lower lip, continued to buck my hips back and forth, and spoke my mind.

"Your…cock's…huge," I said between my choppy breaths.

"It feels like…I'm being fist-fucked…by a midget," I groaned.

"Okay, I didn't need to hear that," he sighed.

"Just…take it…slow," he breathed.

"I'm good now," I sighed.

As I continued to work my hips back forth, his cock began to slide in and out without much discomfort. In fact, it felt incredible. After about the third full stroke, I relaxed with him fully inside of me and had an orgasm beyond compare. By anyone's account, I had lasted roughly as long full of his throbbing shaft as he did when I sucked his cock. For that reason, and that reason alone, I felt no need to advertise what I had done. After relishing in the feeling of having a much needed orgasm and regaining my sexual composure, I began to rock back and forth on my heels. Although this method seemed much less sensual, and a little more boring, it suited me; at least for now.

After a few quiet moments of slowly rocking back and forth, I felt proud I had lasted for a length of time without having another orgasm. With my mind fixed in the feeling, and my body becoming accustomed to the feeling, his cock, and the entire sexual situation, I felt as if I might last long enough to make him reach climax. Still bent over and teetering on the balls of my feet, I opened my eyes and exhaled.

A hand slapped against my thigh, slid upward, and gripped my hip.

A hand gripped my other hip.

Oh shit…

He slowly pulled me rearward, until my ass pressed against his hips.

"Fuck this shit, I'm done dicking around," he said under his breath.

"Okay…" I squeaked.

Sorry, I thought I was doing pretty good.

He forced himself in and out of me, but not without using some caution. I bit my lip again. The momentum of his thrusts increased with each stroke. I braced my hands firmly against my knees as my eyes bulged and my lower lip became my own personal chew toy. His cock began to hit spots inside of me I had no idea even existed.

Good spots.

My legs began to shake. My knees felt like rubber. One of his hands began to fondle my right boob. His fingers found their way to my nipple. Twisting it in between his forefinger and thumb, a tingling sensation shot between my nipple and hyper sensitive clit. I felt his cock began to swell inside me.

Oh dear God, that feels unbelievable.

As his swollen cock continued to slide in and out of my sopping wet pussy, the sound of our flesh on flesh began to resonate through the room. To me, there was nothing sexier *sounding* than skin slapping skin. I felt my pussy begin to contract into an orgasm. As he must have sensed my point of climactic bliss, he held his cock in place as I exploded into a thousand little pieces of *what the fuck just happened.*

My body shaking and my pussy convulsing, the orgasm lasted for an eternity. His cock somehow swelled a little more. Shocked that I could actually *feel* it, my eyes widened and I began to shake. My hands slipped from my knees and onto the floor.

As I felt his cock pulse inside of me, filling me with his warm cum, one last surge of climactic heaven filled my soul.

"Oh my God, that….was…incredible," I breathed as I attempted to stand on shaky legs.

"That was far more than incredible. Holy shit," he gasped.

"What?" I grinned.

"Nothing…" he sighed.

I did my best to turn and look over my shoulder. His face was covered with a smile. A smile I had yet to see. A smile that not only covered his face, but one that exuded even from his eyes. He raised his hands to his face and pressed his palms into his cheeks.

"No, *what*?" I asked.

His breathing still slightly labored, he exhaled a breath. Along with it came his thoughts, "I just really like you."

I shifted my gaze to the floor and stared down at the carpet as I felt his cock begin to become flaccid inside of me.

"I passed that stage a long fucking time ago…" I said flatly.

As I chuckled to myself for my quick witted nature in quoting what he had said earlier, I realized I had truly reached the point of no return.

I reached between my legs with my right hand as I pulled myself away from him. As I cupped my hand against my pussy, holding the proof of his satisfaction inside of me, I turned to face the man I loved. With still shaking legs, I looked up and smiled.

He released his cheeks, placed his hands against my face, and bent at his waist. After a long, sensual, much needed kiss, our lips parted. He gazed into my eyes and blinked. He pulled my face to his, kissing me again passionately. My head began to spin and my mind reeled as the tension inside of me built. Again, our lips parted.

He gazed into my eyes for a long moment.

"What?' I breathed.

He pulled my face to his and again kissed me passionately. Lost in the kiss, I began to feel as if I had been lifted from my feet and was floating in the space before him. I had never been kissed the way he kissed me. I had never felt the feelings I was feeling. This, to me, was completely and utterly new. As our lips parted, I fought for my next breath. I gazed into his eyes.

He narrowed his gaze as his mouth curled into a smile, "I think I'm falling in love with you, Sydney."

TAKING THE HEAT

Falling in love?

I passed that stage a long fucking time ago.

TOAD

"I can't let you go back without me. You know, I had an idea of what I wanted to happen this weekend, but I had no clue where your mind was for sure. I told you I wanted to take you on a date, and I told you how I felt the last time you were here, but I didn't know how *you* felt about everything," I paused and rolled my shoulders.

I raised my eyebrows and turned my palms upward, "I can barely feel it."

She rolled her eyes and shook her head, "The pain's going to kill you, it's a ten hour ride."

"Listen, I've been in a lot of pain before. I can handle it," I assured her.

She shrugged her shoulders and widened her eyes, "What's Otis going to say?"

I walked past her and gripped the door handle in my hand. After turning around and grinning, I I opened the door to the bedroom and stuck my head out of the opening. Otis sat on the love seat watching television.

"Hey O, I was thinking about riding home with you. Having Sydney follow us in the chase vehicle," I shouted over the sound of the television.

He glanced over his shoulder, turned back toward the television, and responded, "Have to buy some jeans, I'm not rolling with ya if you're wearing those sweats."

"So you're alright with me riding?" I asked as I opened the door a little further.

Sydney stuck her head under my armpit and into the opening.

"What about his shoulder, Otis? Yesterday it was killing him, today he wants to ride home," she hollered.

Otis glanced over his shoulder, turned to the television, glanced over his shoulder again, and glanced at the T.V. He pointed the remote at the television and turned it off. After standing and turning to face us, he raised his right hand to his chin and gazed up at the ceiling.

"Well, let's see…What's happened since yesterday? Let me see…" he released his chin and cocked his head slightly to the side.

"You two have been fucking in there like a couple of rabbits. My guess is he likes fucking you, and doesn't want to stop. Be kind of tough to fuck you if he's here and you're there. He's a big boy, Syd. And I'll give you a little advice…" he paused, smiled, and lowered his hands to his waist, "Don't get between a Sinner and his desire to ride, you'll never make it if you do…"

He shifted his gaze toward me, "You wanting to ride that sled of yours, Toad?"

I nodded my head sharply, "Planning on riding it home, O."

"Well, there you have it, Syd. Man said he's gonna ride that sled home," he shrugged.

Sydney pulled her head from beneath my armpit and stepped back into the bedroom.

"Good lookin' out, O," I said.

Otis smiled, pointed the remote toward the television, and sat back down on the love seat. I pulled the door closed and turned to face Sydney, wondering what she'd have to say now. I didn't have to wait long for her response.

"Well, looks like we need to get you some jeans," she sighed.

"Well, let me lace up my boots, and we'll run and get some." I said as I looked around the room for my boots.

"Never been much for riding in a cage; well, unless I had to. I'm sure not looking to have anyone see me riding my bike in sweats, either. Guess we'll take your car?" I asked as I pulled my boots on.

"Sure. You'll be styling with those grey sweats and those boots," she chuckled.

I looked down at the contrast of the light grey sweats A-Train bought me against my boots. I looked like an idiot. At least in Austin no one knew me, and I could make it to the store, buy a pair of jeans, and get home without someone seeing me. Wearing sweats, *not* riding my bike, riding in a cage, and being with a woman buying clothes were all things that were completely different than what I was accustomed to. Strangely, I was comfortable doing it with Sydney. After scanning the room for my cut, and realizing it was in the shop, I exhaled a sigh of almost relief. If a local Sinner saw another Sinner dressed like I was, and wearing a cut, photos would be all over the website.

"Guess I'm ready," I sighed.

"You're going to be okay in a *cage?*" she said with a sarcastic tone.

"I'll be fine," I nodded.

"Going out for jeans," I said as we walked out into the living room.

Otis sat with his eyes glued to the television. As we walked past, I took a second glance toward the T.V. The unmistakable face of Bruce Jenner stared back at me as he stood in the garage arguing with his wife. I shook my head in disbelief. Otis was watching the Kardashian Marathon.

"Is he watching *Keeping up with the Kardashians*?" Sydney asked as we walked by.

"He sure as fuck is," Otis responded over his shoulder.

I glanced down at my sweats and eventually focused on my boots. I turned toward Sydney, shrugged my shoulders, and grinned; two of the most solid Sinners to ever don the cut, one watching the Kardashians, and one wearing sweats and riding in a cage.

If the real world ever knew...

TOAD

Leaving Austin proved to be far more difficult than I ever imagined. The hospitality of the people I had met, the honest unfiltered opinions of Ripp, and walking away from a fellow 2/7 Marine made riding home an emotional journey. The pain in my shoulder throughout the entire trip settled into a dull thud after the first hundred miles, and surprisingly never got much worse. Pain, according to Marines, was the weakness leaving my body. With each hundred miles traveled, I felt stronger. When we finally reached Wichita, I felt relieved, relaxed, and as if I had made a journey not only back home, but to an entirely different place and stage in my life.

A stage I was eager to enter.

Now headed to an emergency call of the Executive Committee, I felt a little nervous about my return, what happened to me, and seeing the Committee. As I rounded the corner of the street toward the clubhouse, it was apparent not only was this a meeting of the Committee, but the entire chapter.

And it looked like I was the last one to show up.

Oh fuck.

I glanced down at my watch as I turned into the parking lot. The 5:50 p.m. time confirmed I should be ten minutes early. I nervously parked my bike and stepped into the empty garage. The fact the shop was vacant, and everyone was already in the meeting room strengthened my suspicion I had either misunderstood the time of the meeting, or something was wrong with my watch. After walking through the empty shop and opening the door to the room, I was greeted by the entire chapter cheering and clapping their hands.

"Alright fellas, make a path and make it wide. Let the man in the God damned room without bumping that left shoulder," Axton growled.

"Settle the fuck down fellas," Axton said as he raised his hands into the air, "Good to have you back, Toad."

Filled with a strange awkward feeling, I wiped the sweat from my brow and wrapped my arms around Axton, hugged him, and slapped my hand against his back. As I pulled away, I reached out and shook his hand firmly.

Axton turned toward the cabinet, opened the door, and pulled what I suspected was my cut from the shelf. As he carefully placed it on the table in front of him, he positioned it perfectly with the edge of the table, and when satisfied, held his hands in the air again.

"Alright fellas, this time I mean it," he shouted, "I need silence."

The entire crowd fell immediately silent. Still somewhat nervous, and uncertain of the need for a welcoming committee such as what he had assembled, I stood a few feet from Axton and nodded at the fellas as I scanned the group.

"This is something I've never had to do, and to be quite fucking honest, I hoped I'd never have to do. There's no President of a club who ever wishes for this day to come," Axton began.

The tone on his voice and the expressed emotion made his state of emotion very apparent. Axton was upset. Slowly, my mind began to work through all of the possibilities. The fact Axton had kept my cut, and his emotional condition could only mean one thing. He was removing me from the Executive Committee and possibly from the club due to his belief of my physical condition. After swallowing heavily, I attempted unsuccessfully to speak. During another attempt to swallow the lump in my throat, Axton continued to speak.

"Fuck, fellas this is tougher than I thought," Axton sighed as he glanced down at the floor.

"Well, there's no better way for me to…to get through this…but to…but to just fucking say it," he said as he glanced up from the floor.

As I finally found Otis in the crowd, I shrugged my shoulders and slowly raised my hands in the air. Otis lowered his chin and winked.

Axton crossed his arms, and scanned the crowd. After inhaling a deep breath, exhaling, and glancing in my direction, he began speaking again, "For the first time in the history of the Sinners, a man has made a commitment to a fellow Sinner, and acted in a manner expressing courage and heroism, risking his life for the safety and the security of his brothers."

He reached down, picked up my cut, and held it in his shaking hands.

"You all need to know this man's name if you don't. Cambio Todelli, known by his brother Sinners as Toad, on August 16th, did hereby save the life of one Axton Bishop, otherwise known as Slice - the President of the Wichita chapter of the Selected Sinners - by willfully and knowingly stepping between a gunman and his intended target, risking his life in the process. For this selfless act, I hereby present him with the first presentation of the Selected Sinners patch of Valor. This patch," Axton paused and unfolded the cut.

"This patch is only awarded to a man for clearly risking his life to save to the life or lives of a fully patched member or members of the club, and must be witnessed by another member of the club. Additionally, it must be voted upon by the president of every chapter. Having met all of this criteria, I now present with tremendous gratitude," he held the cut by the shoulders for all to see.

"The first patch of Valor to your Sergeant at Arms, Toad."

A red and gold patch in the shape of an ornate star with a ribbon around it had been sewn on the left upper portion of my cut, where the bullet hole probably was. As I gazed at the cut, and the men began to clap and cheer, I filled with emotion.

Receiving the patch, the assembly of all the men, the voting by each chapter president, and Axton's emotional state were more than I was prepared for. Now clearly recalling what happened on that particular day, I began to shake as I reached for the cut. Having the men see me in anything but a stable state of mind was not acceptable. I was their Sergeant at Arms, and I needed to act the part. I straightened my stance, pulled my shoulders rearward, and held the cut in my hand.

Axton held his hands in the air, and the room immediately fell silent.

I swallowed the lump which had formed in my throat.

"As the Sergeant at Arms," I hesitated and scanned the crowd.

"I was advised my responsibility was for the safety and security of the club, as well as the protection and defense of all club Members and Prospects. I was uhhm, I was just…"

"I was just doing my job," I said under my breath.

"Let me help you with that cut," Otis said as he took the cut from my hand and slipped it over my shoulders.

"And that, fellas, is why *this* man is your Sergeant at Arms," Axton growled as he nodded his head my direction.

"Now I need every one of you to get your asses out into the shop, and give this man some fucking breathing room. I need one minute alone with him in here, and then we'll be out there," Axton howled.

Slowly, all the men walked out of the room and into the shop. As the dull roar of the crowd became muffled by Otis pulling the door closed behind him, Axton turned toward the cabinet and reached inside. As he turned to face me, he opened his clutched hand. A copper colored, but horribly disfigured bullet mounted to a small swivel and attached to a chain was in his palm.

"I got this from the surgeon in Austin. I know it isn't much, and I understand if you don't want it, hell I got mixed emotions about it," he hesitated and held it from his fingers, allowing the bullet to dangle at the end of the chain.

"You know I make the cuts myself. I take pride in that. Well," he cleared his throat and stared down at the necklace.

He glanced up and narrowed his gaze, "Brother, I didn't know if you were going to make it or not. I truly didn't. I got this bullet, and I brought it home, and I made this damned thing myself. I told myself if you didn't pull out of the coma, I'd wear it for the rest of my life in your honor. Well, you did. So, I guess I'll give it to you; if you want it that is."

Now an utter emotional wreck, I nodded my head and bent at the waist. Without speaking, Axton raised his hands and draped the necklace over my head and onto my neck. I stood, reached for the bullet, pinched it between my finger and thumb, and nodded my head once.

Axton opened his mouth as if to speak. After a few groans and swallowing heavily, he nodded his head and cleared his throat.

He shrugged his shoulders and extended his arms wide. As we embraced, we patted each other on the back. The sound of his hand slapping against the leather cut was music to my ears.

"I love you, Brother," we both said simultaneously.

As I released him from my arms, I realized my gratitude not only for him, but for the club, each of the men, for my ability to have lived through the shooting, and for Sydney's having entered my life in the capacity and at the time she did.

Still filled with tremendous emotion, I turned and reached for the door. After a short hesitation from the uncertainty of whether or not I was ready to face the club, Axton spoke.

"Hold up a minute, Brother, I think I've got something in my eye," Axton said under his breath.

I faced the door and waited. After a short reflection, I began to fill with gratitude, and gave silent thanks for everything I was fortunate enough to have in my life.

"Alright, let's get out there," Axton sighed.

As we stepped out into the shop, I realized for whatever reason, my life, my outlook, and my perception of all things around me had truly changed. I struggled whether or not to attribute the changes, as a whole, to having Sydney in my life, or being shot. I raised my hand to the pendant and pinched it in my fingers.

And quickly all doubt faded.

SYDNEY

Sitting on the couch in Cambio's house was relaxing in a guilty kind of way. Regardless of what our feelings were for each other, our separation by living in separate homes allowed my mind to wander and eventually I would question just what it was we had together. Our frequency of seeing each other helped matters, but it did not eliminate the feelings I had in his absence. There was no doubt in my mind that a woman's thoughts and a man's thoughts progressed at totally different speeds when it came to the feelings of necessity to define a relationship's validity by cohabitating.

"I don't know if it will be as good, but I used your recipe," he said as he handed me the glass of tea.

I smiled as I reached for the tea, "Really?"

He nodded his head and grinned, "Yep."

"So I was thinking," he said as he sat down beside me, "I've got a few things to do here. I don't know, maybe a week or so, and then I think we should head up north."

"Up north?" I asked as I placed the glass on the coffee table in front of the couch.

"To my parents place. So they can meet you," he nodded.

I did my best to hide my excitement. To be quite honest, I suspected we might eventually go to see his parents, but only after a year or so of seeing each other. I realized he had mentioned it while we were staying at A-Train's house, but I had no idea he planned on doing it so soon. Nothing confirms a woman's position in a man's heart like him introducing her to his parents. Considering Cambio's current relationship with his parents, it made matters that much more significant.

"Oh, well, whatever you think is best," I shrugged.

Fuck, Sydney, really?

"Do you not want to meet them?" he asked.

I shook my head and turned my body on the couch to face him.

I lowered my hands to my lap and tried to appear relaxed, "No, I'd love to meet them. I just don't want you rushing into anything for me. I want you to take things at your pace, I'm flexible."

He started to laugh, coughed, and covered his mouth. As he pulled his clenched hand down from his face, he grinned, "I don't have a pace. This is all new to me. You know, I think I know what I want to do, but I don't want you to wig out because I do something you think is inappropriate or something."

"Wig out?" I shrugged.

"You know, flip out. I've got like zero experience at this shit, Sydney. I'm fucking lost," he said as he stood.

"I know what I feel, and I know what I want, but I don't want to do what I *think* I want to do, because I don't know if it's what I'm *supposed* to be doing. Does that make sense?"

"Kind of. I guess if it includes me, and it doesn't jeopardize our relationship, I'm game for about anything. You aren't going to do or say anything that I'm going to think is inappropriate. At least I don't think so. What kinds of things are you talking about? Give me an example," I said as I reached for my tea.

He began to pace in front of the couch and scratched his head almost frantically, "I don't know. I mean, I don't want to make you think I'm crazy or anything. I just know how I feel. I've always said we *think* some things and *feel* others, and sometimes when we think, we make mistakes, but when we feel, it's genuine. I'm talking about feelings."

To have him reveal his feelings to me excited me greatly. Most men never revealed what they were feeling to me unless it was in a fit of anger. Having him be apprehensive to share his feelings with me for fear he was moving too fast made me squirm nervously until I had settled against the arm of the couch and into the cushion, feeling almost trapped. As I nestled into place, I looked up and smiled.

"Okay, give me an example," I said.

"Well, I just know how I feel, and you know. I don't doubt it," he said as he crossed his arms.

"Okay. That really doesn't tell me anything," I shrugged, "At least not about how you're feeling."

"I just told you," he sighed as he shook his head.

"Okay, how about this. I used to always wonder about things all the time. And I'd ride around in the country with Otis or sometimes alone, and I'd just ride around and wonder. Now, I don't wonder. Not about how I feel. Not now, at least now when it comes to us. Now, I *know*, and there's nothing that's going to change it. Well, nothing or no one but you."

He uncrossed his arms momentarily, let them hang at his sides, and crossed them again.

Still feeling like he was a typical male who had no real idea of how he felt, or he had a real reluctance to *reveal* what he felt, I decided to continue to play along until I had received at least a small tidbit of information from him about his true feelings. So far, he had talked in a complete circle, making no sense whatsoever regarding what he felt.

"Okay, so you're convinced how it is you're feeling is how you're going to continue to feel, unless I make a change. Is that what you're saying?" I asked.

"Yep," he nodded.

I shook my head playfully, "Okay…"

"What?" he snapped as he lowered his arms.

"Nothing, sorry. I'm just thinking. So, that's how you *feel*?" I asked.

"Exactly," he responded.

I stared down at his boots, narrowed my eyes, and shifted my gaze upward until our eyes met, "That doesn't really tell me how you feel, though."

He crossed his arms again and exhaled, "I just told you and you said it right back to me."

Exhausted I decided to try a new angle, "Okay. So now we know how you feel, what is it you're thinking might make me wig out? What were you afraid would wig me out?"

He scrunched his brow and looked down at his boots, "I was uhhm. I was thinking, maybe it'd be like. I don't know, might be a good idea if…"

He gazed upward with his face still contorted. He looked like he'd just eaten something extremely bitter.

"If uhhm. I think you should. Well, you should consider maybe moving in. Moving in *here*. With me. I think you should consider that."

Absolutely what I wanted to hear, but nowhere near what I was expecting, I sat, stuffed into the corner of the couch, and stared. I was at a loss for words. Try as I might, I could not speak. I, too, knew what I felt for Cambio, and I knew the feelings were genuine. The way he made me feel when we made love was beyond compare. It was as if we were meant for each other, placed on this earth for no other reason. Living with him would finally give me the feeling of having a family I had never had.

"See, you're wigged out," he huffed.

"No, no I'm not," I said as I stood.

"I was shocked," I said as I opened my arms.

He raised his hands and turned his palms upward, "Same fucking difference, Wigged out. Shocked."

"Shocked in a good way. It's exactly what I wanted, but not what I expected," I explained as I walked his direction.

"So, when would you want to do this, if we decided to?" I asked.

"I don't know," he shrugged, "I mean here pretty quick."

Feeling maybe as if I got the cart in front of the horse so to say, I tried to settle myself down slightly and prepare for the rest of the story. As always, my interpretation of what he was saying, and his intent was two totally different things. Now settling back down onto planet earth, I decided to pry for a little more definite answer. I stepped in front of him, pried his arms apart, I raised my hands up to his shoulders.

"I see. Like how quick?" I said.

He leaned down, kissed me, and shrugged. He turned toward the window and stared out at the street. After walking away from me, and leaving me standing in the center of the living room like an idiot, he peered out the window and into the sky. He turned from the window and smiled.

"We probably still have, like I don't know, three hours of daylight. We could get it done tonight if you want?" he shrugged.

I licked my lips, swallowed, and squeaked out my response,

"Tonight?"

"If you want, yeah. You don't have much stuff. I just. I don't know. When were together, I'm all happy and shit. And when you go home, or I go home, I just sit and look at my watch and try and figure out when I'm going to see you next. Hell, I fucking hate phones, and I'm staring at mine even thinking about calling you and shit. You know, just so we can talk. It's kind of dumb if you ask me; you being in one place and me being in another. It'd be kind of like me saying I have a bike, and I've got the bike here, and the motor over in Otis' garage. It's just dumb, you agree?" he asked.

As strong as I am, I'm still a little girl. I had always told myself I never had a chance to be the little girl I always wanted to be. Now, I felt I was having a chance to be the little girl I never had an opportunity to be. Robbed from my childhood, and never having a place to call home, now I felt like a little girl with the offering for a home to call her own. I stared at Cambio and fought back the tears of the little girl in me, and for a moment attempted to be a woman. Even though I had been in several relationships in the past, I had never been in love. I never even once suspected I was. I was simply filling a void in my life left by my parents, and later my brother. Now, after spending a period of time without anyone, and becoming accustomed to it, having Cambio in my life was something new, something special, something I not only desperately wanted, but something I had spent an entire lifetime without. He was my father, my brother, my mother, and my lover, all wrapped up in one.

He was now doing what he said I was doing to and for him.

He was unbreaking me.

"I agree. It's just plain stupid living in separate places. Let's do it tonight," I nodded.

"Thank God. I was afraid you were going to say no," he sighed.

And I was afraid you were never going to ask.

TOAD

Contrary to what I had always believed, being in love didn't make a man less of a man, or make him soft, if anything, it made him more apt to stand up for what he believed in, all in an effort to preserve his beliefs and protect his understanding of those beliefs for him and the person or persons he loved.

As I stepped out of Tater's truck and toward the house, I feared I would spend the rest of my life preserving my beliefs, protecting the ones I loved, and doing what I believed was best not only for me and the ones I loved, but for society. Some things, I guessed, would never change. As Ripp said, a wolf will always be a wolf.

"Sure you're up to this," Otis asked as we walked up the short sidewalk.

I patted my back pocket and nodded my head, "Just like we discussed."

As soon as we stepped onto the porch, I reached for the doorbell. After ringing it twice, I heard footsteps coming toward the door.

"Something I can do for you?" the man said as he opened the door.

He was dressed in camouflage pants, a wife beater, and flip-flops.

"Actually our truck started running out of gas about a quarter mile back," I said as I pointed over my shoulder, "Damned thing doesn't have a working gas gauge. We're just trying to get back to Wichita. Probably a gallon or so might get us to Winfield to a gas station. I can pay for it…"

"Come on it," he said as he stepped aside.

"Nice place you got here. What's all that fenced in area out back? Turkeys?" Otis asked.

"Dogs," the man responded flatly.

"Must be quite a few, they all yours?" Otis asked as we followed him toward the garage.

"Yep, Pits," he responded as he stepped down the stairs into the garage.

Otis turned, glanced over his shoulder and winked. After rolling his shoulders and stretching, his arms rearward, he expressed interest in the man's response.

"Pit Bulls?" Otis shrugged.

As the man turned to face him, Otis swung a two punch combination into his stomach and chin. As I expected, the man collapsed onto the floor of the garage, unconscious.

Quickly, I pulled the zip-ties from my back pocket and zipped one around each wrist tightly. Another zip-tie tying each of the two together provided a cheap set of handcuffs which would be all but impossible to remove.

"Legs?" Otis asked as he pulled him to his feet.

"No, fuck it. It'll be good if he tries to run. Add to the excitement. I'll open the garage door," I said.

I reached for the remote mounted on the wall, and pressed the button. After the garage door opened, I walked out to Tater's truck, reached in the back, and removed the grocery sack. As I began walking back to the garage, the man was regaining consciousness.

"What the fuck," he hollered as he realized his hands were bound behind his back.

"Shut the fuck up," Otis growled, "Listen carefully, and I do mean carefully. Your life depends on it. I'm going to ask you a question, and you're only going to get one chance to answer me. Only one. Understand?"

"What the fuck's going on? Who are you two? If you're here for that money I owe Pedro, I've got it. In fact, I got it all," he whined as he alternated glances between Otis and me.

"Shut he fuck up. We're not here for money," Otis said, "Again, I'm going to ask you once, and only once. Answer truthfully, and you get to live. Lie, and I'll fucking kill you, so you decide. All I need's the truth, and I can assure you, if you provide it, I won't kill you. Got it?"

Sitting on the floor of the garage, the man looked up, studied Otis for a second, and then studied me. After a few seconds, he turned toward Otis, "Yeah, I got it."

"Pit Bull pup was shot outside of town maybe a month back. He was six months old or so, I don't know. Brindle colored pup with white under his neck. He was shot three times with a 9 millimeter. Did you shoot that dog?" Otis asked.

The man stared at Otis for a long moment and swallowed. After glancing in my direction, studying the sack in my hand, and turning to face Otis, he responded.

"Don't matter what I say, if I tell you the truth, you'll let me live?" he asked.

"I won't kill you if you tell me the truth," Otis nodded.

"Yeah, I shot him. But there was a reason," he said as he tried to stand.

I planted my foot on his shoulder and shoved him back onto the floor.

"Let's hear it," Otis said as he glanced in my direction.

I nodded my head.

"Pup cost me a lot of money. Couldn't fight for shit," the man sighed.

"All I needed to hear, you got anything?" Otis asked.

My blood boiling, and ready for the next step, I shook my head and reached into the bag, "Hold him still."

Otis pulled him up from the floor and placed him in a choke hold. As Otis held him from moving, I opened the packages of hamburger and stuffed the pockets of his pants with the meat.

"What the fuck is wrong with you?" he howled as I shoved the pockets of his pants full of meat.

"Hell his shirt's tucked in, drop some inside," Otis chuckled.

I opened the last package and shoved a handful of the bloody meat inside his shirt and pressed it into his chest. As Otis began to lead him outside the garage, he realized what we were planning.

"Oh fuck no, you can't toss me to those dogs, not with this meat all over me. They'll fucking eat me. Seriously, dude. Dude, I'm fucking begging you, they'll kill me. You said. Holy shit dude, *no*. *No!* You said you wouldn't kill me. You said that," he cried as Otis drug him toward the dog kennels.

The fenced in area had kennels on each side, and a fenced walkway in between that the kennels opened into. It would allow a dog to be taken from a kennel, and into the walkway without coming into contact with the rest of the kennels. All the kennels, however, could be opened into the walkway at the same time, releasing all of the dogs to roam freely throughout the walkway. Each end of the walkway was shielded from an exit by a gate.

"Just like we said," Otis nodded as he dragged the man into the walkway.

After dragging him to the far end of the walkway, the dogs began to bark and howl. I stood at the close end and watched as Otis shoved the man onto the ground and zip-tied his cuffed hands to the wire fence. Now covered in meat, and tied to the fence, the man didn't have a prayer. The dogs, at least in our opinion, would rush to the far end of the kennel after the meat, allowing us to leave without incident.

Although the man lived outside of town, Axton had already spoken to the local police chief regarding our plan, and learned the city had jurisdiction of the area. After we left, we were to call Axton, and he would contact the police. They would respond to a domestic call in the area, and find the dogs mauling him. They'd give him the option of keeping his mouth shut and seeking medical attention, or telling his version of the story to the Fed's while they processed him for fighting Pit Bulls. According to everyone's beliefs, the dogs wouldn't kill him, but having a jaw pressure of over 200 pounds per square inch, the dozen hungry fuckers wouldn't do him any good, either.

As Otis walked past each gated kennel, he opened the door. After opening the last one, he hurriedly walked to where I stood. As the man screamed, I opened the gate, let Otis pass, and stood back to watch the show.

"Let's get the fuck out of here," Otis said.

I shook my head, "I want to see this."

Slowly, the dogs came from their kennels into the walkway. After the first one stepped into the freedom of the 100 foot long fenced area, several others followed. All the dogs appeared scared and extremely shy. At virtually the same time, they lifted their heads and sniffed the air.

Slowly, one began to walk toward the man. After a few steps, he began to run. The others immediately followed.

As they began to maul him in an effort to get the meat from his pockets, immediately things changed from a really good plan to a really disgusting event.

"You sure you want to watch this?" Otis said over his shoulder as he turned away.

"Can't do it," I said as I shook my head, "Fuck, won't be anything left for the cops to find."

I turned around and began to walk to Tater's truck. As Otis and I reached the truck, I turned toward the kennels.

"God damn, didn't quite go as planned, huh?" Otis said under his breath.

"Sure don't look like it," I responded, "Serves the cock sucker right."

"I agree. But holy fuck, huh?" he shrugged as he opened the door to the truck.

"Don't look like the cops are gonna be able to clean this mess up, fellers. Maybe one of ya ought to get a pair of tin snips or Dutchman's out of my tool box, walk around the back of that pen, and cut them ties of that fellers arms; from outside the pen, you know. And the other go close the front door and the garage door. Maybe they can make it seem like he went out to feed them dogs, and it went to hell in a handbasket. Hard to say it's an accident if his arms are cuffed to the fence," he said in a slow southern drawl.

Otis turned toward the kennel, "Fuck I'll do it. Yeah, looks like if they're gonna haul him to jail, they'll need a bucket to carry the pieces in. God damn."

I didn't argue with Otis' offer.

As Otis walked to the bed of the truck and opened the tool box, I walked to the house, careful not to turn toward the kennel. The sound of the dogs alone was more than I was prepared for. My statement to the vet still held true, I didn't kill the man. If Otis got the zip-ties removed through the fence he was tied to, it would truly look like an accident happened during feeding.

As I walked back toward the truck, Otis began walking from the back side of the kennel. We met at the truck at the same time.

"Can't say it enough," he sighed as he leaned onto the bed of the truck.

"What's that?" I said as I opened the door and crawled into the truck.

He reached around the cab of the truck and held the four zip-ties in front of the window for me to see, "Devil looks after his own."

"Amen," Tater nodded.

Amen.

SYDNEY

Life hadn't really offered me a tremendous amount of significant choices. As far as I was concerned, life just kind of happened, and I was along for the ride. I do realize I had made choices in my life, and the repercussion or benefits of the choices were a result of my decisions, but I had never felt any of the decisions were the life altering ones.

I never in a lifetime of lifetimes would have guessed I would make such a statement, but looking at my life now, I wouldn't change any portion of it if I were able. If I never would have been an orphan, I wouldn't have been homeless, and if I hadn't been homeless, I wouldn't have met Cambio. Even my brother's imprisonment brought Avery and I together as better friends, and without her, my life would be free of a having a girlfriend; something I now found essential to being a girl.

"If you can't say it with a picture, it doesn't need to be said," the tattoo artist scoffed.

"You're *Steve*, right? This is *your* shop, isn't it? We are at *Hell Bomb*, right?" Avery responded.

"Yes, yes, and yes," he said as he turned away from us and toward his station.

He looked like a younger version of Pete. He had a shaved head, tattoos down to his wrist on both arms, tattoos all over his hands, and a beard that went almost to the middle of his chest. Although he smiled as he spoke, he looked like he wouldn't take shit from anyone, or be convinced to do anything he wasn't comfortable doing, whether someone was paying him or not.

"Well, Erik Ead told Axton that you'd do whatever we wanted, and that you didn't do stupid tattoos. And neither of these are stupid," Avery said as she walked around the edge of the partition.

"Customers aren't allowed in the shop unless they're getting tattooed," he said over his shoulder.

"Right, and you're going to tattoo us," Avery snapped.

"I close in like 30 minutes, I'm not about to tattoo shit," he said as he looked up at the clock on the wall, "Who sent you?"

"Ead. Erik Ead. *Doc* Ead, rides a Big Dog Chopper, and has a new Street Glide Bagger. He's a psychiatrist here in town, but he doesn't practice. Rides in a club, it's called, uhhm…" she paused and turned to face me.

I shrugged my shoulders.

"Doc Ead? Big snake on his chest? Got a full sleeve on his right, and a half a sleeve on the left arm? Black haired wife, cute as fuck? Mouthy little bitch, uhhm, Kelli?" The tattoo artist asked.

"Yep, that's him," Avery nodded.

"Well, hell. What are you looking to get?" he asked.

"I want a tattoo of script on my left arm, on the back side of it. And so does she. Here," she said as she handed him the piece of paper.

"Veritas Vincit," he said as he looked down at the sheet of paper.

"Looks like Latin. And you both want the same tattoo?" he shrugged as he studied us both.

We both nodded our heads.

"Well isn't that fucking cute," he chuckled, "What's it mean?"

"Truth conquers," Avery responded.

"Hmm. Isn't that the truth. Why this? You sure you want it. You know after I do it, you might have remorse, and there's no removing it afterward," he said as he glanced up at the clock.

"Look. My brother got stuck in prison for saying he'd kill someone in a rival bike club. It looks like they may have entrapped him, like *coerced,*" I hesitated and turned toward Avery.

She nodded her head and grinned.

"Yeah, coerced him to do it. Like forced him to make a decision he wasn't going to make on his own. So, they gave him life in prison, and he's in Big Sandy doing life, and I met Avery, and she said she'd file a legal motion, and she did. Now, well, now," I paused and took a deep breath.

I was almost too excited to speak. After exhaling and collecting my thoughts, I pressed my palms into my thighs and continued, "The upper court, the *appellate* court…"

Avery nodded her head and gave me the thumbs up.

"The appellate court said they'd rehear his case. And her boss is going to try the case and he's never lost. Not a single case. So now, my brother might get let out of prison. And I want this tattoo, I want it more than anything. Because in the end, the truth does conquer. It prevails," I blurted.

"Hell's Fury," The artist nodded, "Club was Hell's Fury?"

I nodded my head eagerly, "Yes. Yes, it was."

"Remember when it happened. Fucking ATF pricks. Hear that Kevin? Remember when the ATF infiltrated the Hell's Fury and set that guy up on conspiracy charges?" he asked over his shoulder.

Without looking up, a man to his right responded, "Sure do."

"His sister's in here. Looks like he may be getting a new trial," he

299

said over his shoulder.

I shook my head, "*Is* getting a new trial."

"Oh, he is getting a new trial. ATF may have entrapped him. And the ladies here want *Veritas Vincit* tattoos to commemorate their…"

"Truth conquers," the man said over his shoulder, interrupting the artist.

"You got it," the artist said.

"I'll donate one," the man he called Kevin said as he looked up.

"Sounds good. You donate one, I'll donate the other. Go lock the door and turn off the sign," he said as he turned to his work station and opened a drawer.

As he began to dig in the drawer, I turned toward Avery and gave her a hug.

"If you mean donate in the donate sense, we don't want a handout," I said, "We've got money and we'll pay you."

"Well, it's bad fucking luck on your part, I guess. Shop's closed now, can't accept money. But if you want this tattoo and want it done right, you're at the right place," he said as he fiddled with what I assumed was a tattoo gun.

"I do, and everyone says you're the best," I said.

"Arguable, but I'm right up there, huh Kevin," he laughed.

"Bigger'n shit," Kevin responded.

"I'm Steve, have a seat," he said as he patted the large leather chair in front of him.

As I sat down, Kevin called Avery to his work station.

After Steve sketched a script onto a sheet of paper, he walked to a copy machine and returned with two copies. He held one in the air for us both to see, "Take a look at this. If it's what you want, fine, if it's not, say so. You won't offend me, it's *your* tattoo. I can draw different versions of this thing all night, but I want *you* happy with it."

"It's perfect," Avery grinned.

"It is," I nodded.

"Sure?" he asked.

We both grinned and nodded.

As he tattooed my arm, I sat in the chair and exchanged glances with Avery. I truly felt as if I now had a real sister. Not only were we becoming the best of friends, we would now forever be marked by the same tattoo, of the same script, obtained in the same place at the same time. It may mean something different to each of us, but the same event brought us together.

Win or lose, we would always be bound by our tattoos and our memory of her attempt at what she believed was conquering her feelings of incompetence. As much as I feared being let down from the cloud I was living in by another *guilty* verdict, I couldn't wait to see my brother at a new trial.

If he was set free, my life, in all respects, would be nothing short of a modern miracle.

Within seconds of each other, the men finished our tattoos. After he cleaned it and wiped the area with a lubricant, he allowed me to go look in the mirror.

The script was perfect, and the tattoo looked amazing. I turned and studied Avery's. Both were identical, and nothing short of perfection.

"Truth conquers, bitch," Avery said as she raised her hand in the air.

I slapped her hand with mine and grinned, "I sure hope so."

"If you two are happy, we're happy. Good luck with your brother, and stop in and let me know how it went after it's all over," Steve grinned as he pulled off his rubber gloves.

I turned to face Steve, smiled, and reached into my purse, "You take tips?"

"Tips are always appreciated," he nodded.

"Well, here," I said as I placed two $100 bills on the counter beside him.

Steve held one of the bills in the air and waved it toward Kevin.

Avery shook her head as she reached into her purse, removing two $100 bills.

"Here's your tip," she grinned as she looked at her arm.

"Wow, thanks," Kevin said as he accepted the money.

"You girls have a nice night, and tell Doc Ead I said hi," Steve said as we walked toward the door.

"I will. We're having a patch-in party in a few weeks, and he's going to be there with several other members of the club he's in. I'll let him know. And thank you," Avery said as he held the door.

"Fire and Iron," Kevin shouted from the back of the store.

"Oh, yeah," Avery chuckled, "That's the name of it, Fire and Iron."

As we walked to the car I looked at my new watch. If we hurried, we could still make it before they closed.

"I have one place I want to stop before we head back," I said.

"Name it," she said as she unlocked the car.

"The Humane Society," I said over the top of the car.

"For?" she asked.

"I want to see if they have any puppies," I responded.

"I love puppies," she giggled.

"So do I. I've never had one, and I was just thinking maybe we could look and see if one's perfect," I shrugged.

"Well, we got perfect matching tats, maybe we can find the perfect puppy," she said as she crawled into her seat.

I hope so.

But he's going to have to be perfect.

Because his master sure is.

SYDNEY

"Well, these pups came from a place up by Winfield. There were several of them. We've had them in quarantine for three weeks, and actually just brought them out earlier today. Sadly, we had to put six of them down, but these are all up for adoption," the helpful worker explained.

Avery and I both looked through the glass excitedly as two of the puppies fought over a piece of rope.

"Can we go in?" I asked.

"Absolutely," the man smiled as he opened the door.

Two of the puppies continued to tug on a long length of rope. The room smelled like a combination of sawdust and shampoo. As we both stood by the door and watched, the two puppies growled and tugged while the others watched. After a few shakes of his head, the spotted puppy gave one last tug, pulling the rope free of the other's mouth. Now running through the room with the rope in his mouth, the victorious puppy seemed very proud of his accomplishment. After half a lap through the room, the puppy tripped over the rope he was dragging and fell face first on the floor.

Avery knelt down and clapped her hands.

All of the puppies looked up, but only the spotted one reacted. He immediately stood up and came running across the floor toward us. As he got close to where we stood, he attempted to stop, and slid across the tile floor until he bumped into Avery's legs. He looked up as if she was in the wrong.

Woof! The puppy barked. Avery put her hands on her hips and stared down at him.

"Is that right?" she asked in a playful voice.

Woof! He responded.

"Oh my God, he's adorable," I said.

"He is, isn't he?" she agreed.

"So what's your name?" she asked.

As if he knew exactly what she had asked, he sat down, stared up at her and opened his mouth. A loud croak-like belch came from deep within him. He almost sounded like a frog.

Or a toad.

I turned toward Avery.

"Uhhm, did he just croak? Like a Toad?" Avery said with a laugh.

"Sure sounded like it," I nodded.

"Is this for who I think it is?" she asked.

I nodded my head, "Sure is."

"I love his white markings down under his neck, he's fucking cute," Avery said as she reached down at patted him on the head.

As soon as she touched him, he flopped onto his back and rolled around in a circle.

"Oh my God, he's…"

"Perfect?" she asked.

I nodded my head, lowered myself to the floor, and clapped my hands lightly, "Come here, little guy."

He immediately flipped over onto his feet, tried to come running, and fell over after becoming tangled in a blanket. After a second try, he came running my direction and fell over intentionally at my feet.

As I scratched his belly, his back leg started shaking with every scratch. I looked up at Avery.

"Normal," she sighed, "They all do it."

"So, what do you think?" the man asked as he slowly pushed the door open.

"This one with the spots, I want him," I said as I pointed down at the playful pup.

"The Brindle?" he asked.

I shrugged my shoulders, "I don't know. *This* one."

"His coloring, it's called Brindle. Are you sure?" he asked.

I nodded my head as I reached down and petted the pup.

"Alright, let me get a crate for him and we'll get him ready for you," he responded.

"You're going to put him in a cage?" I asked.

He nodded his head, "A crate."

"A cage?" I asked again.

"Of sorts," he responded.

"I don't think so," I said, "I want a leash and a collar."

"Very well," he nodded, "We have a store right over there where you can choose any you'd like."

"See if they've got a Marine Corps one," I chuckled, "If they don't, get...I don't know. Get a uhhm, get camouflage."

As Avery walked toward the gift shop, I continued to pet the pup. I knew he was perfect based solely on the fact he croaked when he opened his mouth. He was a special puppy for a special man, and I intended to give him to Cambio on a very special day.

I just needed Avery to help me with one more thing...

TOAD

I had never stepped into a day expecting it to be any different than any other day. A particular date, month, or year didn't reserve a special place in my heart or on my calendar. For me to determine if a day was special, it had to end first, and as I reflected on the events of the day, I placed a value on it. Holidays, birthdays, or days of the week were simply days, regardless of their position within a week, month, or year. Any of them could end up great, mediocre, or just plain awful.

"I was thinking maybe we could go over to the pizza place or something," Sydney sighed.

"And I was thinking we'd stay here and…"

I leaned into her and kissed her neck. I had minimal experience kissing, touching, or even caring about a woman until I met Sydney. Now, based on her comments and expression about what *she* liked and disliked, I truly looked forward to satisfying her sexually as well as sensually.

As I gripped her upper arms lightly in my hands and continued to press my face into her neck and kiss her aggressively, goosebumps rose along her arms. I lightly began to nibble along her heck until I reached her shoulder. As I softly kissed and licked the base of her neck, she sighed and shook her arms.

"Forget the pizza, keep doing that," she said as she exhaled audibly.

I lifted her from her feet and carried her toward the couch.

"You're going to hurt your…" she began.

"Shhh, I'll be the judge of that," I whispered as I lowered her onto the cushion.

I knelt on the floor at the base of the couch and began to kiss her stomach and hips. As she moaned and squirmed, I lifted her shirt over her head. After unsnapping her bra and tossing it to the side, I began softly sucking and licking her nipples. Caressing her breasts as I sucked them, I watched her face as I did. As she watched me sucking her boobs, I observed the expressions on her face. I had learned from simply paying attention that she liked watching me suck and lick her tits as much as I enjoyed doing it. As she began to bite her lower lip and stare down at my mouth, I bit her nipple lightly between my teeth.

"Oh fucking fuck," she sighed as she released her lip and bit into it more aggressively.

I released her nipple and began sloppily kissing and sucking her breast.

"Mmmm," she cooed.

I reached down between her legs, and slid my hand along her thigh and under her shorts. As my finger fumbled underneath her panties, she gasped. She was wet all the way down to the crack of her ass.

I pulled against the waist of her shorts, and fumbled with the button. After finally unfastening the waist, I pulled them to her feet and tossed them aside. Now lying on the couch in only her underwear, I stood and admired her.

As I stood, it was obvious I was beyond ready. My cock was fighting against the fabric of my jeans for freedom. I unbuckled my belt, unbuttoned my jeans, and pulled them down to my thighs. As my swollen shaft bounced upward, and free of my jeans, she leaned forward on the couch and gripped it in her hand.

"Stick it in my mouth," she moaned.

"Oh hell no, you're not tricking me into that bullshit, not tonight," I laughed.

She gazed upward and batted her brown eyes, "What?"

I pressed my hands to my hips and shook my head, "You know *what*. I can't last five minutes with you sucking on my cock. I want to *fuck*."

As I reached down to push my jeans to the floor, she leaned forward and started slurping and sucking the tip of my cock. As I fought with my jeans, she continued. Finally, as I kicked the jeans free from my feet, I leaned backward, and pulled my cock from her very capable mouth.

I reached down and grabbed the hips of her panties with both hands.

"I," I yanked against the fabric.

"Want," I yanked again.

She stared up at me with wide eyes.

"These," I said as I pulled sharply, "Off!"

As the panties snapped in two, I pulled upward on the fabric, pulling the lower part from beneath her ass, and tossed them aside.

"I'm done fucking around, I'm dying here," I said as I pulled my shirt over my head and crawled onto the sofa.

"You just tore my panties off," she said under her breath.

I grinned and nodded my head.

"Maybe we should go to the bed," she said as she tossed her head toward the hallway.

I gripped my cock and guided it between her legs. As I felt the tip begin to penetrate her soaking wet pussy, I gently pushed my hips forward and closed my eyes as she reached down and gripped her ass cheeks in her hands.

After she kicked one of her legs onto the back of the couch, she raised the other, and dropped it over the edge of the couch and onto the floor. I pressed my knees into the cushion and began slowly working my swollen cock in and out of her wetness.

"Oh God, that feels good," she moaned, "fuck me…just like that…. fuck me."

I lowered my chest to hers and began to kiss her as I continued to work my hips back and forth carefully. With each *in* stroke, she exhaled and moaned a pleasurable gasp. Lost in the moment, my love for her, and how it felt to provide her with the deep satisfaction she explained only I could bring, I continued to kiss her and work myself in and out of her swollen mound.

As she released her ass, raised her hands behind me, and sank her fingers deep into my back, I knew she was about to climax. As her fingernails drug across my back, she began to moan.

"Oh…my God….hold….hold it right…"

"There," she moaned as I felt myself bottom out inside of her.

I held myself still as I felt her pussy convulse into an orgasm. After a deep sigh and releasing my back from her tight grip, I slowly began to work myself in and out of her slippery pussy again.

"Oh dear God," she moaned as I thrust myself in and out, bottoming out with each stroke.

"Holy fuck, you know I can't…"

"Handle…"

"This…" she gasped.

I continued to pound myself into her carefully, but with as much force as I had learned she could handle. As the tip of my cock met resistance, I released the pressure, and pulled my hips rearward.

The repetitive motion and her tight pussy soon proved to be too much. I collapsed onto her chest and continued for a few more strokes.

"Kiss me," I said as she arched her back and tilted her head into the cushion behind her.

As she fought to raise her head, I slid my hand underneath her neck, and gripped it in my hand. As I lifted her head upward, I pressed my lips into hers and kissed her deeply until I felt myself begin to reach climax.

As we continued to kiss, her pussy began to contract again into a massive orgasm. She bit into my lower lip and dug her fingernails into my back. As I felt myself explode inside of her, I arched my back, pulled my mouth from hers, curled my toes, and opened my eyes.

"I love you," I groaned.

She opened her eyes as she fought to catch her breath, "I passed…"

"That stage…"

"A long fucking…"

"Time ago," she gasped.

"You little smart ass," I sighed.

"If you move, you're going to have cum all over this couch. Hand me my shirt," she said as she raised her hand in the air.

I reached down and grabbed my tee shirt and handed it to her.

"That's yours," she said.

"Use it, it's cheap," I shrugged, "Ready?"

She nodded her head.

I thrust my hips rearward and yanked my cock from inside of her.

"You fucker," she said as quickly reached between her legs with the shirt.

"I told you, don't snatch the cock away, remember?" she whined.

She had told me countless times not to do what I had just done.

"Sorry," I shrugged, "I forgot."

"You're full of shit," she snapped as she rolled off the edge of the couch and waddled toward the bathroom.

I gazed down at my glistening cock. I had come a long way since I met Sydney. My life seemed to be in order now. I may have been a Sinner, and prone to do things other men would never dream of, but I did so knowing my love for her would never fade. No one on this earth would protect her, provide for her, or keep her from harm with greater assurance than I would. As I heard her washing herself off in the bathroom, I stood from the couch and walked her direction.

"Shower?" I shrugged as I leaned in the doorway.

"Uhhm, sure. Sounds good. I need to see if we can run by the shop, Avery's up there and I want to see her," she said over her shoulder.

"Okay. Well, how about shower, pizza, and shop?" I asked.

She turned to face me as I reached in and started the water, "Shower, shop, pizza. Before she goes?"

"Sure," I responded as I stepped into the shower.

After a shower, fresh clothes, and arguing over the hunger I had developed, we were on our way to the shop. Sydney, as always, rode steady as a rock on the back of my bike. If her hands weren't visible at my sides, I wouldn't even realize she was behind me. As we came around the corner of the block, I noticed several of the fella's bikes at the shop. It was by no means full, but for a Tuesday night, there were more than usual. A few, strangely, I didn't recognize.

After parking the bike, we walked into the empty shop.

"What the fuck? Are they in the meeting room?" I asked as I looked around the shop.

She shrugged her shoulders, "I don't know where you fuckers hang out."

"Follow me," I said as I walked toward the meeting room.

As I opened the door, several smiling faces stared my direction.

Otis, Slice, Junior, Sarah, Kate, Fancy...

I glanced to my right.

Oh God damn.

Staff Sergeant Jacob, my man Ripp, Shane Dekkar...

Avery stepped from behind Axton. In her arms was an exact twin of the pup I had found on the road. He fought in her arms to get away.

My heart, mind, and entire body filled with emotion as I felt a tremendous heat wash over me. I reached up and wiped the sweat from my brow. I turned toward Sydney and stared.

"Happy Birthday, Baby. Sorry, I had to do it," she shrugged.

"Happy Birthday, Mister Toad," Junior waved.

"Junior," I grinned.

"Happy Birthday," Avery said as she handed me the pup.

He looked up excitedly, opened his mouth and belched a sound that sounded like a frog.

I turned toward Sydney and grinned. My heart was racing, and I felt like a little kid again. Similar to what I remembered Christmas being like as a child, it was almost more emotion than I could contain. Holding the wiggling pup in my arms, I turned to A-Train and nodded.

"Fuck brother, we don't have jobs, so it was no big deal. Happy Birthday. How you doing?" he asked as he patted me on the shoulder.

"I'm good, Brother," I sighed as I looked down at the pup.

I turned toward Ripp and Shane Dekkar, "Ripp, Dekk, thanks for coming."

They both grinned and nodded their heads.

"The puppy came from the shelter. If you don't want him, we can take him back. We've got thirty days. Avery and I picked him out," Sydney paused and studied the squirming pup, "But you should give him a chance, he's from *here*."

"Winfield?" I asked.

I hadn't told Sydney anything about what happened with the man who owned the Pit Bulls, and she didn't ask. To think that she may have found the dogs which were confiscated from the home on her own was almost unimaginable. As I held the pup, I studied him. He sure appeared to be a brother of the pup I had tried to save. It had been a month since the dogs were found there and hauled in to the pound. The same caliber of miracle which brought the first pup to me had happened again, bringing another just like him.

"Yeah, the guy at the Humane Society said some guy was fighting them," she shrugged, "They had to put some of them down, and these little guys lived through the quarantine."

"Well, we're keeping him," I said as I patted him on the head.

Otis walked up to me and smiled. As he leaned into me and hugged me, he motioned toward the door with his head.

"Be right back," I said over my shoulder as I followed him into the hallway.

"Remember that pup?" he asked as he reached for him and scratched his neck.

I shook my head, "Nope."

"Last kennel on the right," Otis nodded.

"Well, she said the guy told her they were from here, here in Winfield," I responded.

Otis continued to scratch the dog's neck and shifted his gaze upward, "I got a few questions, Brother."

"I'm listening," I responded.

"What color are Sydney's eyes?" he asked.

"Brown, why?" I responded.

He shook his head.

"Hair color?" he asked.

"Blonde, you know that," I snapped.

"Nail polish?" he asked.

"Nail polish is purple. Well, at least today it is. So are her toes," I responded.

"You cocksucker, I see where you're going," I whispered as I shook my head.

"You've come a long way Toad. She's a fine woman. Hell, *I* didn't even know when your birthday was, because you don't celebrate 'em. She gathered up all the fellas, fuck, she called me two weeks ago; that's a damn good woman. Just thought I'd check with ya, and make sure you knew all the essentials before I gave you my final endorsement," he said as he slapped his hand against my bicep.

"Well?" I shrugged.

"You're good to go," he nodded as he opened the door.

I stared into the room. Everyone stood and smiled as I held the pup. As I lowered him to the floor I noticed he had a camouflage quick-release collar identical to the one I picked out at the vet the day I took the pup in. I glanced up at Sydney.

"You pick out he collar, too?" I asked.

She nodded her head, "They didn't have a U.S.M.C one."

I inhaled a shallow breath and gazed down at the pup. For a short second, I closed my eyes and gave thanks for everyone in attendance, but especially for the woman I loved, Sydney. I glanced upward and clapped my hands.

"Where's the cake?" I chuckled.

"Didn't bring you no cake, bossman. But I gots us some apple pies," Junior responded.

Axton and Junior stepped aside, revealing three apple pies with candles in them. I hadn't had a birthday cake since I was a kid. In many respects, I felt like a kid again. I turned to Sydney and shook my head.

"I love you," I breathed.

She grinned and nodded her head, "I passed that stage a long fucking time ago."

"Quit flirting with the girl and blow out these fucking candles, Toad," Axton huffed, "I've got shit to do."

I turned toward the flaming candles and shook my head, "Like *what*?"

"I've got a dog to train," he responded.

I closed my eyes, inhaled, made a wish, and blew for all I was worth. Fucked up lung or not, I blew out every candle on the three pies.

I guess that means I'm going to get my wish...

TOAD

With the passage of time, things change. Whether we like it or not, or care to admit it, time brings change. Time causes the deterioration of earth, aging of the mind and body, and maturity, amongst other things. In spite of our willingness to accept it, time passes even when we hide our heads from the reality of the ticking clock.

The ride to Philadelphia was pleasant. Warm and without rain the entire trip, it was as if we had planned it based solely on the weather. Truthfully, we merely packed our bags, dropped off Croak with Axton, and hit he open road.

As we rolled along Bainbridge, I gazed in the distance toward the same home I grew up in as a kid. Now feeling a little more apprehensive than I had during the trip, I began to wonder if they still lived in the same house. As we slowly rolled past, Sydney tapped her fingers into my thighs with the beat of the softly playing music. The color of the trim was different, the door appeared to be new, and the landscaping had been altered. Anything was possible. As I reached the end of the block, I turned around and began considering my apology-greeting combination.

Sydney leaned forward and rested her cheek against my jaw, "Close?"

I nodded my head and pointed at the brick home.

She nodded and leaned back into the seat. As I rolled into the driveway, I flipped off the ignition, coasted into the end of the drive, and exhaled. After lowering the kickstand and securing the bike, Sydney stepped off into the driveway. As we stretched our legs and I contemplated going up the walk, the door opened.

"Mio Figlio," he said as he opened his arms.

I bit my lower lip, turned toward Sydney, and blinked my eyes a few times. After extending my arm in her direction, she walked to my side. As I wrapped my arm around her, I turned to face my father and released my lip.

"Buongiorno, padre. Ci si sente bello essere a casa," I slowly began to walk up the walkway toward the porch. My mother wedged herself between my father and the door frame, blinked, and immediately raised her hands to her face and began to cry.

"Mi dispiace per il mio tempo lontano, ma ho portato una donna. Una donna che amo. Semplicemente ho messo un po 'per trovare il suo," I said as we reached the porch.

"English, baby," Sydney whispered.

"I said I'd like you to meet Sydney," I said.

My father wiped his hands against his pants and almost fell down the steps as he rushed to the sidewalk. After wiping his hands again on his thighs again, he opened his arms and smiled.

"He's not going to shake your hand, hug the man," I sighed.

He lifted Sydney from her feet and hugged her as if she were his own. My mother wiped her hands on her apron and quickly shuffled down the steps and grabbed me in her arms. After squeezing me much more than my throbbing shoulder preferred, she released me and grabbed Sydney.

My mother studied Sydney, turned to me, and placed her palms against my cheeks. Softly, and through teary eyes, she spoke, "Lei è una bella donna , ma lei non è italiano."

"Baby," Sydney breathed.

"English momma. English," I sighed.

"I said it was good to be home, and that I brought the woman I loved with me," I said.

My father shook his head, "No, mio figlio, you said you were so sorry for being late, but you took so long to find the most beautiful woman in the world before you came home."

I nodded my head, "He's right. I said all of that."

I turned to face my mother, and grinned as I spoke, "Momma says you're beautiful…"

She shook her head from side to side and covered her mouth. I raised my hands and turned toward Sydney.

"But she said you're not an Italian girl," I chuckled.

Sydney shrugged, "Sorry, I'm not Italian. But no one can love him as much as I do."

"Does she like the meatballs?" my mother asked.

"I don't know, ask her," I replied.

Sydney nodded her head, "I do, yes."

My mother turned and walked in the house. As my father wrapped his arm around my waist, I placed mine over Sydney's shoulder. Together, we walked into the house. As I entered the home, I immediately noticed nothing had changed; the same furniture, the same placement of photos and plants, and the same smell of food cooking. As nervous as I was to return, I was beginning to feel as if I was welcome all along.

I stood and stared into the living room and inhaled a slow, deep breath. A photo of me in my Marine dress blues was centered in the mantle over the fireplace. I grinned as I admired the young man in the photo. A lifetime seemed to have passed since the photo was taken.

"Show her to the kitchen," my father said.

In my father's eyes, Sydney belonged in the kitchen with my mother. It was not a disrespectful thing in his eyes, but more of a traditional family matter. Italian women gathered in the kitchen and cooked together. Men sat and ate, talked, and drank. For him to have said what he said meant to me he had already accepted Sydney as being who she was; the woman I loved.

Sydney followed me to the kitchen. As soon as we walked in, my mother turned toward us and smiled. The aroma of basil, tomatoes, pork, and flour filled the air.

"Let me show you," my mother said as she waved her arm toward the oven.

"She'll want to explain everything..." I began.

"I'll be fine," Sydney said under her breath.

"Sure?" I asked.

Sydney turned toward me and wrinkled her brow, "Yes. Now go see your father."

I kissed my mother on the cheek, and turned toward the door. As I walked away, I heard my mother begin to explain things to Sydney.

"Italian men won't eat pasta from the market. We'll make the pasta inna minute. Let me show you..."

I shook my head and laughed to myself. For the last ten years, I'd eaten pasta from a can. The smell from the kitchen and the thought of once again having my mother's cooking caused my mouth to water. As I stepped into the living room, my father stood from his chair and struggled to speak.

"Sit..." I sighed as I pointed to the chair.

"I'm done sitting. I want to stand," he said as he began pacing the floor.

"I missed you," I said under my breath.

He turned to face me, gazed into my eyes, and eventually smiled. Although his face seemed the same, I knew he had aged since I'd seen him last. Standing before him now, I felt guilty for the time away, and wished I could change the fact I had been gone for so long. There was no way to make up for my failure to be the son to them they had raised and expected, but I felt I needed to try. If nothing else, I felt a desire to explain my version of why I acted in the manner I had.

"I uhhm. Over there," I tossed my head toward the door.

"I uhhm. I did things…"

He raised his hand to his face and pressed his index finger to his mouth, "Shhh."

After another lap across the floor, he looked up and nodded his head, "You know, it doesn't matter. The war, what happened over there, none of it matters. We're proud of you. We've seen the movies. Your momma and I watched the new one; the Clint Eastwood movie with the boy from Texas. That war…."

He shook his head and rolled his eyes, "It was different. I sat in Korea and froze half to death while we waited for an enemy who never came. Your grandfather froze to half to death in France in foxholes while he tried to keep from being shot…"

"You? You fought a man while you looked into his eyes. You fought in cities and in homes. Face to face. You fought women and children. Your war was different. I'm sorry, figlio," he said as he stretched his arms wide.

As we embraced, I found it comforting that although I had not spoken to him regarding my concerns, reasons for not visiting, or my mental state of being, I didn't have to. He was my father, and somehow, he knew. On his own, he had determined through my actions, or lack of actions, what was potentially wrong with me, and what I must be feeling as a result. Over the course of my life with them, they carefully molded me into the man I had become. If anyone knew *me*, my inner workings, my strengths, and my weaknesses, it would stand to reason it would be my parents.

As he released me, I leaned away from him and nodded my head. I opened my mouth with every intention of speaking, but could find no words to say. At a loss for more than the words I wasn't able to find, I stepped to the couch and sat down.

"I like the color of the trim and the new door, they look nice," I said as I sat down.

He shook his head, "Your mother and I fought for a month over the color."

I inhaled a deep breath and looked around the room. The tattered map of Italy from my grandfather's home was hanging on the wall beside my father's chair. I remembered the map from their house on the wall beside where the Christmas tree had always been placed. I smiled at the memories as I studied it, took another shallow breath, and exhaled.

"Meatballs?" I asked.

He shrugged his shoulders, "Sometimes I think it's all she knows…"

"Amo la cucina di mia madre," I sighed.

He nodded his head, "Sono d'accordo."

As I glanced around the room, I realized although time passes and things change in the process, *some* things never changes.

Home is always home.

And I will always be my father's son.

TOAD

More meatballs than I cared to eat, laughing, recalled memories, and countless stories later, and I was in the kitchen spending time with my mother as Sydney spoke to my father. Although I had no expectation of my parents *rejecting* Sydney, I had reservations about their *complete* acceptance of her. She was not Italian, nor was she Catholic. After spending the entire day with them, it was apparent they only wanted me to be happy. Pleased at their understanding, acceptance, and expressed love for Sydney, I felt it necessary to explain to my mother the depth of my love for Sydney.

"Momma, she's the one," I said over her shoulder as I stood behind her.

She nodded her head, "She's a nice girl."

"No momma. She's *the one*," I said as I kissed her cheek.

She wiped her hands against her apron and turned around. I nodded my head and smiled. She raised her hands to her mouth and gasped. Without speaking, she lowered her hand from her mouth, turned her index finger upward, and ran from the room. After I spent several minutes alone cleaning up the kitchen, she returned with her hand at her side.

"Cambio, you ask her proper. For your momma, capisce?" she said as she stood with her hands at her side.

"I will, momma," I nodded.

"And," she paused and raised her hand in front of her apron.

She opened her hand. A small burgundy box sat in the center of her wrinkled palm. With a shaking hand, she reached over and opened the box. A gorgeous ring with a large center stone and several stones along each side, all of what appeared to be diamonds, glistened from its perch on the pedestal in center of the box.

"This was your grandmother's ring. Your grandfather Nonno," she hesitated and raised her hand to her mouth as she inhaled a choppy breath.

"Mother, I can't…"

"You hush, Cambio. You think you know everything. Since you were this tall," she lowered her hand from her mouth and held it two feet over the floor.

"You don't. Your Nonno told me. When he passed. He wanted this for you when the day came. So you hush and you listen to you momma, capisce?" she said.

I nodded my head.

She raised one eyebrow.

"Capisce?" she asked sternly.

"Capisco," I sighed.

"Your Nonno said to give this to you. It's old. He bought if for your grandmother after the war. He couldn't afford a ring before the war, so she wore a metal band made of copper. After the war, he bought this. It's the ring she wore the entire time you knew her as your grandmother," she explained as she gazed down at the ring.

After a short pause, she closed the box, and clutched it in her hand. She extended her arm and softly began to cry. As I reached for her hand and opened my palm, I too began to cry at the thought of one day asking

Sydney to marry me.

Through tearful eyes, she spoke, "You ask her proper, capisce?"

"Capisco," I responded as I wiped the tear from my cheeks.

And she dropped the ring into my hand.

As I clutched the ring in my hand and hugged my mother, it was as if the memories and love associated with the ring began to fill me. Be it from my mother's expressed love through her embrace and her soft crying, or from the thought of the ring and the history behind it, I began to feel as if I were filling with love.

As I released her and kissed her cheek, I realized I had truly reached a point that I could safely say, without reservation, that I was a changed man. As I shoved the ring deeply into my left pocket, there was no doubt in my mind that I had finally reached the point...

I was unbroken.

TOAD

"It's a beautiful spot, here under the tree," Sydney whispered.

I nodded my head, "It's perfect. I put that up there twelve years ago."

"The wind chime?" she asked as she looked up toward the tree.

"It came from his house. He listened to it while he watched the birds. It was relaxing to him. I figured he'd be able to relax here with the sound from it," I said as I knelt down and wiped the dust from the top of the stone.

"I'm really glad you brought me here. And your parents are just precious. I love...I uhhm, I really...I really love your...your mother..."

The emotion in her voice was apparent. I imagined she felt like she was introduced to my family, only to have them stripped away, no differently than her family had been taken from her.

"We'll come back. Often," I assured her as I stood.

After a hug and a long embrace, she wiped her eyes and nodded her head.

"I'm...I'm going to walk over to the bike," she said, "Take your time."

"Thank you," I said, "I'll just be a few minutes."

As she walked away, I admired her. To me, she was the perfect woman. The thought of one day having a family with her, and bringing her in to my existing family, would be my dream come true. As she leaned against the bike and tilted her head toward the sky, I turned toward the head stone.

"Nonno, it's about that time again. I'm sorry, but I didn't write anything this time. You know I love you," I said as I stood.

"Momma gave me the ring, Nonno. She said you wanted me to have it. I'm going to just tell you now, because I may not make it back in time, but she's the one, Nonno," I hesitated and turned toward Sydney.

"I'll take care of her, and protect her like you told me to. You know she saved my life. Well, kind of. No, I guess she really did. She keeps me grounded, Nonno. She makes living life pretty simple. I love her, I just wish you were here to see it when I asked her to marry me, I really do…"

A slight pain shot through my left shoulder as if someone were squeezing it. I spun around quickly and faced the gravestone.

I shrugged my shoulders and gazed at the stone.

"You probably think I'm crazy, don't you old man?" I chuckled.

"Anyway, I'll ask her as soon as the time is right, don't you worry. And she'll wear the ring with pride. I'll see you again real soon, Nonno. I'm sorry you can't be here for all of it," I sighed as I bent down and kissed the top of the stone.

I turned to face Sydney. A hand gripped my shoulder. I spun around and raised my fists.

The stubble on the back of my freshly shaved neck began to rise. I felt a chill run down my spine. My shoulder began to throb. Although I was certain I was going insane, I asked the question anyway.

"Is that you, old man?" I whispered.

My shoulder throbbed as if being squeezed.

My entire body shuddered.

I shook my head.

"Oh…I uhhm. Oh shit…uhhm, you're here?"

The dull pain returned.

"Uhhm. Holy shit, Nonno. You want me to uhhm…you want me to ask her *now*?"

My shoulder felt as if someone patted it twice. Although I knew no one had touched me, *something* did. Be it my mind, his spirit, or be it the good Lord himself, someone was speaking to me. As crazy as it seemed, and as unbelievable as it was to comprehend, I continued.

"I'm glad you could be here, old man. Hold on," I sighed as I brushed my hand along the edge of the stone.

I reached into my pocket and removed the ring. I glanced over my shoulder toward the bike, and Sydney. She stared up at the sky, smiling.

"Come here, I need to ask you something," I shouted as I knelt down in front of the stone.

As I watched her approach, my heart began to race. I slid my hand between my knees and clenched the ring in my fist. As she stepped in front of me and gazed down into my eyes, she looked worried.

"Yes?' she whispered.

"Sydney, I uhhm, I want to ask you something. I uhhm. I was talking to my grandfather, you know how I told you we talk?"

She nodded her head, "I think it's adorable."

I swallowed the lump in my throat.

Come on, old man. Help me out. Don't make me look like a fool.

"Well. Sydney Shephard," I paused and lifted my hand from my knees.

She stared down at my hand. As I opened it, she gasped.

"Will you honor me by being my wife?" I asked as I opened the box.

Tears began to roll down her cheeks. She nodded her head. After looking up to the sky, she gazed down and opened her mouth.

"I will," she responded.

I stood, slipped the ring onto her finger, and pulled her to my chest. After a long, soft kiss, I held her close to my chest and said a short prayer. As she lifted her head from my shoulder, she pressed her arms against my chest, stood back, and lowered herself to a kneeling position.

"Don't worry, Nonno, he's in good hands," she whispered.

Suddenly, she turned and looked over her left shoulder.

"What?' I shrugged.

"Oh, that was *really weird*," she said as she stood.

"I would have sworn you just patted me on the shoulder," she shrugged.

Some things in life aren't meant to be understood. As much as I wanted to, I was never able to understand what happened at the gravesite that day. Not for certain.

But I knew one thing without a doubt.

I loved Sydney Shephard more than I loved myself.

And I'd spend a lifetime proving it.

AUTHOR'S NOTE

If the reader wishes to find out more about Shane Dekkar, A-Train, Ripp, Kace, or Vee, their story is told in the completed Boxer Series.

UNDEFEATED

UNSTOPPABLE

UNLEASHED

And

UNBROKEN

www.ingramcontent.com/pod-product-compliance
Lightning Source LLC
Chambersburg PA
CBHW020904200626
46814CB00001BA/174